ns

The Greenway

'A haunting debut.' Minette Walters

'*The Greenway* lingered in my mind for days. It takes the psychological suspense novel into new realms of mystery.' Val McDermid, *Manchester Evening News*

'Adams's narrative has a simplicity that is misleading. The story is compellingly told and rich with psychological insight.' *The Independent*

'An assured first novel, with a strong cast and a plot which twists and turns without a glitch.' *Yorkshire Evening Press*

Cast the First Stone

'Adams's debut last year, *The Greenway*, hinted at a promising crime-writing talent; *Cast the First Stone* amply confirms that view.' Marcel Berlins, *The Times*

'A powerful and corrosive thriller about child abuse, suspicion and guilt. Gripping, scary, a wonderful read. She could rise to the top of the genre.' *Yorkshire Post*

'The grippingly edgy quality of this *policier*... is tautened almost unbearably.' *Sunday Times*

'Will keep you on the edge of your seat from the first few pages until the chilling climax.' *Stirling Observer*

Bird

'Jane Adams' first two novels of psychological suspense promised a major talent in the making. With *Bird* she amply fulfils that promise with assurance and style.' Val McDermid, *Manchester Evening News*

'The art of the truly great suspense novel, an art which Adams has mastered.' *Crime Time*

'I am a great fan of good commercial fiction, and it rarely comes better than Jane Adams's *Bird*. It is a haunting crime novel and psychodrama pulling all the right strings in all the right places.' *The Bookseller*

Bird

Jane Adams was born in Leicester, where she still lives. She has a degree in sociology, and has held a variety of jobs including lead vocalist in a folk rock band. She enjoys pen and ink drawing, two martial arts (Aikido and Tae Kwon Do) and her ambition is to travel the length of the Silk Road by motorbike. She is married with two children.

Bird is Jane Adams's third novel, following *The Greenway* and *Cast the First Stone*. *The Greenway* was nominated both for the Crime Writers' Association John Creasey Award for best first crime novel of 1995 and the Authors' Club Best First Novel award.

Her fourth novel, *Fade to Grey*, will be published by Macmillan in September 1998.

By the same author

The Greenway
Cast the First Stone

Bird

Jane Adams

PAN BOOKS

First published 1997 by Macmillan

This edition published 1998 by Pan Books
an imprint of Pan Macmillan Ltd
Pan Macmillan, 20 New Wharf Road, London N1 9RR
Basingstoke and Oxford
Associated companies throughout the world
www.panmacmillan.com

ISBN 0 330 35138 9

9 8 7 6 5 4

A CIP catalogue record for this book is available from
the British Library.

Photosypeset by Intype London Ltd
Printed and bound in Great Britain
by Mackays of Chatham plc, Chatham, Kent

For my late father, with love,
and for Stuart's mam – wish you
could have been there.

Prologue

They told me what it was like, but I never did believe them. By the time we'd been there three days I knew they'd lied. It was worse, far worse.

Sun that burned so hot by day it dried the spit in your mouth and baked your eyes in their sockets. And then the sun went down and you froze to the bone. Weeks, we had of it.

I remember that night, Birdie. Remember it when I've forgotten so much else. The sky was so damned clear and so damned black. Black and silver with the stars all studded like diamonds in velvet and the moon so big it looked like I could reach out and hold it in my hands.

And then I looked down, Birdie. Looked down at the ground. At the dead and dying men, and I knew then that there was no God. No final judgement and no fucking order anywhere, Earth or Heaven.

I knew that no one gave a damn about the guilt of one man's heart when there was so much blood. Making the ground black like a spreading shadow.

I don't know how many of us had the woman before we killed her. I took my turn and, I'm shamed to say, I didn't even think about what we were doing or the rights and wrongs of it.

We'd decided they were guilty but there was no logic in it, Birdie. No logic. No mercy and no reason.

I heard her screaming while I tied the ropes. Winding the cord tight. Binding it round the body of the rope the way I taught you to bind a whip handle. Do you remember, Birdie?

Only this time, I left the loops free and didn't pull them through.

She didn't scream when they brought her to me. I think she was past that by then, only cried out, a little cry, like a shocked child, when she saw the others already dead.

And I didn't look into her eyes.

For me, it was like seeing Rebekkah all over again. Seeing her there, rope tight about her neck, like a dirty rag hanging against the moon.

Chapter One

'I knew you'd come, Bird.'

Marcie smiled again and patted the old man's hand. It was the third time he had said those words in the half-hour she had been sitting beside him. She perched awkwardly on Jack's bed, the toe of one foot resting on the floor, the other leg tucked beneath her, Jack's hand clasped carefully in both of her own.

'It's nice here,' Marcie said. Her voice too bright. Too fragile. The hospital visitor's voice, trying to be cheerful; in a desperate hurry to get away before the conversation runs dry.

She glanced nervously at Jack, hoping he hadn't noticed. Then sighed, deeply. Jack didn't notice much of anything these days.

He had closed his eyes as though wanting to sleep, but his fingers still curved around hers, so Marcie stayed where she was and waited.

Four days she had been back. Four days of sitting beside Jack, first at her grandmother's home and, for the last two, here at the hospice.

Four days, and yet each time he had seen her Jack had greeted her like a long-lost friend.

She looked around her. The truth was, it was really very pleasant here.

Four-bedded ward, two others of them occupied. A

large french window opening on to a pretty garden bordered by tall trees.

The sky beyond, summer bright, clear and full of promise.

Jack – the old Jack, not the one lying here in this neat and tidy room, in this hospital smoothed bed – had loved this time of year. His garden in full bloom, vegetables ready for the harvesting and his beloved trees heavy with fruit.

Already, Marcie missed the old Jack so much. She'd never called him Grandfather, even as a child. He'd always complained it made him feel too old.

And he'd never called her Marcie; she'd been 'Bird' from the moment her father had brought her home to live with his parents.

Jack's scrawny little Bird.

'Better here,' he said. 'Much better here.'

Marcie turned to look at him. 'I thought you'd gone to sleep,' she said.

Jack smiled. 'Sleep, my love, and miss all the bit of time I've got with you?' He smiled again, then, as though the effort was too much, his face went slack and he closed his eyes.

'Much better here, you know. They let the sunshine in.'

Marcie patted his hand. 'They let you out there yet?' she asked. 'Or are they scared you'll come over all bossy and tell them what needs pruning?'

With a great effort, Jack shook his head. 'When it's not so windy, Birdie, my love. They say I can sit out, when the weather gets a bit better.'

He turned his face away from her, gazing out at the tall trees. The mature limes and Lombardy poplars.

'All flying away for winter,' he said, softly.

'What are, Jack?'

He didn't seem to hear her. 'Know the winter's coming, don't they? Funny how they all know, my Bird. Flying away before it gets too cold.' He paused, the soft smile at the corners of his mouth creasing his lined face. Then he closed his eyes again, drifting this time into deep sleep.

Marcie watched the even rise and fall of Jack's chest beneath the light blankets.

She stroked his hand. The skin, dry and lifeless as parchment. Whitened by lack of sunlight and marked with purple blisters where the blood pooled beneath the surface.

Then she lifted her head and looked once more at the blue sky and tall trees outside the window.

When the wind dropped, Jack had said. Then he could go outside.

Marcie stared up at the stern poplars, stark, almost black against the brilliant blueness of the sky.

When the wind dropped, Jack had said.

Marcie watched, willing the trees to move.

But the day was calm and still. Not even the merest breath stirring the top-most branches.

Chapter Two

When Marcie arrived back at her grandparents' house Aunt Alice was standing on the doorstep wearing her dark blue house dress, a duster in her hand.

'I heard the car,' she said, 'so I came right down to let you in.'

Alice angled her cheek for Marcie's kiss, then took her arm and led her through to the kitchen.

'Sit yourself down and I'll pour you some tea. I've just made a fresh pot.'

Marcie watched as the older woman busied herself with the tea things. Alice. Granddad Jack's sister, a few years younger and very like him.

Like Jack, her once-dark-brown eyes had seemed to fade with time, becoming hazel with slight greenish lights as she had grown older. Her grey hair was still as thick, though, and she still wore it long, coiled on the back of her head and secured with a single pin. Marcie had watched her braid, coil and dress it hundreds of times and was still uncertain about how she managed to hold so much hair with just the one. It took Marcie all her time to coax her own hair into a tidy pony tail.

'Where's Gran?' she asked as Alice placed the china cups on the table.

'Gone to see your granddad. Your dad's taken her

over there, you must have passed them and not known
it.'

'Ah.' Marcie nodded.

She picked up her cup and sipped the hot tea. It
seemed funny to be using these flimsy china things again.
They'd been part of childhood. Things Marcie had so
consciously left behind. At home with Michael she used
brightly coloured mugs, buying whatever took her fancy.
Here, things had always been so correct. China cups
painted with tiny forget-me-nots and delicately curling
leaves. The table laid properly at every meal, and clean,
crisp linen, spread over thick quilting to protect the polished table.

Marcie had almost forgotten just how precisely things
were done, here, in this place that for sixteen years she
had called her home.

She felt her stomach tighten in response to the memories. The pang, half of nostalgia, half of the fear that
had first gripped her four days before and had renewed
itself each and every time she re-entered the house.

The kitchen even smelt the same. The mixture of old-
fashioned carbolic, of the breakfast toast, of polish and
fresh laundry and, as her aunt reached across the table to
take her hand, of fresh, scrubbed skin and baby powder.

Marcie felt the tightness spreading to her chest and
throat, making it impossible to swallow her tea. The
quiet, claustrophobic correctness of her childhood edging
once more into her consciousness. Possessing her, even
after all this time and all the things that lay between.

'Are you all right, Marcie, dear?'

She managed a stiff smile. 'I'm fine. Just thinking about Jack, that's all.'

Alice nodded, sympathy expressed in the downturn of her mouth; disapproval in the expressionlessness of her eyes.

'How was he this morning?'

'Much the same. He said he likes it there, at the hospice.' Marcie smiled, a little more honestly this time. 'He said they let the sunshine in and he could see the trees and the garden. That seemed to please him . . .'

She trailed off, realizing belatedly that she had said the wrong thing.

Alice sighed deeply and got up, taking her cup over to the sink and rinsing it with unnecessary thoroughness.

'Well, I'm sure that's nice for him. But we all did our best for him here, you know.'

Marcie got to her feet also and crossed to stand beside her aunt. 'Of course you did. I never meant . . .'

'No. No, I'm sure you didn't. It's just that . . .' She paused and snuffled into the folds of a clean white handkerchief. 'It's just, it's so easy for you to judge, Marcie, you haven't been here in all this time. There's been your gran and me trying to cope and your dad helping out when he could. And he's not been all that manageable, you know, your granddad.' She paused again, wiped her eyes once more on the white linen. Close to, she smelt of lavender, sweetly soapy and so very clean. Marcie put her arm around the older woman's shoulders.

'I never meant anything, Auntie. Nothing like that,'

she said. She hugged her aunt tightly, wanting, genuinely, to give some comfort.

Gently but firmly, Alice eased her arms away. 'The hospice have agreed to have Jack for at least a week, so I've put your things in the room he was in. No point you sleeping on that camp bed when there's a proper one to be used.'

'Thank you, Aunt Alice,' Marcie said meekly.

The woman patted her arm. 'Well, I'd better be getting on. They'll be hungry when they get back and lunch won't make itself.'

Marcie turned reluctantly and headed for the door. It was no good offering to help. Alice had made it clear from day one that she did things herself and in her own way. It was a pity, though, Marcie thought. She'd wanted to ask about the things Jack had been saying. About the woman he'd called Rebekkah, about the birds. About Jack's obsession with its being winter instead of high summer. She knew, though, with Alice in this mood, there'd be no chance for conversation. Alice hid herself behind a constant screen of busyness which nothing could penetrate unless she permitted it.

'Oh, I changed the sheets, of course,' Alice shouted from the kitchen. 'And I'm sure you're not going to be silly about things, are you?'

Marcie glanced back down the stairs. Her aunt had emerged from the kitchen, a glass in one hand and cloth in the other. 'I mean, he won't be back for at least a week.' She paused, as though waiting for some response from Marcie, then continued. 'And you won't be staying that long, will you, dear?'

She went back into the kitchen without waiting for a response. Marcie sighed and continued on up the stairs, aware that she'd been put well in her place.

You walked out on us, her aunt was saying. You went away and you've not been back more than twice in all this time, so you've no right to expect anything more.

Marcie pushed open the door to the spare room, the room Jack had been sleeping in, living in, for the last few months, and stepped inside.

She glanced around at the neatly made bed, the old-fashioned, heavy furniture, at her suitcase and travel bag placed on the straight-backed chair.

No. She had expected nothing else from them. Distant, disapproving courtesy and the occasional glimpse of affection, more, Marcie felt, for the child she'd been than for the woman she was now. It was strange and disturbing just how much like a wayward child they still made her feel.

The air in the room smelt close and musty. Over-breathed and unrefreshed. Marcie herself felt much the same. Very, very worn.

Her aunt's comments about the sheets brought a wry smile to her lips. Truth was, the very thought of sleeping in the bed that Jack had not long vacated made her feel sick.

Closeness by proxy. Infection through association. Whatever it was, she didn't want to sleep in that bed in this room tonight or any other night.

'Marcie, take a grip,' she told herself. 'And don't be so bloody stupid.'

She walked over to the bed and pulled the covers back, half expecting as she did so to see Jack's skeletal body lying there with its bone-thin limbs, flesh drawn so tight that it seemed barely able to cover his ribs and that obscenely bloated abdomen, soft and distended.

Marcie turned away from the bed, nauseated by the acutely, painfully remembered image, and crossed to the window, flinging it wide and looking out on to Jack's garden.

He'd packed so much into such a little space. Three small fruit trees. Cordoned blackberries, trained against the south-facing wall. Raised beds of sweet herbs and borders of bright flowers.

Only the tiny vegetable plot, with last year's pea sticks and its unweeded rows, showed the neglect of Jack's absence.

That and the raspberry canes, outgrown and bearing little fruit, and the unpruned roses, straggling on to the lawn.

Marcie leaned on the windowsill.

She'd grown up in this place, helped Jack with his garden, helped to dig and weed and to know when was the right time to plant and when to thin the growing seedlings. She'd taken as much pride and pleasure as he did in the growing and the fruit bearing. In the feeling of the moist earth, crumbling between her fingers with the sun warm on her back and the sweet, green scents rising up from the damp ground.

If she closed her eyes, Marcie could almost taste those other summers, the bright, safe days before everything had gone wrong and she had run away from Jack. From her father, from all of them.

Marcie could feel tears begin to prick at the corners of her eyes. She kept them closed, but the tears fell anyway, on to her hands as they gripped the sill. Sobs rose in her throat and she choked them into silence for fear of Alice hearing her.

Marcie breathed deeply, trying to control the conflicting emotions welling up inside her. She breathed the faint, sweet scents of the garden and the warm, dusty summer air, letting it ease and calm her mind.

And then she exhaled swiftly, forcing from her lungs the sudden, sour, decaying smell.

A slight sound behind her made her turn and that smell grew stronger. Close, overburdened air, suffused with half-identified odours of medication, soiled linen, the sourness of illness and decay.

Marcie retched, covering her mouth with her hands and willing herself not to be sick.

There was a movement, small but unmistakable, as though someone lying on the bed had tried to shift themself. The ghost of a movement in an empty bed.

Marcie shook herself angrily, crossed to the newly made bed and, this time, pulled the covers completely aside.

'No!'

She stared, her hands raised once more to her mouth. There it was. That slight but definite indentation as though someone had been lying there.

Willing herself to move, Marcie reached out and

touched the hollow where Jack's body would have lain.

Then snatched her hand away.

Where she had touched, the linen sheets had been warm.

Chapter Three

'What's the matter with Marcie?'

Her father's voice, strident and somewhat indignant, carried itself up the stairs. Marcie paused, strained to hear Alice's quieter reply.

'Blest if I know, love. She came racing downstairs this morning like she'd seen a ghost; went to see Jack and then spent the rest of the morning mooning about and getting under my feet.'

'Too much imagination, that one. Always did have.'

It was Gran who had spoken that time, her voice heavy with disapproval. 'Too much imagination' had always been one of Gran's favourite afflictions, an ill on which to blame most of the troubles of the world.

But she could be right, this time, Marcie owned. After all, what else but an overwrought, overtired imagination could have accounted for what she had seen? Or thought she'd seen?

She'd let herself get caught up in past regrets. Let her mind drift too far from the present, and scared herself stupid in the process.

But Marcie knew that she was lying to herself. What she'd seen in Jack's room had been so real and so intense there had to be more to it than an imagination working overtime.

When her father and grandmother had returned for

lunch she'd half expected news of Jack's death. That what she'd seen had been some sign that he was gone.

She could have accepted that. It would have made a kind of sense. But as it was . . .

Her father was speaking again, he sounded tired and impatient. Marcie listened. She felt no guilt at eavesdropping like this. Not with them. The younger Marcie had found that if she crept carefully out of bed and sat here, at the bend in the stairs, she could hear a great deal of what went on when she was meant to be fast asleep.

Jack had known. She was certain Jack had known.

But he'd never given her away.

That had been another of their secrets. Another thing that tied them so closely to each other.

'What did she have to come back for? I mean, what does she hope to prove?' Her father, weary now.

'She loved him.' Alice, strident and impatient, as though explaining to a stubborn child. 'For God's sake, Alec, it was your idea to contact her. You agreed that it was only fair they had a chance to make their peace.'

Alec sighed. Marcie couldn't hear the sigh, but she knew her father. Knew the way he would be pacing up and down the room, glass in hand. The way he'd let his shoulders sag slightly when he talked about her, as though the full weight of the problem, Marcie, rested upon them.

'Maybe I was wrong,' he said. 'Maybe we've all been wrong, wanting her back here, thinking we could change anything.' He paused for a moment, and when he spoke again his voice was louder, as though he'd moved closer to the door. Marcie placed a hand upon the banister, ready to take flight if he left the room.

'I don't know,' Alec said. 'I just thought she'd be different. More ... I don't know, less like she used to be.'

'Ha!' That was Gran. 'Bad blood shows, you should have realized that, boy.'

'Bad blood! Oh, for God's sake, Mother, you sound like some Victorian melodrama. Bad blood!' Marcie could hear the shake of his head.

'You can't deny it,' Gran continued. 'She's not strong enough to cope with this any more than she could cope before. No backbone. That's why she ran away from us. And now she's back and you expect it to be all roses. Best thing you can do for Marcie is to pack her off home to her kids and let things be.'

'She loved him.' Alice's voice now, calm and dignified. She'd be seated, Marcie guessed, in the chair by the window. Sewing or knitting or some such, hands occupied as always, protecting her mind from too much thought.

'Loved,' Alec emphasized. 'Loved him in the past, Alice. But now? And you said yourself she was acting strangely.'

He paused again and Marcie could imagine him, standing by the window, looking out over the small, overgrown lawn. 'I should have let things lie,' he said at last.

'She's like her mother.' Gran's voice was harsh and petulant.

'You never even met her mother.'

'No. But I know what she was and I know what she did, and all we tried to do for Marcie couldn't make up for that, and you know that, Alec.'

She could hear them arguing but her mind had switched off to the words now. There was just the buzz of sound from the downstairs room. Another memory of childhood. This anger. This need to apportion blame for something they hadn't even been a part of. And this time there was no Jack to try to bring peace to the proceedings.

That's how she had known. Realized that he'd known about her listening. The way he tried so hard to protect her from their malicious words. From their secrets.

Marcie shifted up a step or two so that she could see herself in the mirror hanging above the first small landing.

Marciella Rose Whitney.

From the exotic to the sublimely ordinary.

What a name to be saddled with.

Marciella Rose Whitney, alias Marcie, alias Jack's Bird, stared at her reflection in the glass. She still looked younger than she was. At twenty-two she could pass for seventeen.

Black hair and dark brown eyes. Too-large eyes, and somewhat heavy brows that she resisted the urge to pluck or shape. A mouth that seemed always to be set in a faint half-smile, even when her mood was anything but happy, and a chin with a too-deep dimple and a funny, pointy look to it. Like a cat, her husband Michael always said. A curious, slightly puzzled cat.

The rest of her didn't fit the simile, though. Far from

being sleek or even elegantly slim, Marcie was small and slightly built, skinny almost to the point of boniness. After the twins had been born she'd lost so much weight that Michael had been truly worried, watching her eat, forcing her to drink milk until she was sick of the smell of it.

Eighteen months on and at least she'd got the curves back. She smiled faintly. Then frowned again as she thought about Michael and the twins. It would be another few hours yet before he would be home and she could phone him.

Marcie sighed.

Maybe Alec had been right. She shouldn't have come. Maybe she should pack her bags and head for home now. She could be there by the time Michael returned with the twins. It was clear that no one wanted her here.

No one but Jack.

Marcie shook her head and dismissed the thought of going home as quickly as it had been born. No, she had to stay, just a little longer. Make her peace and force Jack to make his.

Did he even remember why she had run away from him? If he did, he'd made no sign, spoken no word about it, just greeted her as though it was right and proper that she had come back to him, and talked, when he did talk, of things that Marcie didn't understand.

Marcie stiffened her shoulders and stood up, preparing to go downstairs and join the others. She'd spend another night here, or maybe two. Give Jack the chance to talk, try to get him to remember.

Marcie closed her eyes for a moment, focusing on that night more than five years before when she had left this house. Remembering Jack sitting in Aunt Alice's favourite chair and crying like a child, and Alice herself, hands clawlike on Marcie's shoulders, screaming at her.

'It never happened, Marcie! It never happened! You tell anyone and I'll swear you're lying. We'll all swear you're lying. An ungrateful and deceitful child, that's what you are, and there's no one here will say any different.'

Marcie opened her eyes once more, shivering slightly despite the heat.

'It never happened, Aunt Alice. Nothing ever happened, did it? Unless you all wanted it to. You spent sixteen years writing what you wanted me to see and making me see it.'

And now I'm back, Marcie thought. And you're the ones with the problem, because I know how it was, how all of it was, and I'm not about to let you turn me inside out a second time.

Chapter Four

It was one a.m. when Marcie signed herself in at the hospice reception and made her way to Jack's ward.

There was little of the hospital in this place. None of the drips and tubes and bleeping machines that Marcie had come to associate with sickness; nothing but that faint, distinctive smell, medicines and cleaning fluids, flowers left too long in cramped vases. Dying things.

The lights in the ward had been dimmed. Marcie stepped out of the brightly lit, picture-hung corridor and paused, letting her eyes adjust to the indoor twilight. The curtains had been left open over the french windows and a brilliant moon cast long shadows across the garden and on, into the ward itself. Tall trees, laying themselves down upon the four, darkened beds.

Jack seemed to be asleep. She sat beside him in the big green chair, watching his face as it twitched and grimaced, the slight fluttering of his hands lying outside the blankets, the little movements that told her he was still in pain despite the sedatives, the pain relief and the uneasy sleep.

Oh, Jack, Marcie thought. Why did it have to be this way? Couldn't it have been something quick and easy for you?

She had never realized until now that dying, this great act of uncreating, could take so much time and effort.

All for nothing.

'Would you like some tea, dear?' one of the night staff asked softly.

'Thank you.'

'You must be Jack's granddaughter?'

'Yes.'

'He's talked about you so much. His little bird, he says he calls you.'

Marcie managed to smile, embarrassed now, though she knew the woman meant no harm.

'Just like Piaf,' the nurse went on.

'Sorry?'

'Little sparrow, they used to call her. Do you sing, dear?'

Marcie gave a startled look, then comprehension dawned. 'Oh,' she said. 'Jack taught me songs when I was little. But that's not why . . .'

The woman was not really listening. 'How lovely, dear. I'll get you that tea.'

Marcie watched her go, amusement touching the corners of her mouth.

Little bird indeed. Hardly a songbird, Marcie thought. She could hold a tune, but her voice had no real strength to it.

Not like Jack's.

No, Jack called her Bird in memory of the first time he had seen her. Less than two months old and brought to his house by her father. Such a scrawny little thing and her mouth always open, wanting to be fed.

'It's good to see you smiling. Too many long faces round here.'

'I thought you were asleep,' she said.

Jack shook his head. A slight movement against the pillow. 'No, girl. Just hiding from her.' He gestured vaguely in the direction that the nurse had gone. 'Talk the legs off a donkey, she would. Worse than your gran.'

Marcie laughed, then stifled the sound quickly, looking around to make sure she had disturbed none of the real sleepers.

Jack grimaced, his mouth slack and toothless. He touched his tongue to his lips to moisten them before he spoke again.

'I won't be here much longer, girl. You know that, don't you?'

Marcie began to deny it. 'No, Jack, no, that's . . .'

'True, Bird, very true. And I don't much mind it, girl. I get tired, you know, and I can't do my garden like I used to.'

Marcie felt the tears beginning again. 'It's over-grown,' she said. 'I've never seen weeds in your garden before or the roses not pruned.'

'Forgotten how to do it, have you, Bird? Maybe you could do it for me, before the spring gets here. Too late when the sap begins to rise, they bleed then, you know. Bleed the life out of them if you do it in the spring.'

He closed his eyes again as though the conversation was too much and clutched at the sheets as a spasm of pain crossed his face.

Marcie reached out and covered his hand with her own.

'It isn't winter, Granddad Jack,' she told him. 'It's nearly September and it's warm outside.'

He returned her handclasp, the skin of his palms dry and oversmooth.

'Always were hot blooded, my Bird. Never felt the cold, did you?'

He opened his eyes wide for a moment and stared out of the window at the clear sky. 'Be a frost before morning, I shouldn't wonder, sky clear like that. Break up the ground well.' He moved, snapping his attention back to Marcie. 'Get your dad to help with that rough digging, girl. It's too much for you on your own. We'll have a week of frosts, I shouldn't wonder. If you did that far bed over now and let the frost lie on it we'll have an easier job preparing it come spring.'

Marcie bit her lip and nodded. 'Yes, Jack,' she said, 'I'll get it done for when you come back home.' There seemed no point in telling him again just how far away spring was. That there would be no frost tonight. Jack seemed satisfied and squeezed her hand.

'You're a good girl, Birdie,' he said, his voice cracked and whispery. 'Always told them that. A good girl.'

He closed his eyes and slept. The nurse arrived with the tea and Bird drank it, watching Jack's face, the slack mouth working even in sleep. It confused her. These moments of lucidity – like when he had talked about the nurse – followed so rapidly by disorientation and uncertainty.

She put the cup aside and, slipping her feet out of her shoes, drew them up on to the chair and wrapped her arms around her legs, resting her chin on her knees.

Watching Jack.

*

'Birdie.'

Marcie jerked herself out of sleep and looked around in confusion.

'Oh, Jack, I'm sorry. I must have gone to sleep.'

'Birdie!' There was a nervous edge to his voice now. 'Look, Bird, over there. She's followed me.'

'What?'

Marcie looked over to where Jack was pointing. His hand shook, but he seemed to be waving towards an empty chair that stood beside the opposite bed.

Marcie turned her gaze from the chair to Jack.

'There's no one, Jack,' she said. 'No one sitting there.'

He shook his head impatiently. 'Don't play games with me, Birdie, I don't have time.'

His voice had taken on a sudden sharpness; a strength that took her by surprise.

'She's followed me,' he said again. 'Never given up. Never given up.'

His voice trailed off, but his eyes continued to stare at the empty chair. Marcie could see his hands whiten as they clutched at the covers and the fear in his yellowed eyes.

This was not the time to argue what was real.

'Who is she, Jack?' she asked.

He glanced swiftly at her, relief showing on his face.

'You see her, don't you, Birdie?'

Marcie didn't answer.

'You see her,' he repeated, satisfied now. He eased himself back against the pillows and released his grip on the sheets. 'She comes to me,' he said. 'That damned rope round her neck and her hands tied, and she just looks. Looks at me. Those eyes, Bird. Those eyes.'

Marcie stared at the chair, then looked back at Jack. A half-memory of an earlier conversation wormed its way into her mind.

She felt herself grow cold, the hairs on her arms rising and a sudden chill clenching the muscles between her shoulders.

'Who, Jack?' she whispered softly. 'Who is she?'

At first he didn't answer. He had closed his eyes and his mouth began to work but no sound came out.

'Jack,' Marcie prompted. 'Is it the one you told me about? The woman in the desert?'

He shook his head, a small movement against the pillows.

'So cold,' he said. 'You wouldn't believe that, Bird, just how cold it was at night. Sky so clear and all the stars . . . You can see the moon so close it's like you could reach out and take a hold of it and it's so damned cold.'

Marcie nodded. She'd heard this before, about the moon, about the days full of heat and the nights cold enough for frost.

'In the war, Jack?'

He nodded. 'Out in the bloody desert. Cold, just like it is now, waiting for the frost. Like winter at night, it could be.'

He paused; Marcie waited but he didn't seem able to go on.

'Who was she, Jack?' she asked again, but he wasn't listening now. His mind was elsewhere. Detached from

25

Marcie, separate, even from the woman who sat in the chair and watched him.

'Who was she, Jack?' Marcie asked him for the final time. Then gave up. Jack was sleeping, his breath rasping in his throat and the bone-pale hands twitching as they lay on the cover.

Sharply, Marcie glanced back towards the empty chair. She rubbed her tired eyes.

'Stupid,' she muttered to herself. 'Just stupid.' Even so, she couldn't quite shake off the feeling that something had moved. That there had been a slight flicker at the corner of her vision, as though someone had risen to their feet and walked away.

Chapter Five

'You look like death,' Alec told her. 'Didn't you sleep?'

Marcie shook her head. 'Not well,' she said, 'and I was over with Jack most of the night.'

Alec snorted disapprovingly. He finished the rest of his tea and replaced the cup on the saucer with a loud chink. He pushed his chair back impatiently.

'Well,' he said. 'I've got to go. Some of us have work to do.' He looked sharply at his daughter. 'You'll run your gran over to see Jack when she wants to go?' he said.

Marcie nodded vaguely. She had woken feeling exhausted and horribly homesick. Almost packed her things then and there and fled back to Michael and the twins. The thought of doing so was still with her now. She was aware, suddenly, that Alec was staring at her as though waiting for something.

'I said,' he repeated, 'you'll run your gran over when she's ready.'

'Yes, yes. Of course I will.'

He nodded as though satisfied, but still frowned and did not move. 'Say much last night, did he?'

Marcie looked surprised, then shook her head. 'Not a lot, Da, you know how he is.' She laughed, weakly. 'He kept going on about one of the nurses. Said she talked too much.'

Alec allowed himself a half-laugh in return. He sounded relieved.

Marcie hesitated, then pressed on. 'He says he keeps seeing some woman. Someone he says keeps following him around and watching him.' She paused, gauging her father's expression. 'He's scared of her, Da.'

Alec frowned again. This was clearly something that he didn't want to hear.

'It's the drugs he's on, Marcie. You know that. They make him see things sometimes. And his mind wanders.' He paused. 'He's been ill for a long time. If we'd taken notice of half the crazy things he's ranted about we'd all be halfway round the twist by now.'

Marcie nodded weakly as Alec lifted his jacket from the back of his chair and slipped it on.

'I expect you'll be going soon,' he said. 'Get back to those kids of yours.'

Marcie poured her tea. 'He thinks it's winter,' she said softly. 'I keep telling him it's only the end of summer, but he's convinced it's winter.'

Alec looked angry this time. 'I've told you, it's the drugs he's on.' He shrugged his shoulders into his jacket, settling it better on his shoulders, and straightened his tie.

'Jack won't live to see another winter,' he said brusquely as he turned to open the door, 'so what the hell does it matter what season he thinks it is?' He glanced back and nodded at her. 'See you later, Marcie.' His voice was sharp and businesslike. Then he was gone, the door swinging shut behind him.

Marcie sipped at her tea, gazing absently at the wreckage of the morning's breakfast.

Slowly, she came to a decision.

She would stay today, and, yes, stay tonight. Pack her things late afternoon and spend the whole night over with Jack at the hospice. Then she'd go home. Tomorrow morning, she would go and never come back, not even for the funeral.

'I'm sorry, Jack,' she whispered softly, 'but no one wants me here and you hardly know whether I am or not.'

She put her cup down and got to her feet to carry the breakfast pots over to the sink.

'Then I'm going home, Jack,' she said softly. 'I'm going home.'

I was so proud of you today. Five years old already and so sweet in that pink dress and bows in your hair. I took so many pictures of you that your gran threatened to take the camera away.

But I don't care, my Birdie. She could lose a hundred cameras and every picture I've ever taken of you and I'd still remember.

She doesn't mean to be so hard, my Bird. Didn't mean to snap at you like that and spoil your special day. But she just believes in everything being proper. You know that, and those other children – well, Birdie, she doesn't see them as our sort.

I don't know, my Bird, she thinks I'm stupid sometimes. Thinks I indulge you too much and that isn't good for you. If she knew I wrote you these little letters, I don't suppose she'd understand, would she, darling. She'd have her reasons, too, I suppose. Maybe I do neglect her a little these days, but she makes it so hard. Always distant. Always so busy with things.

But you shouldn't fret, my Bird. There's you and there's your Granddad Jack, and there's nothing can come between.

Chapter Six

Marcie drove her grandmother to the hospice after lunch.

Both her grandmother and Aunt Alice had been very quiet that morning. Marcie had seen little of them. They had been closeted together in what had been her grandparents' room.

As Jack's illness had progressed they had moved him out, into Marcie's old room at the back of the house.

Passing by her grandparents' door, Marcie could hear the two women talking, something heavy being moved across the floor and, once, the sound of her grandmother crying quietly.

Feeling superfluous, Marcie had gone back to her room and slept in the chair.

They had eaten lunch together in almost total silence. Then left the clearing-away to Alice and gone out to the car.

'What's all that?' Marcie asked, noting a stack of bags beside the dustbin.

'The bin men come in the morning,' her grandmother replied. 'It seemed like a good time to clear the rubbish out.'

She seemed disinclined to say more. Marcie looked hard at the stack of 'rubbish'. 'Jack's things?' she asked quietly.

'He wanted to keep everything,' her grandmother

said. She sounded angry and more than a little hurt. 'I always told him, Jack, some of these things just have to go. You don't need them. But no. Insisted on keeping the whole damned lot.'

On keeping what? Marcie wanted to ask her, but the older woman had her lips pursed tight and a strained look about her eyes as though something pained her deeply.

'I'd like time with Jack on my own,' her grandmother said when they parked the car.

Marcie nodded. 'Sure, Gran. I'll take a walk.'

'A half an hour should do it. I can't think what I have to say will take longer.'

She marched off towards the reception, pushing through the swing doors and letting them close with a crash behind her.

Marcie watched her, puzzled. She saw her sign in at the desk, smooth her skirt and pat her hair back into place with the care of someone getting armed for battle.

She'd seen her grandmother in one of these moods before and always, this need to speak to someone alone. This careful mental preparation and physical ordering of herself presaged a row.

Marcie shook her head. What was the point of arguing with a dying man? Unless Gran caught him in one of his more lucid moods, it was unlikely Jack would even understand her.

Marcie turned away and walked across the car park. The sun felt warm on her back but the air had a dusty scent to it, like summer that has lasted just too long. She felt her restlessness growing, like the birds Jack talked about. She knew it was almost her time to fly.

When Marcie arrived on the ward it was plain that Jack and her grandmother had indeed been arguing. From the look of them the quarrel had been a violent one and was, despite the best efforts of staff to calm them both, still going on.

Her grandmother turned accusingly as Marcie walked in. Staring at the girl, she continued to talk to Jack, her words tight-lipped and over-precise, as though each one were designed for full effect. Then, as Marcie reached the bed, she rose to her feet.

'We're going now,' she said.

Marcie stared at her, ready to protest, but Jack reached out and clasped her hand.

'Best take her home,' he said. 'She's got herself in a state. There'll be no peace if you don't.'

'If you want me to,' she said, 'but, Jack—'

She broke off. Jack had slipped once more into his other world. He stared across the ward at some figure Marcie could not see. The grip on her hand tightened, fingers digging in like claws.

'Find her for me, Birdie,' Jack whispered. 'Find Rebekkah for me.'

The air was heavy with the scent of lilacs and the night warm for late April.

Jack stood at the end of his garden, as far from the

house as he could get without passing through the wooden gate and out into the street beyond.

His wife and sister stood close to the lighted window. Jack could see them behind the glass, the curtains still undrawn. They were pretending very hard not to watch him. Two shadow figures with the light behind them, casting furtive glances at the man outside.

Jack turned his back on them. The baby, cradled in his arms, had her eyes shut tight. Well fed and fast asleep, she cared nothing for any of the trio, set in their strange tableau.

She looked so peaceful, Jack thought. So tiny and so fragile in his arms.

'It's a beautiful night, my darling,' Jack told her softly. 'A beautiful night. Sky all full of stars and a great big moon shining down. And just smell those lilacs.' He breathed deep as though to encourage her. 'Blooming just for you.'

I love her already, Jack thought to himself. She's only been with me for this little time and yet I love her as though she'd been a part of me for ever.

He laughed suddenly as a thought struck him and the baby started slightly at the sudden sound. 'I didn't think he had it in him, that son of mine,' he said, his voice full of wonder. 'But here you are. Precious and beautiful and here to stay.'

He smiled down at the child. It wasn't often, he thought, that life gave anyone a second chance. A way to make amends, and yet here it was. This tiny bundle with the stupid name and some trace of his own blood flowing in her veins.

'Marciella,' he said, rolling the word around in his mouth as though getting used to the taste of it. 'Damned silly name, my love, but I suppose you're saddled with it now.' He sighed contentedly. Not that it mattered what they'd called her. She was his now. His little Bird. His to care for, to protect and to mould.

His to love and his to make things right again.

Chapter Seven

They drove back to the house in silence. Marcie tried to speak but her grandmother made no reply, just stared through the windscreen.

It wasn't until they reached the house that she spoke.

'We talked this morning,' she said, 'Alice and I. Then we told your father. We decided it would be best for all of us if you left this afternoon.'

'But why? I don't understand.'

The door opened. Alice stood on the step. Marcie could see her father behind, looking uncomfortable. They must have called him home from work, she thought.

She stood in the tiny hall between the three of them and listened while her father cleared his throat and tried 'to explain'.

'It's not that we don't want you here,' he told her. 'Just that it's harder than we all thought it would be to have you back. And it's upsetting Jack. Upsetting your gran, too.'

'How am I upsetting Jack?' Marcie demanded. 'And Gran? What have I done to bother you? I've tried to help out. Tried not to get in the way ...'

'You don't know when to leave things alone,' her grandmother replied curtly. 'Jack was happy enough before you came back. Settled, he was. Not rambling on about all this nonsense he should have forgotten long ago. Not getting all upset and worrying his head about things that can't be changed. You never did know when to leave well alone,' she repeated.

She paused as though for breath, her shoulders squared indignantly. 'We've done our best for him all this time and not one word from you. And then you come back here, full of your ideas and your questions and your "I'm only sitting and listening to him" and make the lot of us look like we've never cared a damn. And he goes on about his Bird and how good she is to him . . .' She broke off, her lips trembling and her rigid spine beginning to bend under the payload of emotions. 'And it makes it sound like we've been nothing to him. Nothing!'

'It isn't like that,' Marcie told her hotly. 'You sent for me. You told me I'd better come, and, yes, I've sat and listened to Jack. Maybe you've been too busy to do that. Maybe you didn't want to hear what he had to say, I don't know. But he wanted to tell me things. Needed to tell someone and I just happened to be there.' She paused, not really wanting to argue like this. 'But, Gran, no one's suggesting you haven't done everything you could for him.'

'Oh, that's big of you,' her grandmother replied. 'It's nice to know you've noticed all the sacrifices we've been making for him. All the days we've been watching him get sicker and sicker and knowing he's going to die.'

Her voice failed her and she gulped air, trying to force back the tears.

Marcie tried to assimilate the mix of blame and pain in her grandmother's words. 'All right,' she said softly.

'I'll go. I'll go now, just as soon as I've packed my things. But you have to listen to him, Gran, Alice. There's something on his mind. Something that's bothering him and he can't sort it on his own. You have to listen to him.'

She looked from one to the other, but they stood in a tight-lipped, disapproving circle.

'I'll go and get my things,' Marcie said at last.

'We did it for you,' Alec told her. He reached behind him and lifted Marcie's bags from where they sat under the stairs.

Marcie stared open mouthed at this final insult. Then snatched the bags from his fingers.

The front door shut behind her as soon as she was through.

Marcie stood for a moment on the doorstep, confused and deeply hurt. Then she placed her luggage in the boot of her car.

'Damn them all,' she whispered. 'God damn them all.'

Her eye caught sight of the rubbish bags, loosely tied at the neck, sitting beside the bin. Curiosity and not a little anger took Marcie to them. She pulled at the neck of one, ripping the plastic and splitting down the side. Letters and photographs, books and old seed packets tumbled out and fell in a pathetic little heap at her feet.

Jack's things. Jack's memories. Fragments of Jack's life, thrown out as though they meant nothing, even before he was fully dead.

Marcie lifted some of the pictures. Most of them were of her. Marcie at five, blowing out candles on her cake. Marcie at eight in the school nativity play. Marcie as an awkward thirteen-year-old, all legs and skinny arms, standing uncertainly beside the front door.

'What are you doing? Just what are you doing!' Her grandmother's cry startled her to her feet.

'He isn't even dead yet!' Marcie spat at her. 'You've thrown all this away and he isn't even dead yet.'

Furious now, Marcie snatched the bags from where they lay beside the bin, piled them into her arms, spilling fragments of torn photographs and scraps of scribbled notes in her hurry.

She almost ran to the car, threw the armful into the boot and slammed the lid. Then turned again and scooped the remaining stuff, two boxes and another bag, into her arms.

Her grandmother was wrestling with the boot. Her father and Alice had come running from the house and joined the fray. Alec grabbed Marcie's arm as she thrust the remaining things into the back of the car and slammed the door. She pushed at him, hitting out at his face and kicking at his shins as he tried to stop her. She felt her foot make contact with bone. He yelled. Marcie followed through and kicked again; finding his shin once more, she ground down hard with the heel of her shoe, hitting him with her free hand.

'Haven't you taken enough of Jack already?' Gran shouted. 'It isn't yours. I'll have the police on you. I'll have you for assault.'

'Like fuck you will. Now let me go!'

She tore herself free of Alec, flailing and kicking like a spitting cat and almost knocking him to the floor, then scrambled into the car and locked the door. Behind her, she could hear her grandmother pounding on the boot, crying out in a voice that was flooded with tears. Alice was tugging at the driver's door.

'Marcie,' she was shouting. 'You're upset, we're all upset. Now open the door.'

Alec leapt forward as she started the car. For one crazy moment Marcie thought he would jump out in front of her. She revved the engine, dropped the clutch and spun the wheels, screeching away still in first with the engine protesting as she hit the red line.

Alec leapt aside.

Looking in the mirror, Marcie could see him staring helplessly as she drove away.

Watching him grow smaller and smaller in the mirror, Marcie began to laugh. Then, as she turned the corner, the laughter dissolved into a stream of angry tears.

Chapter Eight

Home was three hours away at normal speed.

But Marcie didn't drive at normal speed, at least not this time.

With the boxes and bags rattling about in the boot and tumbling from the seat in the back of the car, she made the distance in a little over two.

Middle-class suburbia gave way, first, to the sprawl of new industrial estates on the very outskirts of the city and then, when she skipped off the main roads, to a network of country lanes left almost unchanged by the centuries.

She slowed, just, for the villages, powered through the bends, foot flat against the floor. Regained the main roads just before the congestion of the rush-hour traffic would have forced her to slow her pace.

She remembered little of the journey. Grief and anger had combined to make her almost blind to the world beyond the confines of the car.

Turning into the side road that led to home and being forced suddenly to grab at the clutch in order to make the bend brought the madness of her journey back to her. A glance at her watch and a quick addition of the time was enough to have her shaking in her seat as she pulled up before the front door.

She sat, motionless, hands gripping the steering

wheel, feet welded to the pedals, for several minutes, before finally coming to enough to pull the handbrake on and switch off the engine.

Only then did Marcie begin to relax. She felt weak, almost light-headed, as she wriggled out of the car and crossed the short stretch of pathway to the front door, fumbling blindly for her keys.

Another hour, two at most, and Michael would be home with the twins.

Shaking now with fatigue and, she realized, good old-fashioned hunger, Marcie let herself in through the main door, made her way down the hall to their own front door at the end of the passage and went inside the muddled, comfortable little flat. She closed the door behind her and sat down on the floor, just inside, breathing in deeply the scent of baby powder and lemon polish, and the warm, indefinable smells that meant comfort. That meant safety. That meant home.

Michael arrived just before the rain began.

Marcie heard him crashing through the house door with the double buggy.

He must have seen the car because he shouted out to her, yelling at the twins, 'Mummy's home! Yeah! Let's go find her.'

Marcie flung open the door and threw herself at the three of them. The twins shrieked and wriggled against the pushchair straps. Michael grabbed at her and pulled her close to him, his arms full of shopping bags and disposable nappies.

'When did you get here?'

'About an hour ago.'

'Why didn't you phone? I didn't think you'd be here until at least tomorrow.'

He hugged her even closer, dropping the bags to the floor in an effort to get a tighter hold.

'I had problems,' she told him, her voice muffled against his chest. 'They didn't want me and I just couldn't take any more. I wanted to get home to all of you.'

The twins' yelling distracted them both. Marcie knelt down, undid their reins and picked them both up in one wriggling bundle of arms and legs and wet kisses.

'I did the washing-up,' she shouted back over her shoulder.

'No time this morning. I was at the centre for the early call.'

'We need shopping.'

'Go to the late-nighter now we've got the car back.' He folded the buggy, dumped it in a corner and shut the door with a crash, reaching out for Marcie and the twins again. 'God, but it's good to have you home. So tell me everything. How was it? Was it as bad as you thought it would be? What's that junk in the back of the car?'

Marcie laughed and deposited the twins on the floor, trying to keep hold of one of them long enough to remove his coat. Michael tackled the other.

'Lord, I'd almost forgotten. I should have brought it in, but I was in such a hurry just to get inside and close the door . . . It's stuff Aunt Alice and Gran threw away. I found it by the bin so I brought it with me.'

'Threw away? The bin?' He reached a hand to touch

her forehead, drew his finger back in mock surprise. 'God almighty, girl, we done get so poor we have to pick the rich folk's bins?'

She chased his hand aside. 'Don't be so daft,' she told him. 'It's all Jack's stuff. Pictures, letters. I don't know. I didn't really get a proper look. But I couldn't leave it there. Not just thrown out like that as though he didn't matter to anyone.'

She sighed and, as though suddenly deflated, flopped on to the sofa, watching the twins distractedly as they found their toys.

'I don't know what's in it, Michael. Three bags and a couple of boxes of stuff.'

She looked at him, suddenly shy. 'Thought you'd help me sort it out,' she said, hopefully. 'Find out just what it was they didn't want me to have.'

Chapter Nine

My Mary.

I could live for ever in that afternoon.

You didn't know your gran then. I know you don't always understand her, Marcie. And I guess she doesn't understand you. Not the way I do.

Oh, but you should have seen her then. That Sunday afternoon.

We'd gone walking. Down Swinhope Hill and along the bottoms out towards the mill.

She was eighteen, your gran. Eighteen, with this mane of long red hair and freckles scattered across her nose.

All dressed in white, with blue piping on the cuffs and collar and a big straw hat, perched on the top of her head, and a long blue ribbon trailing down her back.

Beautiful, she was, Birdie. Just beautiful.

I could live for ever in that afternoon.

It was several days before Marcie persuaded herself to sort through Jack's belongings. She was caught between a need to know what it was she had so impulsively brought with her and a half-fear of the memories stored away inside.

It was the call from Aunt Alice that finally prompted her. An angry, recriminatory phone call, made worse by Alice's inability to reach Marcie in the days before.

Marcie stood in the communal hall, listening to Alice's vitriol and trying to keep her answers calm. Twice, tenants from the upper floors passed by. Twice, Marcie was uncomfortably aware that Alice's voice could be plainly heard.

'You turn up,' Alice almost shouted, 'disrupt our lives, criticize the way we cared for Jack and then you steal from us! And when I try to be fair to you, try to talk to you and clear the air, you avoid my calls! Didn't you get my messages?'

Marcie doubted that there had been any messages. She knew of old that if she herself didn't get to the hall phone first, then Alice would simply ring off, try again later and complain about it.

'I've had no messages, Auntie, and I've hardly been here to receive them anyway. We both have to work, remember. And as to "clearing the air", my God, I think I've heard enough.'

Marcie didn't really listen to the rest of her aunt's complaints. She held the receiver loosely in her hand, gazing around distractedly at the dusty hall.

They had lived here, in this house, since that first night she had spent with Michael.

He'd had the attic room then or, rather, one of them. A cramped little bedsit with a two-ring stove, stuck high in the eaves of the Victorian house. The sloping roof oozed damp and there'd been a cracked pane in the window that must have been ages old. The line of the crack was filled with impacted grime.

A year on, they had moved down to a larger room on the first floor and then to ground level a few months before the twins had arrived.

At the end of the line, Alice's anger raged on. Gently, Marcie replaced the receiver on the rack and walked away.

Michael looked up as she re-entered the room. He was putting the twins to bed in what was laughingly called their bedroom. Marcie suspected it must have been a walk-in store cupboard, a butler's pantry or some such.

Now it had been converted into space enough for two drop-sided cots, an assortment of toys in plastic crates and the children's clothes, packed carefully in cardboard boxes and old suitcases and slid beneath the cots.

A large blue curtain partitioned this 'room' from the rest of the living space. Their own bedroom, small but larger than the twins', led off the main living room and faced the front of the house. A cramped kitchen, hidden also by a faded curtain, was to the rear and the equally tiny bathroom without a bath – there was room, just, for a pink-tiled shower – was through another door to the side. Out at the back, there was a little yard.

'Aunt Alice,' Marcie said. 'Blazing.'

Michael grinned at her. 'That's what happens to witches,' he said.

'Hah! That's an insult to witches. No self-respecting coven'd want Aunt Alice.'

'Oh, I don't know,' he said. 'Useful for the odd exorcism, don't you think? I mean, who needs bell, book and candle when they've got an Aunt Alice?'

Marcie laughed nervously. 'What time are you due in tomorrow?'

'Not till two, so I'll be late back. You'll need to collect the twins.'

Marcie nodded. The temping agency had phoned earlier, to say they had some work for her, but tomorrow she was free. The twins usually went with Michael to the crèche at the law centre where he worked. Somewhere along the line the dreams of big-shot lawyerdom had fallen by the wayside as the need just to earn their keep had taken their place.

Michael put his training to good use, though, working at the centre five days a week. First as volunteer giving the odd hour and now as a paid worker.

Council-run, it was always under threat of closure and sometimes the insecurity of it worried Marcie.

But it, and they, somehow struggled through.

He crossed the room towards her, leaving the twins to grumble and chatter their way into sleep. He took her hands and drew her down beside him on to the sofa.

'She still talking about calling the police?' he asked.

'Nah, knew she wouldn't, though. It's all just talk. She's still yelling about me stealing Jack's things, but,' Marcie shrugged awkwardly, 'I mean, it's not right, is it? Chucking his things away like that.'

'And now, having rescued it all, it's going to stay there, stuffed in that cupboard, is it?'

Marcie laughed. 'No, I guess not. I just don't seem to have had the time since I got back.'

'Or the inclination?'

'That either.'

She paused, listening to the twins making sleepy noises. 'It's funny, you know. Going back and seeing him like that I thought I'd feel something . . . I don't know, something more. That there'd still be all the anger. But it wasn't like that. I just felt sorry for him. Sorry for them all, really.' She reached out and grasped his hand. 'They've spent a lifetime fighting, Michael. Fighting each other till their minds are raw, and you know? I still have no idea what it's all about. What they did to each other, or someone else did. Or what *I* did.'

She shook her head, the dark curls falling forward to half cover her face.

'And you're scared of finding out,' he said. 'Or is it that you're scared of me finding out?' He pounced on her suddenly, grabbing her just under the ribs, tickling her so that she fell back, giggling.

'Is that what you're worried about, Marciella Rose Whitney? Scared dis big black mon will find his momma's secrets?'

She fought him off, beating at his chest with her fists. 'Hush, you idiot, you'll wake the monsters.' She sat up, playfully straightening her hair and clothes. 'Anyway,' she said, 'you had all my secrets years ago. Nothing left to find out.'

'All of them? Oh, I'm disappointed now. I thought at least the odd one might have got away.'

Michael was a large man, grown heavier in the years since she had been with him. He worked out when time allowed, grew muscles almost by thinking about them and with the shoulder-length dreads he'd begun to grow three years ago, and the three rings in his left ear, he looked like the kind of man Aunt Alice would have warned her about.

He wasn't black, not exactly, a white mother had taken care of that, but his skin was richly dark and his eyes brown as melted chocolate.

Michael wasn't exactly the type that blended into the background.

'I suppose I should just take a quick look,' she said. 'Sort out what's in there.'

She looked and sounded so reluctant that Michael put his arm around her. 'Make some coffee,' he said. 'I'll drag the stuff out of the cupboard. You never know, we might find all you've got is kitchen scraps and dirty washing.'

Chapter Ten

' "I'm sorry about the kittens, Marcie, but really, it's the kindest thing . . ." '

'Kittens?' Michael frowned.

Marcie sat on the old sofa, the edge of the quilt pulled over her feet and her arms wrapped around her knees.

'I must have been about, oh, I don't know, eight,' she said. 'We had this big old cat. An old tabby Aunt Alice had adopted when her owners moved. Anyway, the cat had kittens. Five of them. Two black and white. One ginger and two this funny kind of tabby brown like their mother. And then, one morning, the mother cat got hit by a car . . .'

Marcie sat at the top of the stairs listening to the adults talking in the room below.

She didn't have to listen very hard. Gran was mad. Aunt Alice was calm but obviously annoyed, and this time even Jack didn't seem to be on her side.

At eight years old, Marcie knew already that there were rules for adults and other, often incomprehensible, ones for children.

'I can't abide cruelty to animals,' Aunt Alice had declared on more than one occasion. Marcie could clearly recall times when the wrath of Aunt Alice had fallen squarely on the heads of the local children if they teased a cat or ill-treated a dog. 'I can't abide cruelty to animals.'

If that were so, Marcie wondered, her mind confused and her eyes red with crying, if that were so, then why had she been so angry with Marcie over the kittens?

It had happened that afternoon.

Marcie ran through the events in her mind, trying to make more sense of them.

She had come home from school and gone into the garden to look for Jack. And then she'd seen him.

Seen him standing beside the water butt, his hands full of mewling, wriggling scraps of fur. As Marcie watched in horror, Jack plunged them, double-handed, into the water.

'Jack! They'll drown, Granddad Jack!'

Startled, Jack had turned, one hand lifting from the water as he swung around and looked at her. The kittens in his hand, dripping, mewling pitifully, struggling for breath.

'Jack!' Marcie screamed at him this time and ran towards him, arms outstretched, hands reaching to take the kittens from his grasp.

Jack swore and she halted. Watched in horror as he cast the little animals back into the water, cursing audibly now as he swung back towards her, reaching out his hand to grasp her arm.

Marcie snatched the arm away. She spun from him and ran towards the house, crying hysterically for her gran, for Aunt Alice, for anyone to come and stop him.

And then there'd been the lectures.

Bird

Three adults, their quiet world disrupted by an unruly child, telling her that it was kindest in the end. That the mother cat was dead and the kittens too small to fend for themselves. Too small even to lap milk.

'I'd have fed them,' Marcie whispered fiercely to herself. 'I would have done it. All of them.'

You couldn't do it, Aunt Alice had insisted. Not five kittens. Five hungry mouths to feed.

But she would have, Marcie told herself. She'd have fed them all with an eye-dropper, just like she had when they'd found the hedgehog with the broken leg in the vegetable garden.

Sitting on the stairs, snuffling miserably, Marcie heard her aunt moving towards the living room door.

She half rose, clinging to the stair rail, ready for flight.

'You should never have brought her here,' Gran was saying to her father. 'You should have left the child with her mother's people. Saved us all a lot of bother.'

'She had no people. Her parents were dead and I never did know where her brother had gone. There was no one.'

'And if there had been,' Jack was saying, 'who's to say what they would have been like? Her mother was unstable enough.'

'Just like the child.'

'Don't say that!' Jack's voice was sharp and angry. 'Not my Bird. She's sensitive, that's all, But she'll learn. It was just the shock made her act that way. You know how fond she was of that damned cat.'

Alice snorted irritably. 'She won't change and she

53

won't learn, Jack. Lives in a dream world and half the time I think you're there with her.'

Her voice grew louder and Marcie heard her cross the little bit of lino close to the door. She began to move then, slipping off up the stairs and back to her bedroom, trying to control the tears and the running nose and the tightness in her chest, and hoping, in spite of everything, that Jack would come up later. Come and talk to her. Make everything all right.

'I had a dream that night. A nightmare, really, and sometimes, even now, it comes back, even after all these years.' She paused and glanced across at Michael as though to make certain he was still listening.

'I dreamed I was in the garden, watching Jack. He was standing beside the water butt, with his hands in the water, and he was smiling.

'I moved closer to him, expecting to see the kittens. I can remember knowing that this was a dream and thinking that, maybe, in my dream, I could make things different.

'As I got nearer to him I could see that something struggled beneath his hands. He was holding something down in the water, keeping the pressure on tight so that even when the thing fought hard it didn't have a hope of getting free.'

' "There's nothing to be gained by keeping unwanted things alive, Birdie. Nothing at all."

'And then it was me,' she whispered, her eyes fixed and staring. 'It was me in the water. Me struggling to get free. Not able to breathe. I couldn't even cry out. The water flooded into my mouth when I tried and the bubbles frothed all around my eyes and in my hair and I couldn't get away.'

She shook herself as though to shed the dream, but her face was very pale.

'And still you couldn't hate him,' Michael said. He didn't question it, he understood too well that you cannot hate those who also love you. Not completely. Not for ever.

'Oh no,' Marcie whispered. 'I didn't hate him then. Oh no, that came much much later.'

I should have come up to you tonight, after you had gone to bed, and explained.

I'm sorry, Marcie. I feel I've failed you and, God knows, I'd never willingly do that.

Your gran says I should be tougher with you. That it's time you grew up and realized that the world is not always a gentle place. It seems to me you know that, my Birdie, and that it's me and not your gran that taught you.

I'm sorry about the kittens, Marcie, truly I am, but it's the kindest thing . . .

Chapter Eleven

Michael couldn't sleep.

They had gone to bed late and made love quietly and tenderly, glad to be back together. Marcie had fallen asleep curled up close to him, but Michael had lain awake long afterwards, unable to quiet his thoughts.

Finally, he had slipped out of bed, pulled on jogging bottoms and an old shirt and wandered back into the living room.

The twins were sound asleep. Michael drew back the curtain that divided their closet from the main room and stood looking at them. They were so different, Liam and Hanna, even when sleeping.

Liam lay on his side, his favourite soft toy clutched tightly by the ears. The covers neat and tidy, sheets still folded back. By contrast, Hanna was sprawled upon her back, arms and legs thrown outwards as though she had fallen from a great height. Covers thrust aside and escaping through the bars of her cot.

Smiling, Michael pulled them back over her plump little body, then moved swiftly away, knowing that, if she woke, that would be the last any of them saw of sleep that night.

He sat on the sofa, switched on the table lamp and picked up a handful of the letters and photographs he and Marcie had been looking through.

Much of Marcie's childhood seemed to have been contained in those anonymous black bags and battered cardboard boxes. Marcie's birthdays, Marcie's Christmases. Holidays and trips, fairgrounds and fireworks. Jack seemed to have catalogued practically all of it in snapshots – which spoke more of love than technique – and scribbled notes. And letters, some of them no more than a couple of lines, some spreading in awkward prose over six or seven pages. Letters, undelivered, but folded neatly into envelopes, sealed and dated, left that way until Marcie's grandmother and Alice had torn them open and read the thoughts inside.

There was no doubt that Jack had loved Marciella. Loved her with a fervour that bordered on the obsessive. Reading through Jack's 'letters', only half understanding the references made in them, looking at the fastidious detail with which Jack had noted down every important moment in Marcie's life, Michael could not help but feel some faint sympathy for Mary, Jack's wife, in her desire to rid herself of such memories.

Mary and Alice and even Alec, his son, were notable only for their absence in Jack's records. Of course, Michael thought, there must be other photographs, pictures of Jack's wife and sister and son, but they were not here. Maybe, Michael thought, Mary had chosen to keep those. But there seemed to be no group photographs either. No sense of family gathering or family unity. Jack had focused on Marcie, on his Bird, it seemed, to the exclusion of those with at least equal claim upon his love and attention.

Such absolute and total love – if it could be called

that – must have been suffocating to endure. Must have been painful and hurtful to witness and to be excluded from.

Michael wondered if Jack had once loved Alec in that way. If Alec's life, recorded piece by piece, lay treasured in a dusty box.

Somehow, he didn't think so.

There *were* images that were not of Marcie, many in faded black and white. Or even older, sepia toned and ragged edged. Michael gazed at these with keen interest.

'That one's of Jack just before he married,' Marcie had told him. 'And that's of all three of them. God! don't they look young?'

They *had* been young, Michael thought. Early twenties, maybe. Alice not even that. They were in the company of about a dozen others, all crowded close so they fitted into the frame, some perched high on a haywain, some standing in front or clinging to the sides.

All were in work clothes, the women in print dresses with dropped waists, the men in collarless shirts, sleeves rolled above their elbows. Harvest, Michael supposed. There had been horses hitched to the wain, but only their tails showed, the rest cropped from the scene. Michael found it hard to imagine that this was well within living memory. The time when horses still ploughed the fields and brought the harvest in. It was so remote from anything he knew.

He sighed and put the picture down, palmed his eyes to wipe the ache from them. He was tired now, ready to sleep. He was rising to his feet when a strange sound coming from the bedroom first froze him to the spot, then sent him diving across the room.

Marcie was choking, her breath wheezing through her teeth, her hands clutching at her throat as though to pull something free, her back arching up off the bed as she writhed from side to side, gasping and struggling.

'Marcie!' Michael shouted, forgetful for once of the sleeping twins. What the hell! Was it a fit? He grabbed at her wrists, easing them from her throat. The fingers were hooked as though around a tight and choking binding.

'Marcie!'

Hanna woke and began to cry. The crying of one twin woke the other. Michael pulled harder at Marcie's hands, at her arms bent rigidly against her body and her clawed fingers hooked against her throat.

The twins began to wail.

'Wake up, Marcie! God's sake, wake up!'

He was truly scared now. Her back arched like a full-drawn bow, suddenly her legs kicked out and she seemed to convulse, the breath rasping in her throat, her body jerking against the bed.

Then she opened her eyes. He shook her, pulling the hooked fingers and calling her name. She gulped air as if she'd almost drowned and stared up at him, her eyes wide and terrified.

'It's all right,' Michael was saying. 'Marcie, it's all right.' He stared back at her, his own eyes reflecting her fear and confusion. Behind them the twins were standing in their cots, Liam crying still and Hanna yelling for her dadda.

Jane Adams

Michael didn't know who to comfort first, Marcie or the babies. He clasped his wife's hand for a moment, then went swiftly to the twins and lifted them both into his arms, carried them back to the bed.

'Are you all right?' he asked her. 'God, Marcie, I was so scared.'

She didn't reply, just sat up and reached out for Hanna, shaking her head, utterly confused.

'Dreaming,' she managed. 'I guess it was a nightmare . . . all that talk . . . Michael, what is it?'

He had frozen, half bending in the act of lowering Hanna on to the bed. As the child crawled free of his arm and landed herself in her mother's lap, he reached out slowly, a look of horror on his face, to touch the deep-bitten rope mark on Marcie's neck.

Chapter Twelve

The marks were still there the following morning, livid and angry, the twisting pattern of the rope clearly visible on her skin.

The rest of the night had brought little sleep. They had huddled together, all four of them, the twins taking up most of the bed.

'You can't go to work like that,' Michael said, watching Marcie apply concealer to the dark patches under her eyes. 'You've got to go and see the doctor.'

Marcie shook her head at him in the mirror. 'And tell him what?' she questioned. 'That I had a dream that strangled me with a rope and left the marks to prove it? He'll lock me up in a loony bin or have you arrested.'

Michael sighed. Marcie hated doctors anyway. And there was more than a little truth in what she was saying. He caught sight of himself behind her in the mirror. The image of a black Rasta trouble-maker reflected beside that of a small, scared-looking white girl. Even with his considerable skills and experience in dealing with the law, he felt he'd have one hell of a job proving that he'd had nothing to do with the marks on Marcie's neck, no matter what she said in his defence.

'Does it hurt?'

'Not as much as it looks like it ought to,' she said. 'It's a bit stiff and a bit sore, but that's about it.'

She dug around in the drawer for the tube of foundation cream she occasionally used and tried to apply it to the marks on her neck. 'Ow! That stings.'

'Best not to, love. You don't know how it'll react.'

She sighed and rummaged in her drawer once again, this time producing a blue silk scarf. She tied it, wrapped twice, around her neck. It covered most of the marks and didn't look too odd with her light summer suit.

'OK?' she asked him.

'Looks like you're hiding something,' he said, 'but yeah, I guess OK.' He paused for a moment, his eyes meeting hers in the mirror. She looked away first.

'We ought to be getting the monsters ready,' she said, moving towards the twins, who were still fast asleep on their parents' bed.

'Don't go today,' he said to her, reaching for her hands. 'We've got enough in reserve for you to miss a couple of days.'

'I have to, you know that. The trip to Jack's hasn't been cheap, and if I turn down work now at the last minute it's not going to look very good, is it?'

'OK,' he conceded, 'but take it easy. You feel sick or anything you come straight home.'

She smiled at him, squeezed his fingers lightly and then went to see to the twins.

Michael wandered out into the kitchen to start making breakfast. He was glad that he'd be driving her to work today. Dropping her off and taking the twins with him. She'd come to him at the law centre to get a lift home. He was frightened by what he had witnessed the night before, and it wasn't just the weird marks on her neck. At home, one of his foster sisters, Kate, had been epileptic. He'd seen her, several times, convulsed like that. Shaking and trembling and totally out of it. What if the stress of Jack's illness had triggered something like that in Marcie? It wasn't that the illness scared him. Kate had been just fine most of the time once they'd got her pills sorted out, but he knew how dangerous something like that could be if it went undiagnosed.

What if she had a fit while she was driving the car or crossing the road, or . . . ?

Marcie, entering the kitchen with the twins, put an end to his reverie. He managed to smile at her and lifted Hanna into her highchair.

Tonight he'd have another try at getting her to the doctor.

You haven't been here, my Birdie, not for days now. I keep asking for you, but your gran says you had to go away, tells me not to fret. Sometimes she says that I saw you yesterday, that I just forgot, but I know that's not true, my Bird. I've asked them, the doctors, the nurses, and they tell me the truth even when your gran tries to fool me.

You've got a husband, your gran says, and babies. Had to go back to them, I suppose. I can't see it, though, not you with babies or chained to some man. Your gran says you've married some big black fellow with too much hair, but I know she's just saying that. Knows how silly it sounds, but she says it anyway . . . and the winter's coming in so fast, you'd have no time

to go off and get hitched up with anyone, my Birdie.
Not with all the things you have to do, get the garden
ready for the winter.

I wish I could help you. Wish I could be there just
to watch, make sure you get things right.

We none of us always get things right . . . and I have
such dreams, my darling. Such nightmares.

She comes back to me every time I close my eyes,
and sometimes when I open them she's still standing
there, mocking me with that rope tied round her neck
and her hands fastened behind her back and her eyes
never looking at the same place two seconds together.
And sometimes, Birdie, sometimes, like in my dreams
last night, she thinks to cheat me, thinks I won't do it
to her if she changes the way she looks. But I know
different, my sweetheart. I'd know her anywhere. Hang
her just as high and watch her feet kicking at the stars.
I'd know her, Birdie, even when she wears your face.

Chapter Thirteen

Friday was Sophie Lee's party.

They had stumbled through the last two days keeping themselves overly busy with work and children and the usual activities. They'd been afraid to sleep and watched old films on TV till late, finally falling asleep on the sofa. Nothing had happened. The marks on Marcie's neck were still there but were fading fast, and it was almost possible to accept the rather frantic explanations they had come up with.

'I must have scratched myself,' Marcie had said. 'Or maybe even got tangled in the sheets.'

'Psychosomatic,' Michael had stated emphatically.

That made her laugh. 'So I imagined it and made it happen?'

'Well, no, not exactly. But you remember that programme we watched, you know, on stigmata and that sort of thing? There was that case where that man suddenly got rope marks round his wrists. They said that his body must be remembering some previous trauma. Then found out he'd had something happen to him when he was a kid.'

'No one ever put a rope round my neck.'

'No, but with Jack so obsessed with that woman . . .'

They ran the problem ragged, then tried to forget about it. Michael was most relieved to find her so normal afterwards. No sign of the frightening seizure he had witnessed. She had slept fitfully for the last two nights, but without incident.

Maybe that was an end to it. Strange things happen to a stressed body, even stranger things to a stressed mind.

With a sense of rather cowardly relief, Michael let the matter slip, knowing Marcie wanted to do the same.

By Friday night they were both more ready for their beds than for a party. Michael had swapped an evening session for his usual Saturday morning slot, so at least he knew he could sleep late. And they were staying over at his foster mother's house, the one place in the world Michael knew that phantasms and fears would have no place. They'd be out on their ear in a blink.

Anyway, this was Sophie Lee's party. Michael would as willingly have missed this as he would chop off his hand.

Sophie Lee was Adele's mother. Adele was Michael's foster mother. Sophie Lee had been grandmother to all of Adele's children, those she'd fostered for a few weeks or those, like Michael and his brother Leroy, who'd been with her for years.

And today Sophie Lee was eighty. Maybe it was knowing about Jack's illness that brought it home to him, but Michael was acutely aware that there might not be too many birthdays left.

Adele's house was a large three-storey Victorian villa about a mile from where they lived. They were late arriving. Parking wasn't easy in Adele's road and they had walked from their flat after Michael had got home from work. The party was already lively. Music leaked out into the street and a warm blast of noise, perfume and the aroma of food enveloped them when Adele opened the front door. The twins had disappeared within minutes. Marcie glimpsed them in the front living room with some of the older kids dancing to Grand Master Flash, the heavy base beat clear enough even for the little ones to get the sense of. Sophie Lee was in the back room, shielded behind a heavy door that let only the base beat get through. Mantovani shimmered through the quieter air, helped along by the muffled rap. Mantovani with a base attitude, Marcie thought. She bent to hug Sophie and was pulled down beside the old woman, engulfed in arms that were as powerful as they were stick-thin, and a mix of three or four different perfumes. Presents, no doubt, Marcie thought. Sophie Lee would have had to try them all.

'Marciella, my love, and how are you?' Sophie Lee was asking her. 'And that grandfather of yours. How is he? He still living?'

Marcie glanced across at Michael and settled herself comfortably on the narrow sofa next to the old lady, preparing for a good long gossip. Michael smiled back, noting that the tension was gone from her for the first time in weeks. Since she'd first heard that Jack was ill.

'Leroy was lookin' for you,' someone shouted over. 'Think he's with Adele.'

Michael nodded thanks, bent to kiss and hug his grandmother, then went off to find his brother and Adele.

*

'The first time I came to this place,' Michael was saying, 'I was all of eight years old and felt like the weight of the whole world was landed on my shoulders.

'I can remember the smell of the place even now. Adele was cooking dinner and the air was full of rich, spicy scents drifting out on the heat from the kitchen. Leroy was holding on to my hand so tight our fingers had got slick and sweaty and the palms of our hands all sticky with what I hoped was just chocolate. Leroy was just five. Always poking his fingers into something and you never could tell.

'I remember looking up at this great big house with its top windows sticking out from the roof and wondering what it would be like and if, this time, we'd be staying.

'If we'd want to stay.

'This was the third place we'd been dumped in as many weeks. That might not sound fair, but it was the way we felt, Leroy and me. Like there was no one in the world gave a shit about us. And I'd made him this promise. Eight years old and I'd made the biggest promise I could ever think of making. We'll always stick together, I'd told him. Ain't no one goin' to take my bro away from me.

'I'd heard so many things about kids being split up and sent to different places and I was so worried that would happen to us. Just so scared.

'I knew Leroy's dad wasn't my dad. I knew as well that my mom'd spent the best part of the last two years trying to keep us one step away from him. I was just terrified they'd let Leroy go, to his real dad, and that would be it for the both of us.

'Then we came here, to Adele's place. She'd got other kids here and there wasn't that much space left so she asked us if we'd mind bunking in the top room, right up in the roof.

'Mind! That room was magic. She showed it to us, right up at the top of these narrow stairs. Easy to defend from anyone we didn't want, and off on the first landing down there was a door to the fire escape that led down the side of the building and out the back way. I knew then that if things did go wrong for Leroy and me, we could just flit out that way and through the yard. I could keep my promise.

'But it didn't do to look too eager. You know, look too eager and they know they've got you. So I looked round the little room, all casual, like, playing it real cool and I said, "Well, I guess it'll do," when really, deep inside, I was singing. This funny little room with its wooden floor and bright red rugs looked like the deck of a ship and with its twin beds pushed into the sloping corner under the eaves I knew me and Leroy could pretend like we were bears in a cave or pirates in a prison cell or anything else that we might want.

'But I still played it real cold and dumped our stuff on the floor next to the beds, looked all around me like I was inspecting the place, you know, swaggering about like I'd got a real big dose of attitude. The big man.

'Then Leroy here went and spoilt it all, tugging at my sleeve. "I wanna wee, Mikie. I need to do it now!"

'And there I was, Mr Cool, grabbing him by the hand

Jane Adams

and yelling at Adele to tell me quick where the toilet was and as we went charging down the stairs trying to get you there before you peed yourself. And I could hear Adele and that social worker woman we'd come with – what was her name?'

'Mrs Simpson – call me Naomi,' Leroy supplied, mimicking the woman's clipped accent.

'Oh yeah, Naomi Simpson . . . I could hear the pair of them laughing at me and my face was getting real hot and . . .'

'You were mad as hell. Mr Cool! It was weeks before you eased up on Adele for laughing at you.'

Marcie giggled happily, her mood softened by a little too much wine and the atmosphere of Adele's house. She'd heard the story before, many times, slightly different versions from Adele and from Sophie Lee, but she was more than content to listen to it again.

She and Michael and his brother had planted themselves halfway up the first flight of stairs. The kids were still dancing in the front living room, Sophie Lee with them now, Hanna in her arms managing to be half asleep despite the Gangsta rap pounding through the floor.

The door to the second living room was open and Mantovani played on, his shimmering strings competing valiantly against the back-beat and the stomped-out lyrics.

Liam was dozing on Marcie's lap, his head lolling against her arm. She could barely hear it above the noise, but he was snoring contentedly.

She got up, a little unsteadily. 'Best put this one to

bed,' she said, turning to go up the stairs. 'See if you can prise Hanna away from Sophie, will you?'

'OK,' Michael said. He bent to kiss his son, then went off to face the music in the front room.

Hanna had taken longer to settle, objecting to the notion that she might be tired. 'Sophie party,' was still obstinately being declared even as her eyes were closing and her chubby limbs relaxing into sleep.

Marcie sat with the twins until she was certain they wouldn't wake. Then stayed a little longer to chat to Kate, Michael's foster sister, as she came in to lay her own small child in the other bed. A couple of the older ones, children of the generation just ahead of Michael, would be camping out on airbeds on the floor.

Judging by her previous visits here, Marcie doubted either she or Michael would get much sleep themselves. Sitting and talking well past the early hours was just something that happened when the clan gathered at Adele's house.

Later, she made her way back downstairs. The loud music in the front room had been muted now and altered in mood, the sounds drifting out through the half-closed door moody and romantic.

In the back room people were gathered in loose groups, chatting and laughing and teasing. Michael and Leroy sat next to Sophie Lee. A couple of others with whom they had shared bits of childhood had flopped on the floor close by.

Patrick Eaton, who was minister at the local Baptist

church, and a couple of neighbours Marcie knew by sight sat talking near the door.

Adele was seated at the now-cleared dining table, shuffling a pack of cards between her hands.

Marcie had once asked Adele just how many children she had fostered. Adele remembered them all in detailed order, even the ones who'd only been with her a week or so. She kept in touch with most, some only at a distance. Some, like Michael and his brother, had never quite moved out, even if they had moved away. And there'd been those who hadn't quite made it through, who'd slipped through the gaps even in Adele's tightly meshed net. One ended in prison. One turned up cold and swollen in the river. Others who'd just never pulled their lives together after a rocky start, even with Adele and Sophie Lee to help them.

She smiled at Marcie and beckoned her over to the table, spreading the cards in a perfect arc on the cloth.

'I am not seeing this, Adele,' Patrick Eaton said to her, his eyes laughing as he sipped at his drink.

'Don't you fret there, Patrick, you can save my soul again on Sunday.' She smiled at Marcie. 'Come and sit down, child. It's a long time since I read for you.'

'And the last time you did I had twins.' Marcie laughed.

She sat down at the table, not sure that she wanted this, but excited all the same. Adele's cards with their strange pictures held a fascination. Gran and Aunt Alice took a very dim view of anything that smacked of fortune-telling or the occult. They visited their church every Sunday, paid their debts to the unknown that way.

72

Anything else was, at best, frivolous and leading to idle-
ness; at worst, probably even wicked.

Michael had once told Marcie that Sophie's mother
had been an obeah priestess. Sophie Lee herself was a
fervent Baptist, rejoicing with a completeness and
pleasure that had, at first, shocked Marcie. And Adele,
well, Adele managed to pick and choose and take the
bits she liked.

With an expert movement, Adele swept the cards
back into a neat pile and handed them to Marcie.

'I should be stopping you doing this,' Patrick said as
Marcie, less expertly, shuffled the thick pack of cards.

'Ah, Patrick, this is nothing. I could be sitting here
studying the entrails of a chicken, like my grandma used
to. Then where would you be?'

'Hoping you'd roasted the rest of it,' Sophie Lee put
in swiftly.

'Too true. Too true.'

Marcie spread the cards face down in a rather untidy
arc across the table.

She'd wanted to go to a fortune-teller once. They'd
been to the seaside and walked back through the funfair
so that Marcie could ride the carousel. 'Descendant of
Gypsy Rose Lee,' the sign had said, all painted up with
roses and birth signs and with pictures of satisfied –
famous satisfied – customers stuck in the window. A
woman in 'Hollywood Gypsy' dress stood in the
doorway.

'Please, Gran! Please!' Marcie had begged.

Gran had been outraged.

'You're really not old enough, Marcie,' Alice had said, trying to placate.

'Ha!' Gran had spat. 'Old or not, she's having nothing to do with bloody gypsies.'

Marcie had been fascinated to hear her grandmother swear.

'There were gypsies where we used to live,' Jack had said gently, a sadness in his voice.

'Gypsies!' Gran had repeated with an angry shake of her head. She had walked ahead then, scowling, and the carousel had been left behind, unridden and forgotten.

'Pick a card,' Adele was telling her. 'A card for where in your life you are now.'

Hesitantly, Marcie reached out and chose one, lay it face up in the centre of the table.

A horned figure with goat eyes looked back at her.

'Obsession,' Adele said slowly. 'The devil is a card of slavery, to an idea, a person, something you should have long ago outgrown.'

Marcie looked nervously at her, the rosy effects of the wine fading fast.

'Now cross the card and see the cause,' Adele said quietly.

'King of cups.'

'A man who draws you in with loving and fondness.' Adele shook her head. 'Alone, this would be a good card. Not the strongest of men, easily led and easily influenced, but loving and kind. Together with the devil card this is dangerous, my love.'

Marcie drew four more cards, placing them top and bottom, left and right, to form a cross.

'In your past was strength that went unquestioned,' Adele told her. 'See the emperor. Then came the tower and your world was rocked on its foundations, torn to the ground by an act of God.'

'That's close to blasphemy, Adele.'

'Is lightning not talked about as an act of God, Patrick? And here,' she held up the card. 'Lightning strikes the tower and brings it down. And now,' she continued, 'there are choices to be made. The lovers. The old ways and the new, and you must do the choosing. And the choice must be made swiftly and wisely. The sword and balance of justice is coming to or for you soon.'

'I don't think I like this, Adele.' Marcie looked across at the older woman, panic in her eyes.

'Just four more cards to lay,' Adele said soothingly. 'Let's see how you solve this, sugar.'

Reluctantly, Marcie drew the other cards. 'Death' came next.

'Great changes,' said Adele. 'At first you may not like them, but life is full of change.'

The two of swords. 'A divided house. Divorce and sadness. Cutting off the pain that lay in the past.'

Ace of swords. 'A new cycle begins. Something that absorbs you. That demands. That cuts through the bindings and forces you to see clearly.' She paused, then pointed to the final card.

'Judgement, Marcie. The rising of the dead. Ghosts that speak. Something must be finished before you can begin again.'

Marcie had grown pale. Maybe it was just the wine.

Jane Adams

Maybe she was overtired, but suddenly this was too much. Too close to the events of the last few days.

'What's Michael told you?' she asked, her voice soft with the effort to keep it steady.

Adele shook her head. 'Michael has told me nothing, sugar, and remember, you chose each card yourself. I did nothing but tell you the meanings.'

Glancing across the room, Marcie met Michael's eyes and knew Adele was telling the truth. He looked just as baffled and she was painfully aware that she had become the focus for the whole room.

'It's Jack,' she whispered. 'There's this woman that keeps coming back, haunts him. I don't know if it's what you'd call a ghost or if it's just in his mind, but he says she hanged herself, or he was there when it happened.'

She paused, took a deep breath and glanced at Michael once more as though looking for approval, then unwrapped the blue silk from around her neck.

'Then a couple of nights ago,' she said, 'this happened to me.'

76

Chapter Fourteen

Strange how some things stay with you no matter what else in your life you might forget.

Some things remain fresh and clear in memory. Like that afternoon with her. That summer afternoon.

It had been so hot. Almost at the end of harvest and so many extra hands needed everywhere, it was easy to slip away. Everyone would just assume we had been somewhere else, helping in another field or another barn and it was so damned hot.

She stripped down to her petticoat and lay back in the dappled shade with her eyes closed and a half-smile curling across her mouth. I knew that she was watching me, dark eyes peeking out under those long lashes.

I felt awkward. Scared, almost. Like the first time we did it. Winter then, when we first made love in the darkest corner of Manx's barn. It was cold and I held her tight, my hands all over her, trying to keep her warm. The centre of us, where our bodies met, burning. Slick with sweat. My back and Rebekkah's arms rising in goose flesh.

Afterwards, we had to dress quickly. Then we lay there, my coat on the straw and hers spread over us, trying to stay warm.

But in the summer it was different.

She'd wait for me and catch me outside in the sunlight. Tease, with a touch of her tongue across her lip or a sideways look. And I went with her. God, I lost count of the times. I warned her, so many times I warned her that we should stop. But that wasn't Rebekkah's way. Oh no, the fear of someone finding out made it all the better. She would bite and tear at my flesh like she wanted to get inside me. Wear my skin. Take my bones for her own. Bite out my tongue and use it to speak my words for me.

I told her, that summer day, that it would be the last, and she just smiled.

'I'll dance at your wedding, Jack,' she said, 'but you needn't think it will change a thing between us.'

Then she took off her petticoat, slipping it from her shoulders, and let it fall to the floor. Stood there, naked and barefoot, with that black hair falling all around her face and on to her breasts and the sun golden on her skin.

'Come here, Jack,' she said, calling me to her like the witch she was. Beckoning. Her eyes laughed at me.

And then, God help me, I went to her.

It was Adele's Tarot that had led them back here. The talk had gone on long into the night. Questions and answers and speculations. Slowly, Marcie had begun to feel better. If people she liked and trusted could discuss all aspects of something very frightening in this easy, rational way then maybe it wasn't so crazy after all.

They had reached no conclusions, just come to the inevitable decision that Marcie must come back and talk to Jack – for her own peace of mind, and for Jack's. She had to end whatever needed ending before she could get on with her life. And, if it turned out that there was nothing to end, that all of this was caused by a sensitive imagination and love for an old man whose drugged mind was apt to ramble, well, then that would be that.

But if there were something more . . .

So. Sunday morning saw Marcie, Michael and the twins standing in the car park at the hospice, preparing to go inside.

'Their car isn't here,' Marcie said, glancing around. With luck, Alice and her gran would be at church and Alec, Marcie knew, rarely visited Jack alone.

'What if they've said something?' Marcie niggled. 'Told the desk I can't visit him?' She squared her shoulders and took the handles of the pushchair as though it offered some divine protection. 'Only one way to find out, I suppose.'

She need not have worried. Her grandmother's desire to save face had protected her from any problems. They recognized her at reception.

'Oh, he will be pleased to see you. And this is your family?' The woman smiled at Michael and bent to make a fuss of the twins. 'He's kept on asking for you, poor old soul. Though I expect you know that. Your grandmother said you didn't want to go, that you'd no holiday left.'

She cast a sympathetic look in Marcie's direction. 'So hard, isn't it, trying to balance everything when you've got so many demands?'

Marcie smiled and nodded as she signed them all in, writing down the registration of the car and their names.

'Is he still in the same place?' she asked.

'Yes, dear. You know the way, don't you?'

They made their way down the long corridor. It was bright with pictures and painted in a soft shade of peach. A thick green carpet dulled the sound of their feet.

'Doesn't look like a hospital,' Michael commented.

'It's not, really,' Marcie reminded him, 'but it is nice here.'

They turned into a side ward and Marcie paused. 'They've moved him next to the window,' she said. 'He'll like that.' For a moment she hesitated, then gripped the pushchair handles tighter and marched over to the bed.

Jack smiled, a wide, toothless grin that spread even wider as she lifted the twins on to the bed.

'Babies,' he whispered. 'Little tiddlers. Your gran said . . . but I didn't believe her.' He frowned suddenly as he caught sight of Michael. 'Who's he?'

'This is Michael, my husband,' Marcie said.

'Husband!' Jack almost spat the word, his face reddening slightly, his hands moving in agitation. He looked away deliberately, staring out at the tall trees and blue sky.

Marcie stiffened angrily. 'Jack, we've all come to see you,' she said, then waited uncertainly for the old man to give some clue that he had even heard, to make some response.

Then, 'They're pretty bairns,' he said reluctantly, adding with sudden strength, 'God, take them outside, man. It stinks of death and dying in here. You want them breathing that muck?'

Michael glanced at Marcie. He'd not expected a warm welcome, Marcie had told him of Jack's rather random prejudices. But unfriendly though the old man's greeting was, their reception could have been much worse.

The twins were already restless. Michael fished in the baby bag hanging on the pushchair and pulled out a soft red and yellow ball.

'We'll go into the garden,' he said. 'I won't go far.'

Marcie nodded and watched as Michael led the twins away.

'You're not being very polite, Jack.'

'Privilege of age,' he said. 'Anyway, why should I be? Got you pregnant, did he? Just like . . .'

'Jack! I said that was enough. I've not come all this way to argue. You want a fight, pick one with Gran.'

For a moment or two both were silent. 'You sound better,' Marcie said at last. 'More like your old self.'

'She said you'd had to go back to work,' Jack complained. 'Said you'd got kids and a husband. Just another of her lies.'

Marcie sighed. The fight that had brought colour to Jack's cheeks and a light back into his eyes seemed to have faded suddenly as though it took too much strength, and he had now slipped even further back.

'They need me, Jack. My family. Gran and Aunt Alice don't want me here. They think I upset you too much.'

'Upset me, Birdie? How could you upset me?'

He was drifting again, Marcie realized. For a moment

she glared suspiciously at him, wondering just how much of this present vagueness was for real or induced by drugs and illness. How much was just convenient for Jack? She leaned back in the chair and closed her eyes.

'I've been having some strange dreams, Jack,' she said quietly, deciding that she didn't have time to work around the problem.

'Always did, Birdie. Always did.'

'I dreamed . . . I dreamed about that woman, Jack. That woman you say comes to you. Watches you.'

Jack said nothing. Marcie opened her eyes and looked at him. He had turned his head away from her, was staring towards the entrance to the ward. Alec stood there, his face set and tense.

Marcie rose slowly, her eyes fixed on his. 'Good morning, Da.'

'What are you doing here?'

'Visiting Jack. You?'

Alec strode over to the bed and grabbed Marcie by the arm, drawing her aside. 'What right do you think you have?'

'Every right!' She shook him off. 'Oh, forget it, Da, there's no audience here now. You don't have to play the hero for them.'

She glanced back at the bed, but Jack seemed to be paying no attention to them. Marcie's anger bubbled into words.

'You treated me like shit, Da! You expect me to accept that?' she whispered furiously.

Alec glared at her. 'And you stole from us,' he returned. 'Those things weren't yours.'

'And they weren't yours either. Yours or Gran's or Alice's. They were *Jack*'s.'

'And that makes it all right, does it? Have you any idea how upset your gran was?'

'Do you know how little I care?'

She shook her head, aware that the last statement was at least a partial lie. Of course she cared. She'd had a whole childhood's worth of caring for what her family said and did and it was a habit hard to break.

'I'm sorry, Da,' she said softly, 'but what option did I have? I couldn't let her throw Jack's things away, just because he wasn't there to keep them.'

'Jack's things,' Alec repeated. He sounded sad and frustrated, she thought. 'Jack's this. Jack's that. God almighty, Marcie . . .' He broke off, frowning as a movement at the window caught his eye. 'Who's this?' he demanded, much as Jack had done.

Michael stepped into the ward, glancing back as he did so to check on the twins, who were picking daisies on the lawn. He'd tied his locks back with a band of yellow, red and green and wore a faded T-shirt and washed-out blue jeans with hi-top trainers.

'This is Michael,' Marcie told him. 'I'm married to him, remember?' She sighed deeply. 'Can we stop arguing for just a minute, Da, so you can say hello? Meet your grandkids?'

Startled by the thought, Alec stared out at Liam and Hanna, watching as their tiny fingers pulled the heads off daisies. It seemed suddenly to deflate him. He took a step forward as though to go outside. Then changed his mind.

'It's good of you to come,' he said to Michael, remembering his manners and determined to make an effort. 'I mean, yes, good of you to come. You'd better leave, though, Marcie. Your gran was going to get a lift from someone at church. I said I'd meet them here. I'm sure you want to be gone before they arrive.'

Marcie stiffened. 'I wanted to talk to Jack,' she said.

'Jack doesn't look like he's up to talking.'

Marcie looked across at the old man. He seemed to be sleeping, his mouth open, a tiny stream of spittle dribbling from the side. She knew her father was right. It would take time to learn anything from Jack, and, no, she didn't want to be around when her aunt and grandmother arrived.

'Who was Rebekkah?' she asked.

'What? Who was . . . ?' Alec was caught off-guard by her change of tack.

'She was someone Jack knew,' Marcie continued. 'In the war, perhaps. I think maybe she was hanged.'

'Oh!' Alec's face cleared. 'Her,' he said, as though it didn't matter. 'That didn't happen in the war, Marcie. That's just Jack off his head again. Rebekkah was someone Jack and your gran knew. She got herself murdered. Hanged by her husband, I believe.' He glanced back at where Jack lay. 'God! But he goes on. Hours at a time. Gets so you can't stand it.'

He shifted uncomfortably as though embarrassed by such an admission of weakness on his part. Then moved back on to more secure ground. 'Your gran and Alice were really upset by what you did.'

'Oh, belt up, Da. Isn't it time you owned up to how much you resent being under their thumbs?'

She said no more then, neither did she listen to Alec's half-hearted attempts to bluster. Michael stood in the doorway while Marcie got the twins and coaxed them back into their pushchair, accepting the daisy heads and stalks with an enthusiasm that blocked Alec out completely. Michael nodded curtly to Alec and followed his wife back down the ward.

Alec stood, arms limply at his side, and watched them go.

They think I don't hear them arguing. Think I don't know how much they quarrel amongst themselves or how much trouble I've been giving them, lying here like this, not doing my fair share.

I thought I heard my Birdie a little while ago, talking to me, telling me about her dreams the way she used to when she was just a little thing. Must have been Mary going on about babies. Must have dreamed about them being here. Little coffee-coloured bairns. Pretty as pictures, sitting on my bed.

It's late in life to be seeing angels. Dusky little angels with curly heads and big brown eyes. Just like my first-born. Brown eyes and curly hair and dead as my Rebekkah.

Sunlight on her skin like warm honey.

God above! But I'd never known such cold, not even in the deep of winter. Desert cold. Clear skies and stars like diamonds scattered on blue velvet. Like a rag

*doll, she was, hanging there. Hands tied so she couldn't
fight it. The rope pulled tight around her neck.*

*It wasn't my fault, woman! No, no, I'd have set it
right. Wasn't my fault the knot slid tight against your
throat. I'd have set it right, one snap and that would
have finished it.*

*Not left you choking with your feet kicking against
the stars.*

Kicking against the stars.

'Rebekkah?'

Mary halted beside the bed, her words of cheerful
greeting frozen on her lips. Alec laid a hand on her arm.

'Mam, don't upset yourself. He doesn't know what
he's saying.'

She turned away, pacing swiftly back down the ward,
with Alec almost running behind her to keep up.

'He doesn't mean it, Mam. He sees her, she haunts
him, Mam. It means nothing.'

'You're starting to sound like that daughter of yours,'
Mary told him angrily, her voice stiff with unshed tears.
'And how should you know what your father means and
what he doesn't? What does any of it mean to you?'

'Is it my fault if I don't understand? Well, is it? Tried
talking to me, have you? Once in a while you might have
thought about confiding in me. Letting me in instead of
hiding behind this pretence that everything in the past is
dead and gone and none of my concern.'

Mary looked at him, her eyes a mixture of pity and
contempt. 'And so it is, boy,' she said.

'No!' Alec almost shouted at her. 'No, it's not, and neither is it none of my business, Mam.' She had halted for a moment and he reached out his hand, groping for hers. 'If it's all past and gone, why do you keep crying every time anyone mentions this woman? Keep pushing me away every time I try to help?' He paused, then said softly, 'Who was she, Mam? Who was she?'

Mary had allowed her hand to rest in his, had seemed to be listening to him, but now she snatched it away.

'It's none of your concern!' she snapped angrily. 'Not now, not ever.'

Chapter Fifteen

Rather than waste the rest of their Sunday they travelled some twenty miles further on, to the seaside.

This was a first for the twins. They spent the day building castles on the sand, paddling in the shallowest of water and finally, when the incoming tide brought a chill east wind, retreated to the fairground and hooked ducks to win furry monkeys that Marcie would not normally have given house room to.

On Sunday, Marcie buried her hurt and her anger in a day of very childlike pleasure. Monday was more difficult. Tuesday also, though the days passed reasonably enough. Work, home, play with the twins, the usual routines and actions, comforting in their demands. Nothing strange or frightening to disturb them, and the marks on Marcie's neck continued to fade.

Jack was barely mentioned. Alec and her aunt and grandmother not at all. Only once did she pick up the bundle of photographs – the oldest ones sorted from the others – finally gazing thoughtfully into the faces of those standing beside the haywain.

'I wonder if one of these is Rebekkah,' she said.

There were five women in the picture. Two they knew. A young Mary and an even younger Alice. The other three were just as youthful, just as hopeful, on that hot summer afternoon.

'It's a nasty way to die,' Michael commented, and Marcie nodded, looking into those forgotten faces, trying to imagine any one of them with a rope around her neck, an agony of fear in her eyes.

Wednesday, Marcie worked late, dashing home for a quick snack with Michael and telling him that she'd been offered overtime. Stocktaking, double time. They couldn't afford for her to turn it down.

Michael drove her back to work, then read to the twins and saw them into bed, tucking the Little Bear book that was Liam's current favourite in beside his small son.

Then he sat down to make some headway into the stack of case notes he had brought home with him from the law centre. People threatened with bankruptcy, eviction, trouble with neighbours, with landlords, with husbands and wives and local dogs.

Michael often pondered wryly at the way his once-cherished dreams of becoming a fully fledged QC had diminished into this morass of everyday problems. This never-ending stream of folk, out of their depth and needing vital but very often quite simple guidance. Sometimes he'd talk about getting his studies back on line, but the reality of their finances meant he didn't have the freedom to move from what he was doing.

He was buried in the minutiae of a tenancy agreement when Alec arrived.

'One of your neighbours let me in,' Alec said, as Michael opened the flat door and stared in amazement at the stocky figure standing on his threshold. 'Told me this was your door.'

'Marcie isn't here,' Michael told him. 'She had to work late tonight.'

'Oh,' Alec said. 'Oh, I never thought . . . should have rung first, I suppose, but it was, well, an impulse, I guess you'd call it.'

Michael raised an eyebrow. 'It's a three-hour drive,' he said. 'That was quite some impulse.'

Alec shuffled his feet, uncertain of his welcome. 'Maybe I should go,' he said. 'Do you know when . . . ?'

Michael shook his head. 'You'd better come in,' he told Alec, standing aside. 'Just keep the noise down, will you? Hanna sleeps real light.'

He went through to the kitchen to make coffee, standing with his back to the counter and his arms folded whilst the kettle boiled, wondering what on earth had brought Alec here. Considering whether he should be openly annoyed or let the other man take the lead first and see where the conversation went.

When he brought their coffee mugs through, Alec was standing with the curtain of the little alcove drawn aside, looking down at the sleeping children. His expression, the sadness of it, took Michael by surprise.

'I remember her as a baby,' he said, moving away and letting the curtain fall. 'Such a tiny, scrawny little mite. Jack thought she was the most wonderful thing in the world.'

He took the coffee and stood awkwardly as though uncertain of what to do with himself.

'Marcie told me her mother died in a car crash,' Michael said. 'That was why you brought her home to Jack.'

Alec nodded slowly, then sat down before speaking, curling both hands around the mug as though he felt the cold. 'She died,' he said stiffly. 'Took a bend too fast and fell close on a hundred feet on to the rocks.' He bowed his head sadly. 'Italy, up in the mountains. She should have known better, but she always did drive too fast. Marcie never really asked about her,' he added. 'Jack made sure of that. Never gave her space or need to know.'

'You could have told her,' Michael commented. 'She's your child.'

'My child,' he echoed. 'My child, was she? You don't know Jack.'

Michael regarded him thoughtfully for a moment. It occurred to him how little Marcie talked about Alec. When she had spoken of family, it had almost always been about Jack.

Alec drained the still-hot coffee then sat, staring down into his mug. He seemed to have given up on the conversation.

What had brought him here? Michael wondered again. He was clearly very disturbed about something. There was none of the semi-arrogant bluster Michael had witnessed on the previous Sunday. By contrast, he looked lost and bewildered.

The slight sound of Liam turning over attracted Alec's attention. He looked up. 'They're beautiful,' he said, with longing in his voice.

'I guess so was Marcie,' Michael said.

'Marcie,' Alec said, tilting his empty coffee cup towards him. 'Marcie. She was never mine, you know. Not from the moment I brought her home.'

Jane Adams

'You made that choice.'

'Choice!' Alec almost shouted, then glanced guiltily towards where the twins were sleeping and dropped his voice. 'I had no choice. What else could I do? I knew nothing about babies. Nothing. And when her mother died . . . there was no one.'

He glanced up sharply, looking properly at Michael for the first time. Meeting the steadiness of his gaze. 'You don't think much of me, do you?'

'No,' Michael said shortly. 'I don't, but I don't think you rate yourself very highly either.'

'What do you know?' Alec bristled. But it was all posture with no muscle behind it. He leaned back in the chair and sighed. 'These days I don't even think about it much,' he said.

Michael watched the other man for a little longer, but he seemed unwilling to say more. He rose, went across and eased the cup from Alec's hand, then went to make more coffee. He started to talk while he reboiled the kettle, and measured sugar and coffee into the cups. Continued as he came back through to the living room.

'It was when she was pregnant, that's when she told me about that other baby and why she ran away from you and Jack. You did wrong by her, Alec. All of you. What had she done that was so bad? Fallen in love, or thought she had. Had sex with her boyfriend and been daft enough and innocent enough to end up pregnant. Did she do anything that deserved what you did to her?'

He paused, waited for an answer but got none. 'Just what did you hope to prove, Alec? Show her what big men you both were? God's sake! She was just a kid.

Scared out of her wits as it was and all you could do was treat her like she'd committed some terrible crime.'

'What she did was wrong. She let us down. We'd taught her better than that.'

'What she did was stupid. Misguided, maybe, but if we all have to pay so hard for the dumb things we do when we're no more than kids it's a poor future we've got, don't you think?'

'What do you know?' Alec fired at him again. It seemed to be a favourite phrase. 'We'd taught her better than that but she showed no self-respect or self-restraint. And that boy. Do you think a boy like that could ever be good enough for Marcie?'

'You're contradicting yourself, Alec,' Michael goaded. 'You can't have her on a pedestal *and* screwing in the gutters. Doesn't happen.'

Alec rose to his feet abruptly enough to spill the coffee in his newly filled mug. Whatever action he had planned was foiled by the rush of scalding liquid slopping over his hand.

'Damn and blast it.' He stared about him, distractedly.

He was more worried about the coffee spilling on the rug, Michael realized, than he was about the insults that had precipitated his reaction.

'Put your hand under the cold tap,' Michael said, pointing to the kitchen. 'I'll get a cloth.'

Mopping up gave them both a little breathing space. Alec seemed calmer when he sat down once more.

'It was Jack's idea,' Alec said, as though that explained it all.

'Don't suppose you thought to say no to him.'

'You don't say no to Jack. Or you didn't. And my mother . . . I never knew anyone refuse her. Lord!' he said, looking up sharply, 'that sounds pathetic, doesn't it?'

'A little, yes.' He caught Alec's expression and added swiftly, 'Hey, man, I ain't about to start badmouthin' you again. Too rough on Momma's carpets.'

He laughed, this time at Alec's expression. 'Look,' he said. 'It's not my place to pass judgement, only when that judgement affects Marcie. Then I think I got the right.'

Alec nodded slowly, then spoke softly, the words dragged painfully from memory.

'It was a cold night,' he said. 'We really thought, I guess, that we were doing the right thing . . .'

Just past Christmas and the nights had been very dark and very cold, full of snowclouds blocking out the stars.

Marcie had been sick for days, miserably so. Tummy bug, Aunt Alice had said, but even then Gran hadn't been too sure. Marcie, regular as clockwork, had missed her period.

It had taken several hours of argument, of anger and tears and threats of violence to get the truth from her.

'Who is he?' Mary had demanded over and over again, even before Marcie had finally admitted the truth.

'Once, I swear it, Gran, it was only once.'

'Once or many times. What does it matter? You sinned, girl. Sinned.'

'It's not a sin. It's not. I love him, Gran, I love him.'

'Love! You're a child. Fifteen years old. What do you know about love? I'll have the police on him. I'll have him in court and you'll have to tell all of them, judge and jury and everyone who cares to listen just what you've done.'

'I only did it once, Gran. Truly I did. I didn't think anything would happen. Not just once. I didn't even like it, Gran.'

They'd been empty threats, of course. Mary would have never faced the public humiliation involved in calling in the police, but Marcie had been too distraught to think of that. Finally the hours of harassment and anger had paid off. Marcie had given them the name of the boy and the places they had met and told them everything that they had ever done.

Mary had been doubly outraged. 'The Simpson boy! That good-for-nothing layabout. Why, Marcie? Why?'

'I love . . . I like him, Gran. He made me laugh. It was fun just . . . just fun going out with him and then it got serious, you know . . .'

Gran's expression told her that, no, she didn't know. *Wouldn't* know.

'You're old!' Marcie finally yelled at them. 'You don't remember what it's like to be young and to *feel* things.'

Mary had slapped her then, hard enough to send her spinning into the door. She fell to the floor winded and shocked, whimpering softly.

'Now go to your room,' Mary told her. 'Go to your room and don't come down until I say you can.'

Marcie had fled, racing up the stairs and slamming

her bedroom door before collapsing on the bed in tears. Even then there was no peace for her. Aunt Alice came up only moments later and began to empty Marcie's wardrobe and drawers.

'What are you doing?'

'Making sure you don't have any stupid ideas,' Alice said. 'Get your nightdress on and get into bed.'

She stood over her until Marcie had done as she was told, then left, taking her clothes and shoes away with her.

'You'll thank us for this one day,' she told her as she left the room.

Outside it was five below freezing, the sky still heavy with unfallen snow.

'You kept me shut away in that room for nearly five days,' Marcie said softly. 'Brought me food I couldn't eat and only let me out to be sick in the bathroom because Gran was scared I'd make a mess of my room. Then you let me get dressed that morning and put me in the car, took me away to that place where they didn't know or care whether or not I wanted to keep my baby.'

'You were too young,' Alec told her earnestly. 'Marcie, you were fifteen years old.'

'Old enough to get pregnant,' she said softly. 'Old enough to have talked about it.' She came closer to Alec, her eyes burning with a sadness and hatred that Michael had never seen before. 'How much did you pay them, Da, to do that to me without counselling or the proper consents?'

96

'You agreed to it,' Alec objected. 'You signed the forms, you agreed to it.'

'By that time, Da, I'd have agreed to anything just to get out of that room.' She shook her head slowly. 'I forgave you that. I know in your own minds you thought it was for the best, but you were wrong, Da. You were wrong.'

Michael got up from his seat and went over to kiss her. 'You hungry?' he asked. 'I'll make some tea.'

Alec had risen too, awkward now. The door was behind him and he'd not heard Marcie come in quietly, opening the door softly in case Michael had been having trouble getting the twins to sleep. She had stood, signing to Michael not to give her away, listening to Alec for several minutes, her father, staring at the floor, too tied up in his story to even notice her.

'You were wrong,' she repeated softly. 'What are you doing here?'

'I came to . . . I mean . . .' Alec shook his head. 'Been asking myself that all the way here.'

'Had a row with Gran?'

Alec started guiltily, telling Marcie that she'd hit the target.

He nodded. 'She's upset. About Jack. About you. I don't know, Birdie, I don't seem to be making a very good job of things lately.'

It was Marcie's turn to look startled. Only Jack had ever called her Bird. 'Only lately, Da?' she asked him. Seeing the intensity of hurt in his eyes, she relented a little. 'Does she know you're here?'

'God, no!' Alec's denouncement was almost comical.

'Still under Mummy's thumb,' Marcie said, then, 'Sorry, Da, I shouldn't have said that. She has got an awfully big thumb.'

Alec looked uncomfortable, but almost managed to laugh at his daughter's half-joke. 'I'll have to be getting back,' he said. 'It's a long drive.'

'There's a sofa,' Michael said, returning from the kitchen. Both Alec and Marcie looked at him in surprise.

'Thank you,' Alec said. 'But I ought to go.'

He sat down anyway and watched as Marcie checked on her children, covering Hanna gently. Michael poured tea into bright red mugs and offered biscuits. Marcie flopped down beside him on the sofa and closed her eyes, reaching automatically for Michael's hand. The atmosphere of intimacy that surrounded them took Alec by surprise. Casual touch and random affection were not something that had been on offer in his parents' house. Jack had tried, but he'd been bluff and male when Alec had really wanted tenderness and warmth – not that he'd readily put such feelings into thought. Mary had managed quick hugs and perfunctory kisses, seeing her more important duties as being those of housekeeper and maintainer of standards.

It was really only in his brief marriage that Alec had realized what he craved. Only in Jack's love of Marcie that he had really witnessed it.

'I loved your mother,' he said, blurting it out suddenly with all the force of a confession. 'Loved her so much it hurts even now to think about it.'

Marcie stared at him, not knowing what to say. It

was Michael who reached across the coffee table and clasped Alec by the hand.

'Of course you did,' he said quietly. 'That's one of the few things you've still got going for you.'

Chapter Sixteen

There were five of us – me, the Fisher brothers, Sam Nichols and Sergeant Mills – holed up in what was meant to be a safe house.

Her house.

I can remember, when she bent close to me to take my cup, the way she smelt. Clean and warm and her hair scented with sandalwood. Skin like honey, like my Becky had.

Then the shelling got closer. We heard the crashing and the screaming not more than a street away and the woman got shaky. Scared of us being found. Of what would be done to her if they discovered us in her house. So she took us out of there, her and that man she was with. Emile, I think they called him, though I never paid it that much mind . . . out into the dark, with me in the lead and Mills bringing up the rear.

She was scared-careful, I saw her checking that there was nothing left behind. I watched her as she put the cups we had been using back in the cupboard, setting everything neat. Every trace of us wiped clean away.

Backstreets that all looked the same. Tiny windows facing the world and dark gateways that led back into courtyards and alleyways. We kept to the shadows, moving like rats along the walls, nerves strung out by the fear of snipers hidden in the black gaps of the narrow windows.

There was a moon, but it was still low, hung behind the buildings. We caught glimpses of it between the broken walls where the shelling had laid open great wounds. And there was smoke, pluming up in the distance, dark against the dark, and a red glow where the fires were still burning. I remember thinking that the moon was rising over hell.

Like I said, there were five of us. If I think hard I can still recall their faces. Filthed-up and streaked with sweat. Sergeant Mills, regular soldier, big square hands, had a slow, steady way of moving like some big bull elephant. Purposeful, like he knew just where to go and what he planned to do once he'd got us there. Got to regroup, he said. Get back to what was left of our unit, like there was nothing to it, and no doubt we could manage it if we'd only just keep listening to him.

They took us to some bombed-out shell of a house, must have been five or six streets from where the woman lived, and we hid out in what was left of one of the back rooms. I could see the moon, shining down on us now through the gaps in the roof beams, bright enough so we could see each other's faces and for us to read the rough map Emile drew for us. A safe route, he said. Or safe as any place could be in a city of snipers. But they wouldn't take us further. Too scared of getting caught.

So we sat there in the half-light, waiting for the moon to set, hoping to make it out of that bloody little town between moonset and sunrise. Just sat there, *listening to the shells falling, until our thoughts had been blasted into bits by the noise of shattered walls falling and the screams of those who couldn't get away. And the not knowing if it was our lot or theirs doing the most damage.*

And the night moved on, ticking away so slow I could have sworn the moon had stopped and was just shining down, like the star of Bethlehem, pointing the way for them to find us.

Alec drove home in the early hours of the morning, drained and tired and deeply reluctant to go back.

I was fifteen when I left home, he reminded himself. Fifteen. Joined the navy. Did my time on the Ganges. Travelled the world and I was just a kid.

Marcie was right. He'd passed judgement on what was right for her when he himself had made decisions at the same age that now horrified him. He was still convinced that having a baby at that age would have been a crazy act, but they had handled things not just badly but probably with great cruelty.

Fifteen, he repeated to himself, and Jack had been at work on the farm a year younger than that.

And yet, they had been such children. Proto-adults, trying to find their way in a complicated world.

He drove along almost-empty roads. Even the motorway seemed thin and unfleshed by traffic. His mind drifted back to the night Marcie had confessed that she was pregnant and to the night not long after that when he and Jack had taken their revenge on the Simpson boy.

It had still been so cold and the snow had begun to fall again, blanketing the streets with a deadly purity. They had waited for him, waited for Patrick Simpson as he'd come out of the pub, said goodbye to his friends and set off across the park towards home.

Pat Simpson was just turned eighteen. A gangly, slightly pimply boy with overlong black hair and a reputation for making it easily with the girls. Alec couldn't see the attraction, but quite a slice of the female population seemed to find one. Older folk talked of him as something of a Jack the lad, but they did it fondly, as though that were something to be proud of, as though it made up for his lack of job and prospects.

Alec could remember clearly how they'd followed him. The night had been bitter. The boy had walked with his head uncovered, his collar turned up and his bare hands thrust deep into the pockets of his coat.

'We'll just talk to him,' Jack had said. 'Somewhere private, like. Make him see he's got to keep away from our Birdie.'

Even then, deep in disgrace, she was still Jack's Bird. Still on her pedestal even while rolling in the gutter, as Michael had said.

Alec had told himself that Jack meant what he said. That all they would do was talk. But following the boy across the park, moving like trackers from shadow to shadow, even Alec hadn't been able to keep up the pretence completely.

Then Jack had leapt at him, screaming like a maniac, arms strengthened by anger despite his years. He had wrestled the boy to the ground and begun kicking him in the head until the snow was stained with crimson and the boy lay still. Then even Alec had been forced to act.

He couldn't remember the words he had screamed at his father. They had seemed incoherent even then as he had struggled with Jack, pulled him way from the now unconscious Patrick Simpson.

'Oh, God! Oh, my God, you've killed him. You've fucking killed him, Dad!'

Jack glared, cat-like malevolence narrowing his eyes. 'Don't you swear at me, boy. Don't you ever swear at me!'

Then he'd bent down, grabbed mounds of snow in his bare hands and scrubbed the blood from his boots before marching away, his back rigid, arms swinging in strict time to his footsteps. When he moved his arm, Alec could almost see the rifle slung across his back.

'Oh, God. Oh, my God.'

He had bent down next to the body, certain that the boy was dead but too afraid of getting blood on his hands to test for a pulse. 'I could say I just found him. Walking in the park, and I just found him. Coming back from the pub. Yes, that's it. What if they know he's been seeing Marcie? What . . . ?'

There were voices coming from one of the other paths, people, concealed by the still-thick growth of evergreens, who might be heading his way.

With a skill that Jack would have been proud of, Alec slipped into the shadows. Backed down the path they had come in by, moving with a stealth born of sheer terror. Then, as the voices faded, he began to run.

Hampered by the thickly falling snow and by his heavy coat, it seemed to take for ever to reach the park gates.

Alec stood panting. The cold air was raw in his lungs. A telephone box. Oh, please let it be working. 'Yes, yes, I need the police, an ambulance. There's a dead body in the park down near the lake . . .'

He hung up, fought his way through the door, almost slipping on a patch of ice as he began to run again. They would know, they would know. The police would come for him. Be there when he reached home. They would know . . .

Alec shifted back from fifth gear as the final marker for his exit loomed, its white flashing stark and luminous as fresh snow.

There had been no police. No one knew. Marcie and Patrick had been careful, secretive enough in their meetings that there was nothing to connect them.

Patrick Simpson had been found two hours later, covered by a heavy blanket of snow that almost hid the body. His injuries, bloody though they were, would not have killed him. Had he been conscious. Had they found him sooner. As it was, the cold had killed him, wrapped him tight and frozen the life from him.

Marcie knew nothing about it, deprived of newspapers and television, even of the radio. Retreating to her room after returning from the hospital, refusing to eat, making *herself* ill, as Gran had insisted. It had been weeks before she went back to school and knew that anything had happened to Patrick Simpson.

Alec remembered vividly the night she had come

home with a vague story that Patrick had died of cold in the park on a winter's night.

'You did it to him, didn't you?' she challenged Jack. 'You did it to him.' Screaming with fury and despair.

Alec flicked the indicator late, almost losing his turn-off at the island. Remembering Marcie, one of Aunt Alice's kitchen knives clasped in her slim hand, flying at Jack with a wildness in her eyes that matched that in Jack's the night he had killed the boy.

Jack had thrown her aside easily, the knife grazing down his arm then cutting into the bicep as she fell.

And Marcie had seen the blood and her resolve had collapsed. Anger dissolving into fear.

'Oh, no, Jack. Oh, Jack, I'm sorry. Oh, Jack, Jack.'

And Jack had stared at her, then at his arm, and covered his face, blood draining from his features as though for the first time the shock of what he had done had come home to him.

'It was pandemonium after that,' Alec said to himself. 'Sheer pandemonium.'

He was heading back towards the city now, street lights marking his way, flicking by him far too fast. He dropped his speed, watching the needle of the speed-ometer fall from seventy back to forty-five.

He remembered Jack sitting in Aunt Alice's big chair, tears running down his cheeks, face screwed into wrinkles, crying like a child.

And Alice, holding Marcie by the shoulders, shaking her, shouting at her. 'Nothing happened, Marcie! The baby, your relationship with that boy. Tonight. None of it happened. None of it! You hear me?'

None of it ever happened.

They moved out when the moon was low on the horizon.

The shelling had stopped and the streets were quiet but for sporadic bursts of gunfire far enough away to echo. They moved softly, keeping close to the walls, eyes everywhere and nerves strung so taut Jack fancied he could hear them snap.

Then it happened. Two shots and two men down. The others dived for cover as a third shot smashed into brick just inches above their heads. They hit the ground. Sergeant Mills had his rifle in his hands, scanning the building, a three-floored warehouse, from where the shots had come. But Jack was quicker. He'd caught the flash of the third shot and suddenly he was moving, avoiding Mills and his whispered orders, running at a crouch towards the warehouse and the shadow of a side door half hidden in a narrow alley.

The small door creaked as Jack pushed at it, jamming on the debris on the floor inside and opening just enough for Jack to consider sliding through. He shrugged free of his pack, lowered it to the ground, then squeezed through the door, the Lee Enfield held close to his body, sitting easy in his arms. Jack could see a broken stairway leading upwards, and a faint sound reached him from the upper floor.

He took the stairs in long strides, dust rising about

him and fragments of half-rotten wood flying from beneath his feet. He paused at the second flight, ears straining for the slightest sound. The sniper had heard him. Jack knew that; the faint sounds above him had completely ceased.

Jack knew he couldn't turn back. He knew there would be just one chance to get it right and only one if he didn't want to wind up dead.

Then he ceased to think of it.

Jack took the remaining flight at a run, then dived and rolled, firing from a half-crouch as he righted himself, then throwing himself sideways under the sniper's shot and through the open door.

It was pure luck that made the shot go wide, that and the insanity of Jack's run as though some instinct born of blind rage made him know how and when to move.

Jack's weight against the other man brought them both crashing to the floor and Jack had rolled free and fired before the other man could move, a close-range shot that blasted him wide open from groin to ribs, spreading his guts like so much waste across the floor, the stink of blood and shit rising from it to fill the dust-laden air.

It should have been enough, but Jack was beyond that kind of nicety. He moved forward and looked down into his enemy's face. A young face, filthy and grimed with sweat and dirt and, now, his own blood, and then Jack raised the gun once more, this time bringing the rifle butt down on the stranger's face with all his strength, feeling the bone and flesh smash and pulp, wanting to grind it into oblivion. For ever.

Chapter Seventeen

It was a small sound that woke Marcie. A small sound, but after weeks of night feeds, even more months of listening for her babies, Marcie was sensitive to such things.

She lay for a few moments in the dark, listening, trying to work out what it was that had awoken her. If it was nothing but one of the children turning over she didn't see the sense of getting out of a warm bed and maybe waking Hanna into the bargain.

Then the sound came again, the sound of sobbing, soft, as though whoever cried did not want to be heard.

Frightened, but also drawn to the sound, Marcie slipped from her bed, glancing back at Michael and wondering whether she had better waken him. Deciding against, she moved stealthily to the end of the bed, pulled her dressing gown around her shoulders and crept into the main room.

'Oh!' Marcie stopped in her tracks, a hand rising to her mouth to stop herself from crying out. There was no way, she told herself. No way this was real.

'What are you doing here? Get away from there. Get away from there!'

The curtain that covered the twins' tiny room was drawn right back, held by a woman in a white blouse and black skirt. Her dark hair fell down in soft waves over her shoulders and as she turned at Marcie's challenge Marcie could see the rope tied tight around her throat and the tears that ran freely down the woman's face.

Marcie almost flew across the room. 'Get away from there!' she screamed.

'Marcie!' Michael's voice behind her caused her to glance back for the merest instant. He was in the doorway behind her, staring not at her but at the woman standing beside the children's cots. Marcie turned back towards her enemy . . . but there was nothing there. The curtain hung partly drawn aside, otherwise nothing.

Michael was beside her now. 'It's all right,' he said. 'It's all right, she's gone now, Marcie. Gone.'

Weakly, sobbing with fear, Marcie allowed him to hold her, feeling that Michael too was trembling, his skin cold with shock. Then she stiffened.

'Hanna,' she whispered. 'Oh, Michael, Hanna. All the noise we were making. Why didn't Hanna wake up?'

Chapter Eighteen

Adele cuddled Hanna in her lap and let her help herself from the biscuit tin. Liam sat on his mother's knee drinking milk from one of the clown-printed mugs Adele kept specially for them. Both children as content and mischievous as they always were. It was their parents who were suffering, still shaken from the events of the night before.

Marcie and Michael had not slept for the rest of the night. They had spent some time just standing, watching their children, worried, at first, that the noise had not woken Hanna, holding on to each other and trying hard not to be quite so afraid.

Morning had found them camped, early, on Adele's doorstep, looking for sanctuary.

'You ask me if I believe in spirits,' Adele said quietly. 'In ghosts that come haunting the living.'

'Sure she does,' Sophie Lee put in. 'Like her grand-mother, she sees ghosts and angels everywhere.'

Marcie laughed edgily, and Adele smiled across at her, then said more seriously, 'The babes were not hurt, honey. Could be that she meant no harm, only came to look.'

'But why, Adele?' Marcie shook her head. 'I don't believe in ghosts.'

'Then what name do you give to this not-a-ghost?' Sophie Lee asked her.

'I don't know. Imagination. Shock, seeing my dad turn up at our place. Something Jack put into my mind with all his talk about this dead woman.'

'But I saw her too,' Michael objected. 'I mean, I'm as sceptical as you are, but I saw her too.'

'I don't know,' Marcie said again. 'Maybe, maybe I saw her so strongly because of Jack, and I kind of projected her image to you. Maybe we shared a dream. I just don't know.'

'Excuse me if I'm wrong,' said Sophie Lee, 'but my calling her a ghost does seem a whole deal simpler than any of all that.'

'Yeah, I guess you're right.' Frowning, Marcie dragged out the photograph of the haywain once more and gazed intently at the picture. 'It's funny,' she said, 'but I always thought the one on the right, the small blonde one, might be Rebekkah, not that one.'

'You still don't know for sure,' Michael suggested. 'It could be that you just needed to give this apparition a face. That subconsciously you remembered the photograph and gave her one of the faces.'

Sophie Lee rolled her eyes dramatically. 'Oh, off we go again,' she said. 'Why do the young ones never go the simple way, huh? Tell me that.' She sighed. 'Look, my children. Marcie's granddad is dying. He's got something on his mind he don't want to face his maker with. Ain't no way he can sort it for himself, lying in that hospital bed, so his problem come to you to be sorted.'

Marcie stared at the old woman. 'But why me?' she asked. 'I don't even know who Rebekkah was, except that Jack and Gran knew her.'

'And she got herself killed,' Sophie Lee reminded her. 'Most ghosts die a violent death. Maybe Jack knew something about her dying that he didn't tell. Maybe she wants justice, Marcie.'

'I don't know. I don't even know how I'd find out. Jack rambles and I can't ask Aunt Alice or Gran.'

'There's Alec,' Michael reminded her. 'Seems to me he never did get around to telling you what he came for last night.'

Marcie sighed and reached for a piece of kitchen towel to wipe Liam's mouth.

She lifted her hand then to touch the almost-faded marks on her neck. That incident had upset her, but far less than last night. It had been Michael who had seen the image of the rope about her throat, seen her struggling for breath and trying to tear it free. For Marcie that night had been like a bad dream and, apart from the bruises and abrasions on her skin, it had faded in much the same way.

By contrast, last night's apparition reappeared with terrifying clarity each time she closed her eyes or let her thoughts wander.

'She was so young,' Marcie said quietly, looking at the photograph once more. Hugging Liam to her as though for protection, she re-ran the events, hoping that familiarity would somehow soften the image. De-focus it and make it bearable. A tiny gesture Rebekkah had made as she had turned came back to her. The way her hand had moved, touching her slightly swollen belly.

'She was pregnant,' Marcie said. 'When she died, she was carrying a child.'

Chapter Nineteen

They were forced to go to work, Michael and Marcie, and to put their problems aside for the needs of others. Michael installed the twins in the crèche, asking the young woman who ran it to keep a special eye on them, telling her that they had been a little unwell and had had a restless night.

She looked at him strangely as the pair had raced off with their usual show of energy. 'Looks like you're the one that had the bad night,' she said. 'Sure you feel OK?'

'I'm fine,' Michael assured her. 'Just fine.'

By ten he was on the phone to Marcie. She was in a meeting, they told him. Taking minutes. Could she call him back at lunchtime?

He put the phone down after thanking the woman, feeling stupid and ill at ease. Then turned with his work smile back in place, as his next problem of the morning came in through the office door.

Alec's day was no better. He was up for breakfast only a few short hours after getting home and left for work early, to avoid the awkward questions wrapped up in the disapproving looks from his aunt and mother. He closed the front door, more than a little ashamed that he felt unable to admit to them that he had been to see his daughter.

He sat outside his place of work for a good ten minutes before venturing inside and, when he did, he went straight to his boss's office.

Fifteen minutes later he was outside again, aware of the puzzled looks being cast at him from the first-floor window.

For more than twelve years Alec Armitage had been Mr Reliable. Never late, rarely absent. Conscientious and predictable. Booking the same two weeks every summer. The same extra days at Christmas and New Year.

And now, to come in like this, almost demand that he be given some of his annual leave. It must seem to them, thought Alec, that the world was about to end.

But they knew about Jack. Knew about the strain he must be under . . . or thought they did.

He started the car engine and began to drive slowly towards home. It was Thursday. Alice and his mother would be shopping from about ten until around midday. He waited two streets away until ten fifteen, then let himself into the house, packed a suitcase and left again. He tossed the case into the boot of the car and drove away, through the pretty tree-lined streets of nineteen-thirties suburbia.

He was waiting outside the house when Michael arrived with Marcie and the twins. Alec's mood had oscillated throughout the day between euphoria and despair. Just what did he think he was doing? Marcie would have every right to tell him to get the hell out of her life. What did he hope to prove by walking out without a word to Alice or his mother? Walking out and leaving them to cope with Jack.

Walking out. Yes! He was free. For the first time in years he was free. Though free to do what, Alec was not yet sure.

His emotions were on the turn when Michael's car pulled up in front of his. Alec practically leapt out on them.

'I want to take you to dinner,' he announced.

'Dinner?'

'Yes, all of you. I mean, they are old enough, aren't they?' He looked at the twins. 'Yes, of course they are.'

Marcie was staring at him in surprise, while Michael looked puzzled but amused.

'All right,' Michael said at last. 'I know of somewhere we can take the kids. Follow us in your car.' And he bent to re-strap the twins into their baby seats.

Alec got back in his car, his optimism failing once again. God, what was he doing here? Just what was he going to do?

The restaurant was Italian. Marcie and Michael had been there twice before, a birthday and an anniversary. Rare treats, saved for over weeks.

'I'm paying,' Alec reminded her again. 'Please, Marcie, do this for me, please.'

There were no highchairs, but the problem was solved happily enough with big cushions and white tablecloths tying the twins securely to their chairs. The children ate pizza, cut into little bites, and discovered just what breadsticks tasted like dipped into milk and anything else within reach.

The adults ate at first in silence, then slowly unwound over the antipasto. They were relaxed enough by the time the main course had arrived, fresh cooked and so hot it had to be eaten slowly, to begin talking.

'I don't mean to be rude, Da,' Marcie said to him at last, 'but just why did you come?'

Alec put down his fork and regarded the others sheepishly. 'It sounds so silly,' he said awkwardly, 'but I guess you could say that I've run away from home.'

'You've run . . . Oh, Da, you can't be serious.'

'You said you'd got a spare sofa,' Alec went on. 'I just hoped . . . Fact is, Marcie, I couldn't take it any more, Jack and Mam, and not being able to say a damned thing without she leaps down my throat, and I didn't have anywhere else to go.'

He paused, looking hopefully at her. 'Marcie, if you don't want me, I understand. I can't expect . . .'

Marcie looked away from him and spent several moments studying her plate.

'It will only be for the night,' he said. 'Or if you like, I'll book into a hotel.' He hesitated. 'I've got to find myself somewhere then, near to work. I've taken a few days off so I can look around. Get myself sorted out. Fact is, I'd like to talk, Marcie.'

She was slow to answer him and when she did her voice was thick with tears. 'No sense paying stupid hotel bills,' she said.

'Thank you,' Alec started to say. 'I really—'

'But if you want to talk,' Michael interrupted him, 'then we really do talk. Sort some things out. And to start with, we talk about what happened last night.'

'Last night?' Alec questioned. 'I don't understand.'

'No,' Michael told him quietly. 'Neither do we, Alec, that's the whole problem.'

Alec listened in silence as they rather hesitantly described to him the events of the night before. His first reaction was incredulity. 'Imagination,' he declared. 'Marcie's always—'

'Had too much for my own good. I know.'

'Oh, I didn't mean . . .' Alec said, suddenly contrite.

'Funny sort of imagination, Alec,' Michael reminded him. 'I saw it too. Saw her standing beside the cot as plain as I'm seeing you now. I could see every hair, every tear running down her face. She was real, Alec. Real . . .'

Alec shook his head slowly, trying to work it out. 'And you say she was in the picture.'

Marcie reached into her bag and withdrew the photograph. 'This one,' she said, pointing to the dark-haired woman. 'It was this one, Da.'

He stared thoughtfully at the photograph for a moment, then nodded. 'Yes,' he confirmed, 'that's her. God, I haven't seen this in years. It used to be in a frame, standing on the sideboard in the living room.' He pointed to the figures in turn. 'There's Jack in the striped work shirt, and there's your gran and Alice and that must be Joe right at the end there.' He shook his head. 'I used to know,' he said, 'used to know all their names. Mam still talked about them in those days. Then something changed and it was as if she wanted to forget them all. Rebekkah was suddenly "that woman", and you know Mam, she never did feel the need to explain.'

'Who's Joe?' Marcie asked him.

Alec looked puzzled. 'Oh,' he said, 'of course, you wouldn't know. Joseph Armitage was Jack's brother.'

'His brother!'

Alec nodded. 'Died years ago, so I understand. When I was still in the navy, I think.'

'Jack never talked about him,' Marcie said incredulously. 'Why did Jack never mention him to me?'

Alec sighed. 'There were a lot of things we never talked about,' he said, 'and to be honest, Marcie, I'm not sure there's much I can tell you. I know that's Rebekkah because I vaguely remember being told who everyone in the photo was. Like I said, it used to be framed and standing on the sideboard. But I know almost nothing about her.'

He sighed deeply once more. He seemed drained, as though the events of the day had begun to tell on him.

'I feel like a coward,' he said suddenly, 'just walking out like that. And you,' he looked across at Marcie. 'Why the hell should I expect you to care?'

'I don't know,' Marcie told him, returning his gaze steadily. 'But maybe, if we try hard enough, we can find a reason.'

We found them, the woman and the two men, hiding out on the upper floor. And, in the dust beside the window, marks where the sniper had knelt, looking down into the street. The bodies still lay there, dead and growing cold.

I've asked myself a hundred times, Marcie, why we didn't kill them then and there, and I still don't have the answer clear in my mind. Mills said we should have a trial, but what a farce that was. I don't know why we waited, Birdie, but it felt good, after all the death and killing and pain, to let our anger grow inside and plan the way to end it.

Darkness came and we moved out. Walked for what felt like hours, following Mills. Like a bloodhound, he was, knew where the others'd be almost like he could smell water. And we found them, what was left of our unit, camped out in an olive grove near a water-hole. A tiny village shadowed one side of the oasis, its buildings burnt out and deserted, but there was water there and others like us and it felt like coming home.

'Traitors,' Mills said. It was all he had to say. They were as good as dead.

Chapter Twenty

Alice phoned early on the Friday morning, demanding to know if Alec was there.

Michael, up first, took the call. He parried her questions as politely as he could; lied as convincingly as possible, resorting to half-truths that they had seen Alec but that he had stayed in a hotel somewhere. All of that seemed to take a very long time. Alice didn't question so much as interrogate, her next question forming before Michael had fully replied to the first.

Returning from the hall to the living room, Michael found Alec with Hanna planted in his lap. He was reading to her, making funny voices as the toy mouse squeaked and the big teddy waved his arms. He looked up, slightly embarrassed as Michael came back in.

'She woke up,' he said. 'And Marcie was so tired last night, it seemed a shame to get her out of bed before she had to.'

Michael smiled at him and bent down to take Hanna, who was now reaching out for her father. 'Thanks,' he said, then to Hanna, 'but we've got to wake your momma now, haven't we, sweetness? And I bet you want your breakfast.'

'Is there anything I can do?' Alec asked. He sounded anxious to be of use.

Michael nodded. 'Yeah, I'm sure there is. Always

rushing around like lunes this time of the morning. Oh, and that was Alice, by the way.' He turned towards the bedroom. 'Wanting to know if you were here.'

'What did you tell her?' Alec asked cautiously.

'That you'd gone to a hotel. That we'd seen you, but you'd left and I didn't know where to find you.'

'Thank you,' Alec said, almost fervently. 'I'll go and put the kettle on.'

The breakfast-time activity made Alec feel distinctly out of place. They were so busy, so purposeful. Feeding and dressing the twins, sorting things for the crèche, taking turns to watch the babies whilst the other showered and dressed. Alec did his best to help, but knew he was getting in the way. Finally he opted out and sat down on the old sofa, half hoping that Hanna would come and reclaim her book and her place on his lap.

He watched Marcie as she applied her rather minimal make-up and pinned her hair into something resembling order.

'I thought I'd go flat-hunting,' he said.

'Good idea.'

'Somewhere near to work.'

'Right.'

She turned to check that they had everything they needed in the twins' bag, automatically moving her lipstick out of range as Hanna reached up for it, then casting her glance about the room as though to make some assessment of their readiness.

'This isn't easy, Birdie,' Alec pleaded.

She straightened, looked at him. 'Did you expect it to be? Look, Da, we never were close, not even when I was this age.' She gestured almost angrily at Hanna.

'Jack . . .'

'. . . made it easy for you not to be a parent.'

'It wasn't like that.'

'Wasn't it?' She glanced quickly at her watch, then shook her head. 'Look, Da, we talked last night maybe more than we'd done in my first sixteen years. And I'm prepared to say that's good, you know.' She paused. 'Michael, we should be going now, love. Come on, sweetheart.' She scooped Hanna into her arms and went to persuade Liam away from his toy bricks.

'I'll be going too,' said Alec, lamely.

Marcie turned back to him, her dark eyes deeply troubled and, he thought hopefully, not without sympathy.

'I want us to make up for lost time, Birdie. I want to say I'm sorry.'

Her eyes hardened and for a moment she said nothing, then, as Michael appeared from the bedroom, she spoke. 'We go across to Adele's Friday nights. Come with us if you like, you'll be made welcome.'

Then she turned and headed for the door. Alec cast Michael a puzzled look. 'Adele?'

'My foster mum,' Michael told him. He reached into his pocket and withdrew a door key. 'Spare,' he said. 'Let yourself out when you're ready. OK? Don't forget to close the street door.'

'No. No, I won't,' Alec said, taking the key, feeling

somewhat bemused by this sudden kindness. 'Er, thanks,' he added as Michael followed Marcie and he heard the street door slam.

I remember it was late October and we'd had the first of the frosts. I'd been up in the top field checking on that bay gelding that had gone lame with a bruised tendon. We'd decided to bring him down into the stockyard. The swelling wasn't going down and I'd got a compress ready for it. Hog's lard and rye flour and camphorated wine. God, but it's a funny thing, Birdie, it's the hands that remember these things, not the head. It's the hands and the eyes that remember the measuring and the mixing and the feel of a good poultice. And the heat of it. Not so hot the fat and camphor would blister the skin, but hot enough to get into the cloth and bind well about the hoof.

I'd gone to get him from the top field. Put him out to grass, they'd said. Rest him, but they didn't know. Needed doctoring, poor old fellow. Getting past the work, you see. Too old for it.

I was leading him down, taking it careful along the back road, keeping him slow and easy. And there she was. Standing in the road and waiting for me.

Rebekkah. Black hair shining with those dark red lights dancing in it, though she looked pinched and sick with the cold . . .

*

'You've been avoiding me, Jack.'

'I told you, girl. It's over between us. This time for real, Becky.'

She came closer to him, laid a long slim hand on the rough cloth of his jacket. 'You don't mean that, Jack,' she said. 'You've said it many times before and never meant a word of it. You don't mean it now.'

'I mean it.' He patted her hand gently, squeezing the cold fingers before pushing them aside and tugging gently at the horse's leading rein. 'Walk on.'

'Jack! Jack, I've got to talk to you.'

'Nothing to say, Becky. It's over, I keep telling you that. I'm a married man now.'

She laughed at that. Bitter laughter that seemed to echo. 'That's never stopped you! A half-dozen times or more you've been with me since your wedding night. Disappoint you, did she, Jack?'

He turned sharply, hand raised as though to slap her. She had made to follow him but she stepped back now, her eyes shadowed with hurt.

'No more, Becky. No more! It's got to end and I'm ending it now. It was always crazy and now I've got too much to lose. Much too much.'

'Now?'

'Mary's pregnant,' he told her shortly. 'My wife is pregnant, Becky.'

She stared at him, her cheeks flushing and then growing pale.

'So am I, Jack,' she told him softly.

Chapter Twenty-One

Alec spent the morning trawling estate agents and the small ads in the local papers, managing to find Thursday's editions still in the town centre library. It had been a depressing task, places either too high in rent, or too small, or too far from where he worked . . . Or too close to home. By two he had found three possibles, all, it seemed to him, overpriced. He'd made appointments to view with the agents and signed on at an accommodation agency, a shabby basement office in the backstreets close to the university. It didn't inspire much confidence, but it was something else he could tell Marcie he had done, and it seemed important, somehow, to have positive things to tell her.

It's not easy, he told himself, to know that your daughter thinks you're a complete failure as a father and probably as a human being too.

He caught sight of himself in a shop window as he was leaving the last agent. The reflection startled him. He'd never been tall, but middle-aged thickening around his waist made him look even shorter, even stockier. And did he really brush his hair back over the bald patch quite that obviously? And when, oh when, for Pete's sake, did he go that grey?

Turning away abruptly, Alec tried to remember a time when he had actually felt good about himself.

He was still straining for the memory when he got back to his car. He ought to check on Jack, he decided. Take a chance on Alice and his mother's being there. He drove to the hospice still trying to think of the last really positive feeling he had had about his life. He recaptured the moment as he turned into the hospice car park. The night Marianne had agreed to be his wife. And when he had found one positive time, he was surprised at the others that followed quickly on its tail.

He was smiling as he signed himself in. Still smiling as he walked the length of the ward to Jack's bed, relieved beyond belief to find that his mother and Alice were absent. He sat down beside Jack and took the old man's hand as he had seen Marcie do.

'I've come to see you, Jack,' he said as his father turned to look at him. 'Come to talk to you.'

His father tried to smile, but the dry lips seemed ready to crack with the effort of it. Alec hesitated, his own smile fading as he looked at the old man's face, realized that Jack was much, much worse. Wondered what his mother had said about him and if he had been right to come back.

But it seemed that it was Alec's week for acting impulsively. He leaned forward, resting his elbows on the bed and bending his head close to Jack's. Breathing in the scent of dying and decay, he began to speak.

'I never told you, did I, about Marcie. Really told you about my . . . about my wife, about Marcie's mother. About how we met and about how beautiful she was. How much I loved her, Dad. How much she made me feel alive and wanted and so strong, just because she cared about me. Loved me, wanted to be happy with me. I never told you, did I? You only knew the bad parts, about how she died. How she got so depressed after Marcie was born and how we didn't realize just how serious it was.' He paused, looking intently into Jack's face. 'She drove too fast, Dad, but I've never believed she meant it. Never believed what Mam and Alice tried to push at me, that she'd taken her own life. You didn't know Marianne, Dad. If you had, you'd know it was all lies they made up about her to make them feel better. To make it seem right when they insulted her and I was too damned stupid to tell them no. I loved her, Dad. I don't care what she was or that she had nothing, or even that she went with other men. I loved her and she gave Marcie to me and that's all that matters now. All that really matters now.'

Jack's eyes flickered towards him and he moistened his lips with the tip of his tongue.

'Rebekkah,' he whispered, his voice cracked and arid like a whisper of dry autumn leaves.

It was not long after she'd told me she was pregnant. I knew her husband was away and it was pitch black when I crept round the back of their cottage and scratched on the window.

She'd hardly talk to me at first, was sly and bitter and only let me in for fear I'd make a row.

But I knew I could win her round if I just gave her time. Truth was, I liked the thought of it, two women with my bairns growing inside them. Yes, I have to say, I liked the thought.

She let me sit by the fire for a time, working me hard when I tried to make conversation. But I could tell she felt lonely in that house all on her own and needed someone to comfort her.

She didn't say no when I took her by the hand and led her upstairs, and didn't fuss either when I laid her on the bed and started unfastening her clothes.

Beautiful, she was, and now I knew about the baby I began to see the little changes in her, compared them to those I saw in Mary. Her breasts had grown heavier, the nipples huge and dark against the pale honey of her skin, and her belly was no longer flat. I stroked the slight swelling of it, gliding my hand down between her thighs.

'No, Jack,' she said, but she made no effort to stop me and when she cried afterwards I held her tightly, knowing that was what a woman needed at such a time.

Afterwards, I lit the lamp and set it on the wash-stand, stood behind her, watching her in the mirror while I brushed her black hair. Long slow sweeps of the brush down the length of it until it gleamed in the light.

In school we read a poem about a man who killed his lover with her own long hair, and I twisted Becky's in my hands, twining it about her throat and laughing at her in the mirror whilst I pulled it tight across her neck.

She lifted her hand to cover mine.

'You'd miss me, Jack,' she said, and her voice was sad. 'And I promise you, Jack, kill me and I'll never let

*you be free. I'll be there always, even if you can't see
me clearly. I'll be there, just off the corner of your eye
or in the shadows waiting for you to fall asleep.
Watching everything you ever do.'*

*She said it lightly, showing me I couldn't scare her,
but I knew, even then, that she meant the words and
I let her black hair fall. I stroked the soft skin of her
throat gently with both my hands, watching her in the
glass.*

Chapter Twenty-Two

Saturday morning was bright and clear. They set off in Alec's car, leaving the twins with Adele and Sophie Lee. It seemed wrong to drag two small children on a longish journey that might well turn out to be a wild goose chase. Anyway, Marcie still felt shaken by the apparition she had seen standing beside the cots. Chasing after this thing, whatever it was, seemed bizarre and risky enough, without having to worry about its effect on her children.

In spite of everything, though, she still felt she had an obligation to Jack. More than that, the image of Rebekkah, standing beside her children's cots, preyed on her mind.

Finding out where Joseph Armitage, Jack's lost brother, was buried. Maybe finding someone who remembered him, had known Jack, even known Rebekkah, seemed their only way of finding the root to Jack's obsession. Adele had offered to have the twins and the agreement was that they would give up their weekend and possibly Monday to the project, Marcie having no work that day and Michael taking the precaution of swapping to the late call at the centre in case they needed the extra time. If they found nothing in that time, then they would consider it a lost cause.

Their journey took them north from the Midlands where Marcie had settled and back into Lincolnshire, where Jack and Mary had lived until just before Alec had been born.

'They moved just after they lost their first baby,' Alec said. 'Mam couldn't seem to rest after that and Jack was offered work so they uprooted and shifted to Harrelton. Been there ever since. Alice came to live with them when I was born. I think Mam was ill for quite a while.'

'I didn't know they'd lost a baby,' Michael said. 'That's really sad.'

Alec nodded. 'She was only a few days old.'

'When did Joe die?' Marcie asked.

Alec shrugged. 'I don't know,' he said. 'I was away for a long time. After I got back, I was told that he'd died, but your gran didn't seem inclined to talk and, well, you know what she's like. I never knew him anyway.'

'Did you never visit?' Michael asked.

'Not that I remember. There were Christmas cards, that sort of thing, but not much other contact. It's as if they wanted to sever all connections with the family. With everything.'

'Didn't that seem a bit odd?' Michael questioned.

'God, no,' Alec said. 'Perfectly normal. I think "keep ourselves to ourselves" was a phrase my mother invented.'

'So, where do we start?' Marcie asked.

'Louth, I think. It's a sizeable town and we take our bearings from there. I know they lived out at Ludford for a while when they first married and that my gran retired to a village called Binbrook. Mam moved back in with her during the war. Has some right horror stories to tell. It was surrounded by airfields, apparently.'

133

'They called it Bomber County,' Michael put in unexpectedly.

Alec shot him a surprised look through the rear-view mirror.

'Aw, bass, dis nigger boy know history,' Michael drawled at him.

'Sorry,' Alec said and flushed.

'I dare say we'll get used to each other.' Michael laughed.

Marcie shook her head at them. 'So, what are we looking for when we get there?' she asked. 'Someone with a memory like an encyclopaedia?'

'I guess so, Birdie,' Alec told her. 'I guess so.'

Mary was sitting at Jack's bedside.

'Everyone I've ever loved keeps leaving me. Not that there've been that many, Jack. Only, with you, it's like it's happening a second time. I knew about her, you know, but I told myself, Mary, he loves you. What does it matter what's past and gone?

'But it was never the same, was it? Not after our Margaret died. I felt you blamed me in some way for that, never quite forgave me for losing our baby. And when Marcie came to live with us, well, that was it, really, wasn't it? It was as if you didn't have enough love to go round. Never realized, did you, that love isn't sold in pound packages? You don't run out of it just because one person needs so much. There's still plenty left to go round, if you let it.

'And now Alec's gone too. Left us. Both my babies gone, it seems, and you getting ready to go with them.'

'Alec?' Jack's voice was cracked and hoarse.

'He's not here, love. There's only me. Only me.'

'Been dreaming. Long road and my horse . . . lame. Three parts hog's lard. Three parts . . . and camphorated wine . . .'

'It's all right, Jack, you were only dreaming. There've been no horses now, not for years.'

'Must be rye flour, Mary. Rye flour. Soaks up more, ground really fine so it's nearly black.'

'All right, Jack. I'll remember. I'll remember, love.'

'I told her, Mary, but the horse was lame and I couldn't leave him. Up ahead of me, standing there. Hair like soot with the fire dancing on it and I couldn't tell her no.'

'Jack, oh God, Jack, that's enough. Please, love, that's enough.'

She bent forward, her hands covering her face, weeping. Her tears falling on the neat, white linen sheets.

'I remember you,' Jack told her softly. 'Red hair and freckles on your nose and the sound of church bells. Lovely . . . got to be rye flour, promise. Wheat flour just won't do . . .'

Marcie had always thought of Lincolnshire as being flat. She'd been to the east coast a few times, crossing the fens to the seaside resorts, but she had never encountered the ridge of hills with their twisting, switchback roadways that formed the wolds.

'It's beautiful,' she said. 'Really gorgeous.'

'That's Louth, over there. See the church spire? I remember coming for picnics here when I was a little kid. A place called Hubbard's Hills. It's like a country park just on the edge of town. All trees and grass and not much else. Funny, though, I never realized that Mam and Dad came from around here, not for years.'

'Was it a market town?' Michael asked him.

'Hmm, yes. Must have been pretty wealthy too in its day. Let's find somewhere to have coffee then figure out where to start.'

It was ten in the morning and the streets were narrow and packed with pedestrians and too much traffic. Parking was difficult. Eventually they found a small café tucked away in a backstreet and settled themselves at a table by the large window.

Alec sat watching the passersby. His memories of Louth, apart from the quiet times spent in the hills above, were connected with the hustle and bustle of crowds pushing along the narrow streets. He remembered Jack talking about the place. One of the few times he could remember Jack talking freely and happily about his childhood.

'They held the hiring fairs here,' Alec said. 'Twice a year.'

'Hiring fairs?' Marcie asked.

'Most farm labourers were practically itinerant,' Alec said. 'They'd come here with their families and all their bits of possessions and stand in the market place with their . . . I don't know,' he laughed briefly, 'their CV, I suppose, pinned to their jackets. I remember Jack telling me about it. He'd come here with Joe and the uncle they lived with . . .'

It was spring. A year, almost to the week, since our folks had died in the last throes of the flu epidemic that had swept the country after the war. It had taken a few extra years to get itself our way, but in the end it had come north hard enough to take our parents.

This day, we'd gone to Louth with our Uncle William. He had chickens to sell and we'd piled on to the carrier cart, William up front with the drivers, me and Joe in the back. Mack's cart had wound its way from village to village. We were packed in the back with sacks of onions and casks of salted pork, Uncle Will's chickens squawking and fussing in a basket and me and Joe chucked in amongst the lot of it.

It was a warm day for April and we were still well stitched into our winter underwear. It was getting itchy and sweaty, but Aunt Emily wouldn't dream of letting us free of our winter clothes at least until the month end. We wore cord trousers and flannel shirts over the top and our oiled boots, newly hobnailed, which we clattered against the side of the cart, beating time with the horses' hoofs.

This was a special trip. First time we'd seen the hiring fair and the crowds of labourers and their kin vying with each other for work.

By the time we got to the market place and jumped down from the cart it was close to noon and Joe was complaining that he was hungry. The day was warmer, with some real heat in the sun, and I remember scratching and pulling at the thick woollen underwear and wishing that Aunt Em would let us out of it. But even that couldn't take the excitement away. It was a place that seemed made up of sounds and smells. The noise of cattle and fowl and voices announcing what they'd brought with them and the scents of spice and gingerbread all mixed up with the cow shit and the sweat of overwintered bodies.

I remember, we wandered through the narrow streets and crowded alleys, threaded our way across the market, filled with noise and heat and the crush of people. Eating the bits Aunt Em had packed up for us and backhanding the odd bit extra when anyone was careless enough not to be looking our way.

Life was good that day, secure and happy and sunny after a winter of hard graft and bad weather and months before that full of grieving when we'd lost kin.

I felt, and I swear that Joe felt the same, that we were coming out of a long, dark dream and that life was not so bad on that soft spring day.

There was a thing that happened, though, that brought all the pain and trouble back to us with such force.

We'd come to see the hiring fair, but in the interest of all the other things around us we'd almost forgotten that. Then we came upon it in a quiet corner close beside the church and the sight is one I swear I never will forget.

It marked me, Birdie, and I decided then and there

it would never be a part of my life, of my family's life, no matter what I had to do.

They stood there like so many head of cattle, their possessions crowded in a heap around them and their womenfolk and kids keeping to the background, silent and hopeful while their men sold themselves – or so it looked to me. They stood with their names and skills written on card, or scraps of paper, pinned to their jacket fronts for all to read. Stood solid and with as much pride as you could hope such a man could have while the foremen and the farmers and the petty land-owners walked along the rows inspecting them. Reading what they had to say, examining their hands and barking questions about their past employ.

I expected, almost, that they'd make the men break into a trot, or that they'd open their mouths and look at their teeth to find their age.

Every so often, one would be called forward and sign his deed of contract, then leave with his new employer and a backward glance at those still left behind.

I know this was just the way of things, Birdie. That it had gone on, twice a year, for maybe hundreds of years. But it seemed to me hard not to feel degraded. That this way of doing things left a man with little worth or honour and I wondered, then, what would happen to those left behind at the end of the day. Where would they go, those who no one claimed? Would they just be swept away with the night's rubbish, like rotten cabbage and broken eggs at the end of a market?

We didn't watch for long, Joe and I. We went away then and tried to return to the excitement we had felt at having the day off. But it would not come back. I dreaded that I had glimpsed my future in those men. Standing with all they owned gathered at their feet, selling themselves to whoever would buy.

'I know it affected him,' Alec said. 'I was never certain what it was that bothered him so much. It was only like going to the job centre.'

Marcie laughed. 'There speaks a man who's been in the same job more years than he can remember,' she said.

Michael looked thoughtful. 'When Sophie Lee was a little girl,' he said, 'she met a woman who'd been born a slave.'

'It's hardly the same thing,' Alec argued, inexplicably uncomfortable with the analogy.

'No,' Michael agreed, 'it's not. But in real terms I wonder how much more choice those men really had. From what I understand, a lot of them were bonded labourers. They had no rights to even leave their employer until their time was up, however badly he treated them. It's not so far from slavery in my book.'

The thought sobered them. By the time they'd finished their coffee they had decided that maybe Louth was not going to be much help.

'They didn't actually live here, then?' Michael asked.

Alec shook his head. 'No, I just thought . . . Well, I guess this is the place I was most familiar with, but it's been years. I'm not sure this is such a good idea.

Binbrook's better. The last address we had for Joe was there.'

They left soon after, drove out past Alec's fondly remembered Hubbard's Hills and on up the switchbacks, the road twisting and turning like a snake across the backbone of hills.

The village of Binbrook, settled in a dip between hills, was quiet and small. They got out of the car, parked beside the walled garden of what looked to be an old manor house and scanned around, wondering where to begin. A couple of teenagers lounged inside the bus shelter, but otherwise the heart of the village seemed deserted. The kids glanced their way, their looks curious but unconcerned, then returned to talking.

Four roads led off a central open area, not quite a village square, more of an elongated triangle. A large pub, the Marquise, stood to the side of the apex. It was boarded up and deserted, Alec noted. The long wall of the manor house gardens ran along one full side, with a butcher's shop between the roads at the base, and other, smaller shops making up the third side.

The place had a prosperous, satisfied look to it that Alec recalled from childhood visits.

'There were two churches here once,' he remembered. 'Two churches and a chapel and at least two pubs. The Plough was the other one, I think.'

'Well, I guess we should look at both churchyards,' Marcie said.

'No need,' Alec told her. 'One burned down a long time ago. There's just St Mary's and St Gabriel's now.'

Michael glanced along the empty roadway, bleached white in the strong sunlight.

'The pub might be a good starting place,' he said, a trifle wistfully, Marcie thought.

'Later, maybe,' she said, smiling. 'We don't even know where to find that yet. We do know where the church is.'

They had passed the church on their way in, a walled graveyard visible to one side.

'We'd get more done if we split up,' she suggested. 'I'll take the shops, you and Michael try the churchyard.'

'All right,' Alec agreed. 'I wonder if it's still in use.'

'Well, you might find someone to tell you. Anyway, Joe died a while ago. Could be it was when he was here.' She flashed a quick smile in their direction and headed off towards the nearest shop.

Alec glanced at Michael. 'I think we're being organized,' he said.

Michael laughed. 'To the churchyard, Watson,' he said.

It did not take them long to realize that Joe wasn't buried there. The modern stones were easily recognizable; they checked the older-looking ones just in case, but there was no sign of a Joseph Armitage anywhere amongst them. They spent much of the remaining time on their knees deciphering moss-covered monuments decorated with the masonic equivalent of copperplate and reading the inscriptions on the airmen's graves, planted in a straight avenue of white behind the church, a reminder of the airfield so close by. Some had not even left their teens, Alec noted, remembering his own time in the forces, and, paradoxically, how happy he had been.

But there was no sign of Joe.

When Marcie appeared an hour later it was obvious from her expression that she had something important to tell. She hurried over to where they stood beside the churchyard's high north wall.

'You've found out something?' Alec questioned excitedly.

Marcie nodded. 'I tried everywhere, but there're quite a lot of new people. You know, been here less than a lifetime and still foreigners. Then I found an old lady at the post office, she overheard me asking the man behind the counter about Joe. Wanted to know why *I* wanted to know. Well, I told her who I was and that we were trying to find out where Joe was buried – made up a story about Jack wanting to be buried with his brother.'

'And?'

'And she thought it was hilarious. They were still having a laugh about it when I left.'

She paused, milking her story for all it was worth.

'And?' Alec asked again.

'Joe isn't dead,' she said. 'He's very old and not very well, but he was still alive two years ago and no one's heard about him being dead, so . . .'

'So where?' Michael demanded.

Alec looked shaken. 'Not dead,' he repeated.

'Lincoln. A sheltered housing place or something.'

'No clues to which one, I suppose? Lincoln must be quite a big place.'

143

'Something with "woods" in the name, that's all she could remember.'

'Still alive,' Alec said again. 'Why would they lie about something like that?'

Chapter Twenty-Three

*I can remember her, Alec, when she was nine years old,
how tall she'd grown, all long legs and long black hair.
Pretty as a picture. We'd been on the beach all day. She
was brown all over, long brown legs, long brown arms
and that black hair. She wanted to ride the carousel.
Always her favourite. Only horse she ever rode, painted
and wooden with blue glass eyes.*

Couldn't ever go lame, a horse like that.

*Rye flour and camphor and . . . and I'll remember
soon . . .*

In the back seat of Alec's car, driving towards Lincoln,
Marcie read from one of Jack's letters.

> I remember a day, my darling, when you were
> nine, when we'd been to the seaside.
>
> We'd played on the beach all that day, just you
> and me. The others had gone off somewhere,
> sightseeing. But the two of us, well, we'd played
> and paddled and got wet and dirty and sticky
> from all the bad things we shouldn't have been
> eating.
>
> Then your gran and the others came and found

us. Time to go back. Time for tea. You know what a stickler your gran is for time.

Well, I'd promised you a ride on the carousel. We'd picked out the horse. A big white brute painted with red and blue swirls on his flanks and neck and with glassy blue eyes and we made Gran promise that we could go there first.

Then you saw that damned woman. Gypsy Rose something or other, standing on the caravan steps, and you wouldn't be satisfied. Wanted to know your fortune. And your gran, so against all that sort of thing.

'Gypsies,' she said. 'Gypsies.' Wouldn't have you dealing with any gypsies.

Forgets the past, your gran. Rewrites it when it suits. All of us gypsies at one time. Dealers and horse-traders, all the old families. The villages were founded by the gypsy folk. But she doesn't like remembering that, my Mary. Too much of a lady to remember her past. So she changes it to suit.

But, then, I guess we're all a little guilty of that, aren't we, my Birdie?

Anyway, she marched us off, said it was time to go, right there and then. No arguing with your gran when she'd got the bit between her teeth. Not ever.

You never did get to ride the carousel . . .

Marcie blinked the tears away. 'I remember that day,' she said softly.

Always hoped I'd teach you to ride, Birdie. Ride for real. I could see you racing through my dreams on some great white horse, with eyes like blue glass.

I see her in you, Bird, see my Becky. The baby we'd have had if life had been kinder, if I could have found a better way . . . Must be rye flour, Birdie, remember that. Rye flour and camphorated wine and three parts hog fat.

Remembered it, didn't I? Memory in the hands and in the eyes, Birdie. In the hands and in the eyes, even when the words forget how it should go.

They arrived in Lincoln just before one thirty and parked up behind the castle. The early-afternoon sun shone brightly on the massive bulk of the stone walls and slanted through the narrow alleyways leading to the tourist centre around the cathedral square. They wandered, like tourists, admiring the mellowed stone and mish-mash of styles left by centuries of patchwork growth, feeling relaxed but somewhat bemused.

Where to start looking for one old man in an entire city?

Alec took them up on to the city walls. Looking out towards the cathedral, the sun hot on her bare head, Marcie gazed down on the beautiful, muddled roofline of the old city.

'I like this,' Michael said, gazing at the cathedral's twin towers. 'Look at the height of those things.' He glanced at Marcie. 'Think we'll have time to go in?'

Marcie shrugged, lethargic in the afternoon's heat.

147

'Oh, I should think so,' Alec said. 'I don't know about you pair, but I'm starving.'

They stifled hunger with ice-cream and then walked the rest of the walls, climbing the tower from where prisoners were hanged, the gibbet suspending them out over the walls in full view of the town.

'If you look down there,' Alec pointed, 'there's a pub, called the Strugglers. Offered the best seats in the house for an execution. Jack used to say they laid bets from there on how long the hanged man would keep twitching.' He grimaced as though the thought left a bad taste.

Marcie stared down at the pub sign as he spoke.

'They've changed the sign,' he continued. 'Now it's just somebody struggling with a barrel.'

'Too much reality,' Marcie said. 'Maybe bad for business.'

Alec snorted. 'I doubt it.'

The image of Rebekkah as she had seen her in their flat drifted once more into Marcie's mind, Rebekkah with a rope pulled tight about her throat. Rebekkah weeping over her own lost child.

Finally they climbed the many steps to the Lucy tower, the walled graveyard. Burial place for prisoners executed by hanging from the high tower. Even in death there was no liberty.

Marcie walked slowly between the stark rows. Graves marked with tiny slates, inscribed with no more than the initials of the dead and the year their lives had been ended. The whole overshadowed by a giant, spreading yew.

She shuddered with the cold that seemed to permeate the walled garden even in the heat of the afternoon.

'We're wasting time,' she said at last, squaring her shoulders in a fashion so reminiscent of her grandmother.

Alec nodded. 'Let's find some lunch,' he said, 'and think what we should do.' He shuddered in his turn as they left the stone-walled circle and retraced their steps. 'It's been a shock,' he said at last, 'finding out about Joe. Thrown me, rather.'

Marcie touched his arm. 'Yeah,' she said. 'I know it sounds daft, but I was almost counting on not being able to find anything. I sort of thought that if we tried and failed, well, that would be an end to it.' She looked sideways at him, the unease of her little confession showing on her face.

'I know what you mean,' Alec acknowledged. 'Nothing to let us off the hook now, I suppose. I feel,' he paused, trying to find the words, 'manipulated,' he managed at last. 'Just because one old man is dying and another hasn't. Cheap of me, isn't it?'

'No, Da, not cheap. It's just so hard to understand. Why tell you that his brother's dead? I mean, people lose touch all the time and no one thinks anything of it. They might regret it, but they don't generally lie.'

They walked back through the castle gates and across into the cathedral court. The two men waited for her there while Marcie found a telephone to call Adele. They said little. The afternoon lethargy seemed to have spread and even conversation seemed too much effort.

'There's no one there,' Marcie said when she came back.

'Probably shopping, or Adele's taken them to the park.'

'I had a quick look in the phone book. There're literally dozens of homes and sheltered housing set-ups.'

'Register of electors,' Michael said. 'That's our best bet. If he's been here a couple of years he should be on it.'

'Right! Of course.' She frowned. 'Where do we find that?'

'Police stations, post offices, some of the bigger libraries. It shouldn't be that hard.'

'It's Saturday afternoon,' Alec commented. 'Post offices will probably be closed. We could ask where the nearest library is at the tourist information back near the castle, but maybe the police station would be easier.'

'Though what do we tell them?' Alec worried. 'I mean, surely you can't just walk in and say you want to see the register.'

'Well, you can in theory,' Michael told him, 'but it might be best to have a reason.'

'Why not the truth?' Marcie asked. 'You two really are making this complicated.'

'The truth,' Alec considered. 'Jack is dying and he keeps seeing ghosts. Now he's got other people seeing them too. We want to get rid of them, so we're trying to find Jack's brother, who, until a couple of hours ago, we all thought was dead, in order to get a fix on this ghost so we can make it go away.' He paused. 'That do?'

Marcie laughed at him. 'No. I mean we just say that we're looking for your father's long-lost brother. That they quarrelled and lost touch and now Jack's dying he wants to kiss and make up before it's too late.'

'Flexible view of the truth you have,' Alec commented.

Marcie grinned wickedly. 'I had some very creative teachers.'

At the police station the desk sergeant listened thoughtfully to Marcie's explanation, then stood for a moment regarding them curiously. Alec shifted uncomfortably, suddenly aware of what an odd trio they must seem. He had quite forgotten his own first reaction to Michael. But the tall black man with his tied-back locks and faded jeans was part of his family now and was rather put out by the officer's scrutiny. Marcie was used to second looks. She slipped her hand into Michael's and smiled sweetly. 'We'd be really grateful if you could help us,' she said. 'We've come a long way today and if I could phone home and tell them that we've found Joe, it would be a real weight off my gran's mind.'

The sergeant smiled, and Alec glanced at his daughter, impressed at how glibly the half-truths slid off her tongue.

'Well, I'll see what I can do for you,' he said. 'But it might take a few minutes, all right?'

'Thanks,' Marcie said.

'Couldn't we look through the list ourselves?' Alec asked. 'I mean, we don't want to put you to any trouble.'

'We're computerized, mainly,' the sergeant explained. 'Provided he's filled in his registration forms and he's lived here more than, say, a year, we should be able to track him down for you.'

They waited in the reception area while the officer spoke to someone in an inner office. Waited quite a time longer watching the sergeant deal with a string of queries and complaints, document checks and lost motorists, feeling awkward and out of place, as though somehow they were awaiting judgement.

Eventually, a young WPC came through and handed the sergeant a slip of paper. He looked up at them. 'You're in luck,' he said. 'Sorry it took so long, but it appears the old boy moved earlier in the year and he hasn't been logged on the general register yet.' He gave them the same speculative look as before. 'Would you like me to phone the home for you? Make sure he's still there?'

It looked like the only way he was going to let go of the piece of paper, so Marcie nodded.

'That would be very kind,' Alec said. He stood up abruptly and fished his wallet out of his pocket. 'If you could tell them that Alec Armitage and his daughter and son-in-law would like to see him, I'd be very grateful.'

He laid his wallet open on the counter, to display his driving licence and the passport-size photo on the name tag he wore at work. 'I know you have to be careful,' he said softly. 'We could be anyone. But if you could just phone them.'

The sergeant scrutinized the documents for a moment, then nodded. 'All right, Mr Armitage,' he said. 'You just hold on and I'll give them a call.'

It took time, again, for the call to be put through, for someone in charge to be found to take it, for them to confirm that, yes, Mr Joseph Armitage was a resident at Hill Grove.

Finally the policeman put the phone down and spoke to Alec again. 'Mrs Silverman wants you to go over and see her, then she'll introduce you to Mr Armitage. He's not been well, she doesn't want to shock the old man, so she asks that you let her prepare him.'

'Yes,' Alec nodded. 'That's fine, more than fine.'

The desk sergeant took another sheet of paper, scribbled the address and some directions on it and talked through them, checking that Alec understood.

'Thank you,' Alec said. 'You've been a big help. I thought we were going to have to work our way through the phone book.' He laughed nervously, then waited for Marcie and Michael to follow him out, thanking the officer in their turn.

'God!' he said as he left and walked swiftly away from the big glass doors. 'I hate police stations. Make me feel as though I've committed a crime.' He coloured slightly and glanced at Michael, who looked back, his eyes non-committal.

'Thought I was the one with the right to have a complex,' he said.

Alec laughed again, just as nervously, and got into the car. 'Goes back to when I was about five or six,' he said. 'We still had this local station, couple of streets away from where we lived, it's part of the community rooms now. Anyway, there was this local bobby. Looked like Dixon of Dock Green but he had a voice that would cut steel and a way of talking that put the fear of God into me.'

He shifted into first and began to negotiate his way out of the overcrowded station car park.

'Mam used to threaten me with him. Bit like the bogeyman only far worse. The bogeyman lived miles away; PC Edwards was round in our street twice, maybe three times a day.'

'Sounds like good solid neighbourhood policing,' Marcie commented cynically.

Alec checked the road then pulled out, shifting into gear and driving down towards the lights, the first direction they'd been given.

'Yes, well, your gran, being your gran, she got on just fine with the old bugger. Cups of tea, cake, the works, and when I'd been a bit too much of a handful she'd threaten to call him, get him to lock me in the cells.'

'And did she?' Marcie asked.

'Damned right she did. I'd been playing her up or something. I don't even remember the reason. All I recall is coming home past the station and being dragged inside and her telling this big fat man who scared me so much that he was to lock me in his cell until I said sorry to her.'

Michael laughed, but it was a sound of disgust and disbelief. 'And did he?' he asked.

'Well,' Alec conceded, 'I'm not sure the place even had cells, but he shut me in this little room and left me there. I remember screaming the place down. Pulling on the handle and throwing myself at the wooden door trying to get out. I was convinced she'd just left me there and was never coming back. God, I was scared.'

Marcie stared at him with a mixture of recognition and sympathy. 'How long did she leave you?' she asked.

Alec shook his head. 'Look at those directions again, will you, Marcie? I think it's next left.'

He was silent as Marcie checked the scribbled instructions on the paper and relayed them back to him.

No, he thought, it probably hadn't been long. Ten minutes, maybe, but it had seemed like for ever and the panic had grown worse with every minute. At last he had become hysterical, beating against the walls with his fists, no longer even able to scream as his lungs locked tight and his head began to spin. Suddenly, he had felt the warm spurt of urine soaking the front of his shorts and flowing down his legs, forming a little puddle on the station floor. He had been even more terrified then, fearing his mother's continued anger, fed by the shame that he'd disgraced himself, disgraced her even further.

Alec remembered little more after that. Just the confused images of his own panic and desperation, blurring into a fog of pain, and his mother's voice, hot and angry, as PC Edwards finally opened the door to let him out.

Chapter Twenty-Four

Hill Grove was trying hard to live up to its name. Certainly, it was on the top of a small hill, and whoever owned it seemed to be attempting to construct the grove. Two mature trees in the front garden of the big Victorian house had been joined by younger, newly planted shrubberies and dense, overdressed flower borders. Everything appeared dusty and wilted in the summer heat. The grass was parched as a result of the hosepipe ban and even the brick pathway that led to an impressive black door with brass fittings was bleached and desiccated.

The front door stood slightly open to let what little breeze there was make its way into the hall. There was no one at the reception desk, but a bell sounded as Alec pushed the door wider, and a woman came through from what looked like a dining room; tables laid with check cloths and little vases of flowers could be seen through the open door behind her.

'Can I help you?' she asked, but she gave the impression that she knew already who they were and why they were here.

'I'm Alec Armitage,' Alec said. 'My daughter, Marcie, and my son-in-law, Michael Whitney.'

'Martha Silverman,' the woman said, extending her hand towards Alec. Then, 'I don't mean to be rude, but could you . . .'

'Of course,' Alec said. He produced his wallet once again and identified himself.

Michael reached into the pocket of his jeans and found his pass card for the law centre, giving his picture and his job description. 'You're a legal adviser?' the woman said. 'That must be a fascinating job. Is it like being a solicitor?'

She seemed satisfied then, not really waiting for Michael to reply and passing up on Marcie altogether.

'I'm sorry,' she said, 'but, you see, Joe has always told us that he has no family.'

'My father told me that Joe was dead a long time ago,' Alec said, as though to confirm this. 'They quarrelled, I understand. But Jack's dying now. He's not expected to last much longer and I think, well, I think he wants forgiveness.'

The woman regarded him thoughtfully, then she nodded. 'I told Joe you might be coming,' she said. 'I don't know if he took it all in but he's agreed to see you.'

They followed her out through the back of the house, through what had once been french doors – now widened and with a shallow ramp leading on to a terrace. A further shallow ramp with handrails on either side led down on to a broad, sun-parched lawn. More trees, more flowers, chairs and tables and an elderly man taking practice swings with a golf club and a tethered ball. The rear of the house had been added to, nicely, but with little reference to the original architecture. Two single-storey wings extended its width; living accommodation, Marcie guessed, with level patios running along the full length.

As they stepped on to the lawn a large tabby cat uncurled and stretched and looked up expectantly, then wandered off to find a better place in the sun, its tail in the air.

There was a quietness to Hill Grove, a sense of peaceable decay that both pleased and saddened. There must be, Marcie thought, far worse environments in which to spend your final years, but for all that it was melancholy.

Joe was seated at a small table under the shade of a massive lime tree. He wore a cardigan with leather buttons despite the day's heat, and a bright red Chicago Bulls baseball cap shading his eyes from the late-afternoon sun. A chess set, carved wooden pieces on a wooden board, was placed in front of him and he seemed to be concentrating on a half-finished game.

'Joe,' Martha Silverman said gently. 'These are the people I was telling you about.'

He looked up. It wasn't that their faces were all that alike, but the faded brown eyes that met Marcie's – their gaze curious and alert – could well have been Jack's.

'Joe,' Alec began, 'we've, er, come to . . .'

But Marcie stepped forward, her eyes fixed on the old man's, her hand fumbling inside her bag. Slowly, she removed the photograph of the summer harvest from her bag and laid it in front of him.

Chapter Twenty-Five

They drank tea and ate digestive biscuits, gathered around the tiny table. Alec had helped Mrs Silverman to get more chairs and she had brought the tea and biscuits on a tray, which Joe had insisted be placed on the ground and not on the table. 'I'm in the middle of a game,' he objected.

'You're always in the middle of a game, Joe.' She turned with a confidential air to the others. 'The trouble is, he has no one to play with here. He's beaten everyone who can play and now he says there's no opposition worth the name.'

'Well, there isn't,' he declared irascibly.

'I play,' Michael said.

Joe regarded him thoughtfully. 'Do you?' he said. 'I mean, do you *play*, or do you just know how to move the pieces?'

Michael was regarding the board carefully. He reached behind him and pulled up a chair, sitting down with his eyes still fixed on the board. 'White knight to king's bishop four,' he said, his hand hovering over the board. 'May I?'

Joe's eyes had lighted with sudden interest. 'Go ahead,' he said. 'Well, now. You pour the tea for us, there's a good girl,' he said to Marcie, rubbing his hands together in anticipation and studying the board with deep

Jane Adams

interest. 'Well, now,' he repeated. 'Looks like we may have ourselves a proper game here.'

Marcie rolled her eyes at Alec, then knelt down beside the tea tray and began to arrange the cups and saucers and pour the tea. Joe seemed almost to have forgotten them. For several minutes they sat in silence, watching the deliberations of the chess players and politely sipping tea. Marcie used the time to take a good look at her great-uncle.

Sitting down, it was hard to tell, but he looked to be about Jack's height and build. His hands were knotted by arthritis, blue veins stood out through the mottled, suntanned skin. His face was weathered with far more lines around the eyes than Jack had managed to collect, but there was a vibrancy in his movements, and especially in the brightness of his eyes and in his smile, that Jack had lacked, not just during his illness but for many years.

She found herself thinking back to her beloved, child-hood, Jack. The one who could make the whole world right with a single word. The Jack who had arranged her birthday treats and taken her to the zoo, to the seaside. To see the latest Disney at the pictures. It occurred to her, not for the first time, just how rarely anyone else featured in these memories. Usually, it was just Jack and Bird, walking down the street hand in hand, the man's head bowed to hear the little girl's chatter. Gran and Aunt Alice and even her father had always been distant figures, watching from behind the curtained glass. Lips growing tighter and eyes sadder with the passing years and the exclusiveness of an old man's love.

160

Marcie looked across at Alec, meeting his eyes, seeing the tiredness in them as if for the first time.

There was so much bitterness in her heart directed at these others who had made her life with Jack less than perfect. She could not forgive them, any of them, Jack included, for all they had done. But she began to wonder, for the first time, just how much less than perfect had she in turn made their relationship with Jack. How much of their lives had Marcie swallowed whole and never realized. Never thought about until now.

Her reverie was interrupted by Joe clearing his throat, about to speak. With his hand still hovering over the board, still assessing his next move, he said, 'So, what have you found me for? Martha spun me some yarn about that brother of mine wanting to make peace, but I don't believe that.'

He made his move swiftly, his twisted hand swooping down with sudden agility and shifting his bishop two squares.

Marcie heard Michael whistle admiringly, but, glancing at the board, could only make a guess at who was ahead.

'What makes you so sure?' she asked him. 'Why shouldn't Jack want to be reconciled with you?'

The old man looked at her, his eyes shadowed beneath the peak of his cap. 'What makes you so sure I want to be reconciled with him?' he asked sharply. 'Believe me, my dear, I could see that so-called brother of mine burning in hell and I wouldn't even give him the grace of pissing on his balls.'

Marcie stared hard at the old man, who'd now turned

his interest back to his game. She looked at Alec; her father's round face wore a shocked expression that matched Marcie's own. Michael was laughing to himself. His eyes were fixed on the board and his face was admirably blank, but there was no mistaking the humour that shook his shoulders and twitched the corners of his mouth.

'I hadn't really thought of that,' Marcie said slowly. 'That you might not want to be contacted, I mean.'

Joe snorted rudely. 'Well, you know now,' he said. He cocked an eyebrow in Marcie's direction. 'And does he want to make peace? I mean, has he actually said so?'

'Well, no,' Marcie admitted. 'Not exactly.'

'So what is this all about, eh? I hear nothing from my so-called family for close on forty years and then three of you turn up out of nowhere and talk like UN peacemakers. I mean, lass,' he said, a smile easing the sternness from his question, 'you got to admit it's a bit of a conundrum.'

Marcie took a deep breath. 'It's a long sort of story, Joe,' she said, uncomfortable with the prefix of 'uncle'. 'I'm not too certain where I should begin.'

'Well,' he told her, the smile getting broader. 'Choose somewhere. If I need to go back a bit then I'll tell you. Be like Alice, begin at the beginning and carry on until you reach the end. Then this pair can help you fill in the gaps. Maybe you could start with how I've got myself a great-niece with a name like Marciella.'

'Italian mother,' she said with a smile. 'She died when I was just a baby and my da brought me home to live with Jack and Gran and Aunt Alice.'

Slowly, hesitantly, and with a great many interruptions from both Alec and Joe, Marcie pieced together the story of how she'd lived with her aunt, father and grandparents. And then the hardest part, trying to explain that Jack, this shadow-Jack who lay in some half-world of his own making, had found no peace in dying.

Instinctively, Marcie had not named the woman that haunted Jack's waking dream. Had kept the details sparse and made no reference to her own nightmares. Joe made no comment at this point, but, watching him, she could see his hands begin to tremble at each move he made on the board, and there was a curious, expectant tension in the set of his shoulders as he bent forward studying the game.

Marcie pushed the photograph towards him once again.

'The woman Jack keeps seeing,' she said. 'I think I know who she is. I know she died a long time ago. My father told me that much.'

Joe leaned back in his chair, his eyes fixed on the board as though still planning his move.

Not sure what to think, but knowing that the old man was deeply disturbed by what she had been saying, Marcie pointed to the woman in the picture.

'That's her,' she said, moving the image so that the dappled light, filtered by the spreading tree, illuminated Rebekkah's face. 'Her name's Rebekkah, Joe. We wondered, maybe. You must have known her. Do you know why Jack's so obsessed? What's eating him so much?'

Joe didn't look at the image she had set before him; instead he reached out and moved his queen, placing her to block the check that would have been Michael's next move.

'Oh, yes, I know her, lass. I know her. You see, Rebekkah was my wife.'

Chapter Twenty-Six

*We moved to Naples after Monte Cassino. Days of
being pinned down, flat on our bellies in the mud while
the world exploded all around us.*

*Then Naples and the quiet shock of relative peace
for a little while. The town clinging to the hillside with
views of a calm blue sea and Capri on the horizon,
beautiful and grey in the empty distance.*

*The thing I remember most, Birdie, was the kids.
Dozens of the little mites, begging in the streets. There
was one little thing, a little girl about six years old with
great dark eyes and long black hair. She was just like
Becky looked as a child and she had that way with her
of looking at you. Young as a baby and old as the first
woman ever born, and I knew that she was the one.*

Jack watched the child.

He stood in the filthy street between narrow houses.
The sky was an unearthly, polished blue and the sun beat
down on the tiled roofs and battered, whitewashed walls.

The town might have been beautiful, Jack thought.
At a different time and if his mind had not been so full
of ugliness and dying. He could see with his eyes the
loveliness that might have been there, even though he
could not feel it in his heart. And there were signs here

and there of the kind of normality that dominates even at the height of war. Someone had grown flowers in a stone jar by a door, and washing hung across the street, bright and clean, blowing upward towards the red-tiled roofs.

And the child, she seemed caught between war and non-war. Dancing her way down the dirty street, hopping and jumping, hopscotch without the numbers chalked upon the floor.

Bright and lovely she was, and untouched. The kind of child that he and Becky might have brought into the world.

But the world of war touched her as totally as it did Jack himself. Sullied the brightness he perceived in her. Earlier, as they had passed by, she had held out her hand and run along beside them. Two words of English she seemed to have by heart: 'Soldier give! Soldier give!'

These marching troops might be her parents' enemy, but her smile was bright and she had learned that few people could resist a pretty child.

They had stopped for a time then, sitting on the broken walls and smoking stubs of cigarettes, waiting to find out where they'd be camped. Jack wasn't sure what made him follow her a few brief steps as she ran back down the hill and disappeared into an alleyway that led towards the harbour.

Staring down at the way she had gone, Jack could see the clearer signs of passing war. Bombed-out buildings and charred ruins, stark and ugly against the clear blue of the sky and sea. And he lost sight of her, the dancing child, lost her amongst the confusion and rubble of broken buildings and blocked roads.

Her image danced in his mind, even as they were called to order and marched on.

And Jack smiled.

Chapter Twenty-Seven

They found bed and breakfast accommodation for the night a few streets away from Joe's home. It looked expensive, Marcie thought, here in this rather select and proper Victorian backwater.

'I'm paying,' Alec informed her abruptly. 'Least I can do.'

They were a little late if they wanted dinner, the woman at reception told them. It really needed to be booked, though she was certain something could be arranged.

Alec shook his head. 'No, we'll just get ourselves tidied up,' he said. 'Then probably go out for a while.'

The woman nodded, took his credit card details and signed them in.

'I'll meet you in the lounge,' Alec said. 'Say forty minutes. Give you time to get yourselves sorted out. Then we'll go and find somewhere to eat.'

Marcie flexed her tired muscles. The day seemed to stretch for ever behind them and she felt extraordinarily tired.

'I must phone Adele,' she said, suddenly pining for her children and wishing herself back at home.

As it happened, both Michael and Alec were ready early. Alec was sitting by the window reading the evening paper when Michael found him. He sat down opposite and gazed out of the window, listening to the soft rustle of pages as Alec read and the clatter, distant and comforting, of the other guests in the dining room.

'Marcie's just getting changed and calling home,' he told Alec. 'I think she plans to call the hospice as well.'

Alec nodded, then put his paper down and folded his hands comfortably in his lap.

'Do you think he killed her?' Alec asked. It hadn't seemed quite polite to ask the old man they'd just taken tea with if he'd killed his wife.

Anyway, the revelation had thrown them off balance.

'I don't know,' Michael said. 'He doesn't look like a murderer . . . but I suppose they don't, do they?'

Michael laughed, then stopped and looked at Alec strangely.

Alec went on.

'That boy I was telling you about. The one that made Marcie pregnant . . .'

Michael held up a hand to silence him. 'I don't want to know, Alec. Marcie told me all she could, long ago. Told me the official line was that he'd been attacked, mugged, probably, and died of hypothermia. She wasn't sure whether or not to believe it . . .'

'That's exactly it, Michael. I want to get this out into the open. All these years I've . . .'

'Then go to a priest. Go to the police. Salve your conscience elsewhere. That's not what I'm here for.' He paused and sighed. 'Look, Alec. I'm going along with this for Marcie. Given time I could even get to like you. But you've got to grow up, Alec. You can't make it better by piling your guilt on to someone else's lap. It's bad enough that Jack's doing that. I don't think we can handle your share as well.'

For a moment Alec was indignant. Then he nodded slowly. 'You're right, of course,' he said. 'But at the moment I don't know what to do.'

'Alec, you've done nothing all these years. A day or so won't make no difference.'

'And when I decide?'

'Decide what?' Marcie asked, coming up behind him.

'How's things?' Michael spoke as she bent to kiss him, covering for Alec's startled look.

'Twins are fine. They all went to the park this afternoon. Sophie Lee, Adele, Kate and her two and Leroy. Must have looked like a coach trip.' She faltered slightly.

'And Jack?'

Marcie shook her head. 'Much worse. They've got him on a morphine pump. He can't last much longer.' She looked helplessly at Michael, and he reached for her hand, gripping it tight.

'Well, then,' he said softly. 'We'd better get this right, hadn't we?'

Alice had stepped out into the hospice garden for a breath of air, leaving Mary alone. The day had been even hotter than expected, without even a breath of wind to stir the treetops or brush against the curtains.

It was eight thirty in the evening. The sky had begun to darken, but not with night blackness. 'There's going to be a storm, Jack,' Mary whispered, bending close to him but keeping her eyes fixed on the gathering clouds billowing iron-grey across the sky. 'You always loved to watch the rain. See the lightning and when the thunder cracked you'd count the seconds. Do you remember, Jack? Do you remember?

'Marcie must have been two years old. Such a tiny little thing, more like a baby doll than a toddler. That night the storm wrecked those climbing roses you loved so much. You held her in the window. Tiny little doll standing on the sill while the rain streamed down so fast that was almost all you could see through the glass. A world viewed through water and bright flashes opening up the sky . . .'

'She'll be scared, Jack, bring her off there.'

'No, she won't, not my Bird. Look at that, my darling, like fireworks. Just like fireworks.'

The child's eyes opened wide. She was trembling, whether with fear or with the chill coming off the glass Mary couldn't tell, but Jack held her tightly, his body pressed close to hers and one arm circling across her small, baby-plump body.

'Lights. Lights, Ganda Jack.'

'Yes, my darling, pretty lights.'

Mary had stepped back from them, watching. Excluded. As a child, Alec had been frightened of the storms. Had hidden under the table or behind a chair and never overcome Jack's disgust of such cowardice.

'Lights,' Marcie said again, small hand reaching out

as though to seize them, bring their brightness into the room.

Jack stroked her gently, his voice soft and full of praise, his face close to her dark curls.

A second small hand reached out for the lightning, the urgency of the child's desire transforming her entire body. She seemed to grow taller, bigger with the strength of it. Jack held her even tighter, his arms circling her as though he could never bear to let the moment go.

As if on cue a massive lightning flash crashed with full violence right outside the window. Mary cried out in fear and leapt instinctively towards her husband and grandchild.

Then she let her hands fall back to her sides and stood, still and despairing, watching them both. The crack of thunder followed swiftly on the lightning's tail and Mary watched, cursing her own despair. Her own unheeded need to love, as the child, hands still raised towards the heavens, laughed aloud.

'Your granddaughter just called,' the nurse told her, startling Mary back to the present.

'Are you all right, love? I didn't mean to make you jump.'

'Yes, yes, I'm fine.'

'I told her you were here, but she was in a payphone and didn't have much change.'

Mary nodded. 'Yes,' she said. 'I see. Thank you.'

She sighed deeply and reached across to take Jack's

bony white hand in her own. 'Even now,' she said softly. 'Even now, she's trying to take you away from me.'

They had found a pizza restaurant and been too tired to look for anything else. They ordered Pizza Margherita with extra toppings and salad from the salad bar. Marcie had eaten half of her salad and was wondering if she could sneak back for a second helping long before the pizza arrived.

'How come you don't get fat, eating the way you do?' Alec asked her.

Marcie shrugged. 'I get hungry. Normal, healthy appetite, that's all.'

'God, I can remember a time when we couldn't get a damn thing down you.'

He broke off, suddenly embarrassed. After the abortion, Marcie had just refused to eat. Even when she'd recovered a little and had gone back to school, she seemed to have no appetite. And then, when she had found out about Patrick Simpson, things had gone from bad to worse. Her emotional outbursts had become daily events. She refused to believe anything any of them said. Would barely even look at Jack, and her appetite had diminished to almost nothing once again.

Finally, she had fainted at school and they had had no choice but to get medical advice. The doctor had diagnosed eating problems, possibly anorexia. Had pressed for the family to let Marcie see a psychiatrist, wanted her to attend a special unit at the local hospital.

Outraged, and for once in harmony, Mary and Jack had refused.

Marcie had grown progressively worse. Underweight, lethargic but for the fierceness of her temper. Bitter. Then there had come the night when she had found the papers Jack had kept hidden in his garden shed. He'd bought and clipped out every report he could find about Patrick Simpson's death. Pasted each account into a scrapbook.

Marcie had brought the book up to the house.

The back door had slammed open, smashing against the kitchen counter. Eyes blazing, more life in her body than she had had in a long, long time, Marcie almost hurled herself through the living room door and threw the book into Jack's lap.

This was not like the time when she had first found out about Patrick Simpson. This time there was no hysteria, no rage, just a quiet despair

'Did you kill him, Jack? Did you? Did you?'

And Jack had stared at her, dumbfounded, as though even to think such a thing was madness.

'No, my Birdie. No, I swear to you. I never laid a hand on him.'

'You're lying to me, Jack, I know you are. Oh, Jack, I don't know what to think about you any more.'

She stood in front of him, dark eyes burning as though she had a fever, not wanting to believe. Begging Jack to explain, to tell her beyond doubt that it wasn't like that. That she could still salvage something of her old life.

Then there was Mary, holding Marcie in a fierce grip, her fingers digging deep into the thin flesh of her arms.

'He did nothing, Marcie, nothing. What do you think you're doing, bursting in here like this? Hysteria, girl, that's what it is.'

'I'm not . . .' Her voice rose as she began to protest. It was all the cue that Mary needed.

She slapped Marcie hard across the face, holding her steady with her other hand.

'I don't believe you,' the girl was whimpering now. 'Don't believe any of you. Oh, Jack, I want to believe.'

The following day Marcie was admitted to hospital. She had wandered into the emergency room in the early hours of the morning, clearly distressed, frozen. Dressed for bed with just a coat around her shoulders despite the bitter cold. She had been close to collapse. The hospital had informed the police, who had in turn contacted her family. Jack and Alec had rushed down, only to find their access denied.

'She doesn't want to see anyone,' they were told. 'You see, Mr Armitage,' the houseman told them carefully, 'your daughter is severely underweight, and possibly in a psychotic state. She's certainly very distressed. It's best if we go along with what she wants, for the moment, at least.'

Alec stared at him. It was the first and only time that anyone had addressed him, and not Jack, when they had talked about what was best for Marcie.

'I want to see her. When can I see her?'

The doctor shook his head. 'I'm sorry, Mr Armitage, but she doesn't want to see you. Any of you, I'm afraid, and we do what's best for our patients.'

Marcie had been sixteen and a half. It was almost a year since Patrick Simpson's death.

'You put yourself in hospital, didn't you?' Alec asked her now. It was something he had wanted to know for a long time. 'I mean, all that stuff about you being anorexic. It was just your way of getting back at us.'

Marcie didn't respond immediately. She stabbed viciously at a piece of new potato, heavy with mayonnaise.

'It got me away from all of you,' Marcie said at last. 'Anorexia, I don't know. Seems to me that's a word that labels a lot of problems and I saw a lot of kids that really couldn't help what they were doing. Me, I didn't want to eat. I didn't want to live. I certainly didn't want to be with any of you. It wasn't about the way I looked, I mean not even superficially about that. I'd given up thinking how I looked by then. It was about, I don't know, about what I didn't want to be.'

She looked across at her father. 'Look, Da, I don't think I'm ready for this now. We've other things to think about. Maybe another time, but not just now. I guess the reason I'm here, now, talking about this at all is because I want to move on. I can't, you know, not with Jack the way he is.' She paused, shook her head as though confused. 'I want to be free, Da. Free of all the things I think I owe the old Jack. The one I loved when I was a little kid. Stuff I owe all of you, I guess.'

Alec nodded slowly. 'Do you still love him?' he asked.

'What do you think? Oh, God, Da, you don't stop loving someone, not really. I've still got most of a lifetime tied up in memories of Jack. Memories of all of you.'

Alec said nothing. He felt that the last part had been added in deference to his feelings and wished it wasn't so. He was about to say more, but Michael, noting the tension in Marcie's voice, moved the conversation on.

'What do you think about Joe?' he asked.

There was silence for a moment, then, 'I think I could like him,' Marcie said.

'Do you think he killed her?'

Marcie shook her head. 'I don't know.'

'Jack always said that Rebekkah was killed by her husband. If Joe was her husband . . .'

'Jack also said that Joe was dead.'

'Well,' Alec went on as their pizza arrived, 'we see him tomorrow. Maybe we'll be able to talk about it then.'

'He plays a damned good game of chess,' Michael said, his voice admiring.

'Oh well, that's all right, then,' Marcie replied.

Michael smiled across at her, his look intimate. Alec watched them, feeling like an outsider. His mind drifted to Marianne, to the two short years they had had together. If she had lived, how would things have been? Would they have always been so happy? Would he always have felt as complete as he had back then?

Or would they have become like Jack and Mary? Disappointed and frustrated by a life that failed to deliver?

He thought of Joe, old and alone with only the memories of a woman long gone. A woman who had died by violence as great as that which had taken Marianne, but far more sinister.

Sighing, eating his meal with little awareness of how

it tasted, Alec thought of Joe as they had last seen him. An old, slightly awkward figure, walking with an ornately twisted stick, making his way across a parched lawn checkered by deep tree-cast shadows.

Alone. Alone for a long time now.

Alec shuddered suddenly as he found himself remembering the old man's face, and in his mind seeing not Joe's eyes but his own gazing back at him.

Chapter Twenty-Eight

It wasn't hard to get away. A few extra cigarettes slipped to the guard and that was it. They knew me. Knew I'd do the same for them some time.

I went back to where I had last seen the child disappear amongst the blasted rubble. It was a test, you see. If I hadn't found her that night, well, that would have been an end to it. Same, if Benny hadn't come back so soon, or that boy hadn't been there ... A test, just circumstances.

But I knew the child would be there. Knew for certain.

I caught sight of her in the half-light, playing amongst the dirt and bricks and broken tiles, the moonlight bathing her skin so that already she looked ghostlike against the dark sky.

She looked up, scared at first, when she saw me. Then smiled widely as she realized who and what I was and came forward with her hands outstretched and her begging eyes fixed on mine.

I gave her money and the little bit of chocolate I had in my pocket and sat talking to her while she ate it.

Such a pretty little thing. And I could see Rebekkah, watching me all the time, standing in the shadows, just at the limit of my sight. Waiting for me.

I was sorry, you see, Bird, though I'll never get the

chance to tell you. Sorry for what had happened to
her, and sorry, most of all, for the child that never got
a chance to live. I knew she must be lonely.

So I knew she'd understand when I reached out and
tried to smooth the tangle of curls back from the little
girl's face, then took the comb from my pocket to ease
away the cots. I knew Becky understood when she
came closer so that I could see her clearly, and I knew
she didn't mean me to stop, even though she held her
hands out as though to hold mine still, her shadow
blocking out the light as I tightened my grip around
the child's throat.

Marcie drove. The roadways were twisting and narrow,
at times with an almost alpine drop into deep green
valleys.

Much of the road was over-arched with trees and the
dappled shift of light through leaves confused Marcie's
vision. Shadows took flight at the corner of her eye as
the car sped by and she thought of Rebekkah, running
with the shadows through the trees. Rebekkah, dancing
with the shifting sunlight. Laughing, dreaming her
dreams.

Rebekkah, dying in the cold darkness.

They took Joe to Ludford, but he had no wish to
stop there, so they went on a mile or two and found a
narrow place to park beside a little church set back from
the road and sitting atop a bank. The bank was faced by
local stone. Once, maybe, the graveyard had sloped
down, level with the road, but the years of burials had

built it high, and only the wall kept it from washing across the road in the winter storms.

Marcie couldn't guess how old the church was, but its stone was mellow and weathered and the path was shiny with the wear from centuries of feet. The church was locked and they couldn't get inside, but a notice in the porch gave the times of service. One Sunday in three a vicar could be spared for worship here, and this was not one of them.

Joe walked slowly, leaning on his stick. He wandered through the graveyard, Michael holding his arm when the going was hard. Joe pointed out the graves of people he had known or been related to. It was just past mid-morning, but already the day was growing warm. Joe wore the same thick, oatmeal-coloured cardigan with the leather buttons as he had the day before. It was buttoned closed, his only real concession to the heat the Chicago Bulls cap that shielded his eyes from the worst of the sun.

They made their way around to the back of the church. The graveyard, where it faced the road, had been well trimmed and the grass and plants cut back. At the back, the graves looked older and less ordered. Joe pointed to a place to the rear of the walled graveyard where long grass had not yet been cut and where brambles and nettles fought to dominate.

'She's buried there,' he said softly. 'My Becky.'

Michael helped him walk over the uneven grass towards the trees that bordered the graveyard.

'How long since you've been here?' he asked.

'Too long,' Joe told him sadly. He frowned in puzzlement, then shook his head. 'I can't quite remember. She's here somewhere, but I can't see.'

He edged closer to the overgrown foliage, his movements stiff and awkward. His distress that he couldn't pinpoint his wife's grave was serving to make him even more unsteady.

'Stand still,' Michael told him. 'I'll see what I can find.' He began trampling down the nettles, gingerly pulling the brambles aside.

'Should we be doing this?' Alec asked.

'Haven't noticed that you're doing anything,' Joe told him. 'Here, come and let me hold your arm. Here, girl.' He handed his walking stick to Marcie. 'Let him use this. I know she's there, my Becky. I know she's there.'

It took time for Michael and Marcie to clear the undergrowth away and expose the grave. Time in which Joe watched in excited silence and Alec glanced about him, fearful that they might be seen. At last, Marcie uttered a little cry of triumph. 'It's here, Joe!' she called out, as though until that moment she hadn't quite believed it.

She and Michael stood up, their hands covered in scratches from the brambles, their clothes stained with the ripening fruit. They held the long briars and runners aside for Joe to see beneath.

He stared in silence at the low mound of raised earth and at the simple headstone, muddied and stained.

'Read it to me,' he said as though he needed confirmation. Michael knelt, his fingers brushing away the dirt and grime, reading as much with his hand as with his eyes.

Rebekkah Armitage. Born May 4th 1914. Died
February 14th 1937, aged twenty-three. God
enfold you in his arms.

He looked up at Joe as though expecting some
response, but there was none. The old man's eyes had
filled with tears, but he said nothing. Instead he took his
stick from Marcie, reclaimed Michael's arm and pointed
back the way they had come.

'Take me over there,' he demanded. 'I want to show
you something else.'

The something else was a tiny grave marked by an
equally tiny stone. The grass was clipped and neat and
the headstone cleaned, the words easily visible.

'That's where Mary's child is buried,' he told them.
'It lived long enough to be given baptism. Margaret, they
called her. Poor little bugger. Cursed before she was even
born.'

'Cursed?' Marcie asked, wondering if he was
speaking metaphorically.

Joe nodded sadly. 'They said that was what did it. I
weren't here, of course. Locked me up by then, they had.'

Marcie shot a quick glance at her father, but Joe
didn't pause in his narrative.

'It was Becky's mother cursed her. 'lizabeth. Took me
years to find out what had happened and why she'd got
it in for Mary and Jack. Then Jack told me and it started
to make sense.'

He paused, shaking his head as if denying some
memory. They almost held their breath waiting for him
to go on.

Looking down once more at the tiny grave, Marcie frowned. The grass might have been clipped as part of a general measure to keep the front of the graveyard tidy and presentable, but that could not explain everything. Although Margaret died, the inscription said, in 1937, and her parents had long since moved away, fresh flowers in a little vase had been newly placed upon her grave.

Mary sat in Alice's big chair. She had moved it back from the window and sat in shadow, made deeper by the shaft of sunlight streaming through the window into the centre of the room.

She had been too hot, taken off her soft pink cardigan and sat down in the chair, her mind wandering. The cardigan lay in her arms now. She hugged it close, one hand stroking its softness as she rocked gently, singing a lullaby:

> *When you wake, you will have*
> *all the pretty, little horses . . .*

It had been a Sunday. Coming out of church on Jack's arm, the pleats of her best blue dress stretched tight over the swelling of her stomach. The baby kicking and squirming like a fish inside her.

So happy she had been. So very happy.

'Here, it's chilly, love, slip your coat on,' Jack had said. He'd been content lately and so attentive. Now the baby was almost due and the terrible events of the winter could be put aside.

Mary took his arm and they promenaded together down the churchyard path to the little gate, greeting friends, enjoying the watery spring sunshine glinting through the trees.

So happy, at peace, the man she loved beside her, showing her off to everyone. Proud, of her and of the child she carried.

Then out of nowhere she appeared. Elizabeth Lacey. Her black hair in tangles about her face, her clothes disordered and her youngest daughter tugging at her arm, trying to pull her away.

It was as if she owned the moment. The silence that fell all about her was unbroken but for her breathing, heavy and laboured, and her cry of pain as she caught sight of Jack.

'You!' she cried out. 'You. You killed her. You killed my Becky!'

Mary was stunned. She stood still beside Jack, clinging to his arm.

'Away with you, woman,' someone told her. 'Jack hadn't nothing to do with it.'

'You can't blame one brother for what another did, 'lizabeth.'

The vicar stepped forward trying to calm her, summoning help to assist her daughter, Ann, in easing Elizabeth Lacey away.

'She's mad,' Mary said. 'Mad or drunk.'

'Mad, am I?' Elizabeth hurled back at her. 'Drunk, is it? Let me tell you, I buried my child here in this churchyard. Mad with grieving if I'm mad at all. Drunk on it, I am.'

She broke free of those holding her and pointed a finger directly at Mary. 'And I'll tell you this, woman. You'll know what it's like to grieve for a lost one. That child of yours will not draw breath before you're burying it.'

A stunned silence fell once again over the gathered company. Mary stared, shocked. She placed her hands over her swollen belly as though to protect the unborn child.

'Mam, come away, Mam, please.'

People were protesting and trying to intervene.

'That was cruel, Elizabeth. Cruel and undeserved.'

'Mary, it's all right, love. It's like she said, the woman's mad with grief. She doesn't know what she's saying.'

Elizabeth was calmer now. She stood at the centre of a hostile circle, her eyes fixed on Mary.

Then she let Ann lead her away from the crowd, but she turned back towards them, looking over her shoulder, her eyes fixed on Mary's face.

'Mary? Oh, Mary, what is it, love?'

Alice set the tea tray down on the little table and went to her sister-in-law's side.

'Oh, sweetheart, please don't cry. Please don't, I think it's more than I could bear.'

She took her hands and pulled her from the chair and into her arms, folding her tightly.

'Oh, Mary. Mary, I know, my love, I know.' Tears flooded her own eyes then and ran unchecked down her face. Tears Marcie and the men of the house would never have been allowed to see.

'I was thinking about Margaret,' Mary sobbed. 'About my baby.' Her voice trailed off into a thin stream of crying. 'I could have loved her so much, Alice. So much, if there'd been room for me.'

Alice held her tightly, stroking her back and kissing her grey hair. 'I know, love, I know you could,' she said, uncertain if Mary still meant Margaret, or if she spoke of Bird.

'What did Jack tell you?' Marcie asked him at last, when she could bear the waiting no longer.

Joe closed his eyes for a moment. Then opened them again and looked back to where his wife was buried under the deep shadow of the ancient trees.

'About him and Rebekkah,' he said slowly. 'Always knew there was someone but I didn't know who. There were rumours, of course, all over the village about Becky being unfaithful. She had that look about her that men couldn't seem to resist and, God above, but she was beautiful. Black hair and dark eyes that could melt your heart, and skin like honey with the sun on it.'

'And Rebekkah and Jack...' Marcie whispered, beginning to understand. Understand a whole lot of things.

'They were lovers,' Joe said. 'And, likely as not, that baby she carried was his.'

'How can you be so certain?' Michael asked him.

'I can count, lad. Because when she got herself pregnant, I'd been away a month or more.'

He shook his head sadly. 'Things were bad. Work wasn't easy to find and I wanted the best for her. Not just a farm worker's wage. Often enough there wasn't even that. And if you couldn't work, you ended up on the parish given a pittance that wouldn't even pay the rent.

'I'd gone away after most of the harvest was brought in. A week or so after that picture you showed me, lass. That was taken early August. I was gone by the end of it. Two months without a break I was away, then I came home for a couple of weeks. She should have told me then. She must have known. But never a word.'

He sighed deeply and stared down at the baby's grave.

'Jack was full of it, how his Mary was in the family way . . . I should have come back at the Christmas, but I'd found a place on a merchantman. They needed unskilled hands. Hard work, long hours. But the pay was good. I came home on February the eighteenth. She'd been away, staying at her mam's since Christmas. Not well, everyone said, she'd seen no one. I went to fetch her from her mother's and then I realized why she'd kept herself hidden. Five months, she must have been, though she wasn't big with it. Barely eaten enough for one, let alone for two, and she could still almost hide it under her winter things.

'Everyone reckoned I must have found out she was pregnant and known that I wasn't its father.'

'And did you kill her?' Marcie asked gently.

Joe turned his gaze back on to her face, his faded brown eyes, so like Jack's, regarding her sadly.

'No, lass, I didn't. And I wouldn't have let on it wasn't mine. They'd have all known. Laughed behind my back for a bit, no doubt. But, you see, I loved her. I didn't care what she'd done. I knew how it was before I wed her. She'd have settled, given time. I knew right from the start that she loved me back. It was just temptation, getting in the way, and with me not there I should think she was lonely.' He shook his head. 'I loved her. I can't explain it away or make excuses for her. I loved her and that's the long and short of it.'

Alec looked quickly away, swallowing hard, his eyes fixed on the tall trees standing black against the summer sky.

'And if you'd found out earlier, about her and Jack?'

'Then they might well have found him hanging in a tree instead of her,' Joe said angrily, his jaw set and tense. 'One thing you've to understand. There's been no love lost between the two of us, Marcie. Right back from when we were kids, Jack was an evil bastard.'

Chapter Twenty-Nine

They took Joe to lunch in a little pub, then drove him back to Hill Grove. Michael spent the afternoon playing chess with him and they talked, but not about Jack and Rebekkah. Mostly, they chatted about the twins – Marcie had photographs of them – about Michael's job. About the dreams he had once had of being a QC. About Alec's time in the navy, and after, when he'd lived and worked in Greece and then in Italy.

Most of this was new to Marcie. 'I picked olives,' he told her. 'I caught fish. I worked two seasons in a taverna and I learned the language.'

Then in Italy he had found a job with a builder, managed to get permits and visas and he had settled, starting as a labourer and learning the trade from the foundations up.

'He restored churches,' Alec said, 'and built schools and houses. Even a railway station. I started off scraping bricks. Finished up doing his accounts.' He laughed. 'I'm not sure how I got from one to the other, it must have taken years, but now . . . it all crowds into a very small yesterday.' He looked across at his daughter, his rather bland face softened by a smile. 'Then I met your mother. Marco Benelli, the man I worked for, his daughter was getting married and Marianne was one of the extra workers they'd hired. And that was it. I followed her around all that night, pestered the life out of her until she agreed to go out with me.'

'I'd never figure you to be that determined,' Marcie said, smiling.

'Once upon a time I must have been,' Alec said quietly.

'So? What happened?' she pressed him, trying to keep her voice light in case he took offence.

'I don't know,' Alec told her wearily. 'I suppose I just gave up when she died. Gave up and came back home and it was all the same, just as if I'd never left.'

Thoresway was a tiny village hidden amongst a nest of hills where Jack and Joe had grown up and where Rebekkah had died.

The village ran along a single street. A few cottages, a church, a school now converted into a house with neat, arched windows, and a couple of larger houses, one of which looked to be the vicarage, half hidden by trees and almost neo-classical in design. It would not, thought Marcie, have been out of place on the set of *Gone with the Wind*.

They parked the car close to where a spring bubbled from beneath the hedges. Marcie reached down and dabbled her fingers in the water. It was cold and clear. Hot from travelling, she plunged both hands up to her wrists in the water, then lifted them to her face, watching the drips course their way down her arms and gather in the folded crook of her elbows.

Alec looked long at her, reminded of the infant daughter he had hardly known.

Joe had drawn a map for them and they walked back through the village, past the cottages and the white-washed house that enclosed a massive mill wheel. Then, turning through a gate at the other end, they trekked across fields up to the remote clump of trees Joe had marked on his rough map.

The hill was steep. Marcie found herself breathless. She thought of Rebekkah, pregnant and desperate, making the same climb. No one could have carried an unconscious woman up here, she told herself. If Rebekkah had been murdered, then it had been done here, on this ridge, with its backdrop of ash trees the only shelter from the open sky.

From the top of the hill, Marcie turned and looked back across the valley. Perspective seemed to be distorted; hills rose opposite and to the sides of them, billowing out, concealing features that could be clearly seen from lower down the slope.

'Down there,' Alec said, 'must be what they call Roman Hole. That's where the gypsies camped, in that hollow.'

'You've been here before?' Marcie asked in surprise.

'Must have been,' Alec confirmed. 'But I was just a child, I think. I have this memory of the place. Of Jack telling me about it and showing me different things, but I didn't connect until I saw the spring.'

Marcie nodded. Michael had gone further up the hill. He stood beside the grove of trees, Joe's sketch map in his hand, looking down towards the millhouse and the reservoir behind it half hidden by a small copse.

'Joe said it was an oak tree.' He frowned slightly. 'I don't know my trees very well, but these look like ash to me.' He glanced at Marcie. 'Sure we've got the right place?'

'Yeah,' she said softly. 'I'm sure.'

He sat himself down on a fallen branch and slipped a Pathfinder map from his pocket, glancing about him to get his bearings.

From the opposite hill, back across the road, two figures in bright clothes came hurtling down on mountain bikes. They didn't pause even as they crossed the road, instead came racing up the track, out of their saddles, heads down, legs pumping and bright clothing flashing in the sunlight. As they came closer Marcie could hear their breathing, laboured and excited, as they neared the top.

She moved aside to let them pass and looked down once more into the little village, noting, with amusement, Alec's anxious half-frown at the two children. She heard her husband ask them about the tree, knowing with a sudden intuition that Michael was sitting on all that remained of it.

Alec had moved closer to her. She half heard the conversation continue between Michael and the boys. They knew all about the 'hanging tree', revelled in the chance to share the story.

'It was her husband that killed her,' one of them said, with the certainty of common knowledge. 'And my granddad says no leaves ever grew on the branch she hanged from ever again.'

'Oh, that's stupid. It must have caught a disease or something,' said his friend.

'My granddad says it's the blood. Like that bit of fence that won't stand down in Roman Hole.'

'Don't talk wet, there's no blood when you hang . . .'

Marcie smiled across at Michael, who was encouraging them to tell him more. A good listener, was Michael, Marcie thought. Alec was speaking again, softly now as though not to attract attention.

'The fence,' he said, 'down at Roman Hole. They killed a child there. A baby.'

'Who did?' Marcie asked him.

'Gypsies, long ago. Some blood feud or other. A child had been murdered, I think, and this was the justice. They killed it and flayed it and hung its skin on the fence. Sent what was left back to its parents.'

He'd not intended the two boys to hear, but, of course, they did.

'My granddad says they skinned it alive. He says the doctor said if there'd been one scrap of skin on it then it would all have grown back. But they left nothing. Skinned it clean like a rabbit.'

'Aw, come off it. It would have died if you just took one bit of skin off. Like people do when they get burned. They lose body fluid,' the other finished triumphantly. He turned to Michael. 'That's right, isn't it?'

Marcie shuddered. 'I remember Jack telling me that,' she said softly. 'Gave me nightmares for weeks. I kept seeing this skin hanging on the fence and the poor child, bundled up like so much meat.'

She smiled wryly. 'For some stupid reason I had this idea it had been posted back through the letterbox. I tried it with my dolls, but only the Barbie would fit.'

Alec held her gaze.

'The dreams sort of changed then. I dreamed of this blood-soaked Barbie doll in the postman's bag, all wrapped up in brown paper and Aunt Alice finding it on the mat one morning and her saying to Gran that she'd forgotten to cancel the butcher's delivery that week.'

'God almighty! You were a strange child,' Alec told her. Then he reached out and touched her hand. 'I had nightmares about it too,' he confessed.

'Someone will see,' Jack whispered. 'For God's sake, Becky, get under the trees. You must be mad following me up here.'

She laughed, her dark eyes sparkling and her long hair lifting in the breeze. Then she sobered, sat down on the ground with her back against the oak and looked thoughtfully at him.

'Don't you ever get tired of sneaking around like this? Why can't we meet out open, Jack?'

'You're mad, Becky! My brother's wife. God! It would be close to murder round here the way our people would see it.'

She sighed and closed her eyes, tipping her head back to look through half-closed lids at the blue arc of sky.

'Do you never want to be away from here?' She

switched her gaze back to him abruptly. 'There's a whole world out there, Jack. So much to see. A whole big world and the two of us never been further than Lincoln.' She spat the word contemptuously.

'I ask you, Jack, what is there here? What future? I'm a wife, I'll one day be a mother. And what for? To breed another generation of farm workers and farm workers' wives.'

'You married Joe, you must have felt something for him.'

'Oh, I did! I do!' Her eyes softened in a way that turned him to water inside. 'He's a good man, that brother of yours, and one day I'll make him see sense and we'll be gone from here.'

Jack laughed out loud. 'If he's so good, then why is it that you're here with me? Joe's weak, always was. He'll never make anything of himself.'

'And you will? What's the great ambition, then? Foreman, maybe? Stockman? That the beginning and end of it, is it, Jack? And as for Joe being weak, when was the last time you took him in a fight?'

Jack looked away, angry with her. They both remembered the last time Jack had put Joe down.

Marcie watched as the two children hurtled back down the hill, yellow and orange streaks disappearing into the distance. Beside her she could feel Alec wince at the speed they were doing.

She moved into the shadow of the other trees, resting her eyes in the gloom, and stared hard at the fallen tree, trying to see where Rebekkah would have hung. Imagining her body, limp and lifeless, tied to the thick branches, her belly swollen. She saw in her mind the woman standing beside the twins' beds, one hand touching her abdomen in a way that both protected and despaired.

Joe said he'd played no part in Rebekkah's death, but he had refused to speak of it further. Marcie didn't blame him. Seeing him in the churchyard she had realized how much pain he still carried with him and she had no wish to add to it. He had convinced her that, whatever the courts might have said, he had not killed his wife.

'So,' Marcie asked herself, 'if Joe didn't kill you, then who?'

Only one name came to mind. One person who had so much to lose and whose conscience clearly burned him now . . .

In the afternoon Alec drove them home. It was a little later than they had intended and Michael decided he ought to go straight to the law centre. Alec took Marcie to collect the children from Adele's.

'She's, er, quite a character, Michael's foster mother,' Alec said, remembering his first meeting with Adele the Friday before.

Marcie nodded. 'One of the strongest women I've ever met,' she said. 'And one of the kindest.'

They arrived as Adele was cooking the evening meal. The kitchen was full of people helping and getting in the way. Liam and Hanna were at the table playing with dough – half of it seemed to be in their hair – and Sophie Lee was helping them to make pastry 'cakes', decorating them with bits of currant and chopped cherries.

They squealed at the sight of Marcie, demanding to be picked up. She hefted them both into her arms, trying vainly to keep the dough out of her own hair, and smothered them in kisses.

'Come along in,' Sophie Lee called out to Alec, who was standing nervously in the doorway. 'Leon, put the kettle on, my love.'

Alec sat down amid the chaos, looked around him with an air of bewilderment. The noise was incredible, everyone talking at once and asking questions and Adele calling out instructions.

'Is Michael not with you?' Leroy asked.

'No, he's gone straight to work.'

'Knives and forks on the table, if you please,' Adele called out. 'And how is your grandfather, Marcie?'

'A lot worse, Adele. They don't expect him to last much longer.'

'But you found the brother . . . ?'

'Oh yes,' Marcie said. 'We found Joe.'

'Stay the night here,' Adele invited. 'What point is there findin' a hotel or sleeping on a lumpy couch when we've got a good bed you can use?'

'Oh, I don't want to put you out,' Alec protested. 'Really.'

But Adele had made up her mind. 'Leroy, will you find clean sheets for me, please?' she said. 'There, now.

There's no bother and you can begin fresh in the morning.'

It was getting late and Alec had to admit that he was tired. They had talked for hours, both over the meal and after. Telling Adele and Sophie Lee about Joe, about the child's grave and about Jack and Rebekkah.

'It sounds like he has a guilty conscience,' Sophie Lee declared of Jack. 'You think he killed this woman who carried his child?'

'I don't know,' Marcie said. 'I don't want to think so, but it would explain so much.'

'I'm going back to Lincoln tomorrow,' Alec said. It was something he had decided as they had been talking. 'I've still got some time and I think we ought to find out what we can.'

'I don't think Joe will tell you much more,' Marcie said, frowning.

'No, maybe not, or at least not yet,' Alec agreed. 'I mean, he's trusted us with a great deal so far and I really don't want to push him. No, I thought I'd find the local newspaper offices, try and get a look at their archives. They're bound to have covered a murder trial.'

'I thought you were looking at a flat tomorrow?'

'Oh, damn, so I was. Well, I'll have to postpone it.'

Marcie looked at him thoughtfully. Alec had changed in these last few days, become more decisive, more in control. Even his manner of speaking was different. And it was odd, she noted, but Jack was no longer 'Dad', or 'my father', but merely Jack, as though he had removed himself in some way even while he chased the old man's interests.

'Why are you doing this?' she asked. 'I mean, there's no reason for you to do anything more.'

'No,' Alec agreed. 'I don't suppose there is. But it's like what you were saying the other night about unfinished business. Whatever happened between Jack and Rebekkah and Joe, and even my mother, it's affected us all ever since. It's embittered and frustrated and made lonely people who shouldn't have been that way.'

'There've been more victims in this than that poor girl and her baby,' Sophie Lee said, nodding sadly.

'Yes,' Alec agreed. 'We've all been victims. Jack and my mother. Joe. Me. Even Marcie. I'm not a superstitious man. I don't, if I'm honest, have the imagination for it. But it's as if Elizabeth Lacey's curse has lasted, right through the decades, and someone has to end it. Turn it back, or whatever it is you do with curses.'

Sophie Lee nodded wisely.

'Something I can't make fit,' Adele said. 'That woman Jack keeps talking about. The woman in the desert. Where does she fit into all these things?'

'I don't know,' Alec admitted. 'I'm afraid I never really listened to Jack when he went on about her. I've only what Marcie's told me.'

'Maybe he's got things confused. Maybe the woman in the desert was just a symbol.'

'I don't know, Birdie. I really don't. I remember him when he came back from the war. I didn't like him, not one little bit. I kept telling my mother to send the horrid man back.' He laughed harshly. 'Mam said he came back changed. He'd seen too much he couldn't forget. Kids begging for scraps, women and old people tortured and dying. And just so much death and destruction. He came back brutal and angry and I hated him. It took me years to realize that it might not have all been his fault. That he just couldn't cope with it, with being back, any more than we could cope with having him.'

Alec drove Marcie to the flat and helped her transfer the sleeping twins from the car and into their beds. It was late – Michael shouldn't be more than a couple of hours at most – but after Alec had gone the flat seemed to Marcie very quiet and terribly lonely.

She tried to watch the television, but nothing held her interest. She felt edgy and nervous, the slightest sounds making her jump. Finally, she went out into the hall, leaving the flat door open so that she could hear the twins, and phoned the hospice.

'There's been no change,' they told her. 'He's still hanging on, but he's barely conscious now.'

Marcie thanked the nurse and replaced the receiver. She stood in the darkened hallway, staring at the patch of light that flooded from her door, and tried to make sense of all the feelings she had about her father and about Jack. Alec seemed to be emerging from the shadows almost as fast as Jack was retreating into them. It was quite a revelation, after all this time, that she could actually like her father.

But what about Jack? What if she found out that Jack had killed Rebekkah?

She wandered back into the flat and, feeling suddenly cold, dug around in her drawer to find a sweater. In the bottom of the drawer was a folder, kept from schooldays, full of letters and cards and notes from friends, song lyrics. Even the odd picture, cut from magazines, of pop stars she'd once admired but whose names she could barely remember now. The usual debris of teenage years. It was the one thing she had taken with her when she had left her grandparents' house that night.

Marcie took it out of the drawer and looked inside. There was one other thing there. The clippings book, with its records of Patrick's death.

'I wanted to believe you, Jack,' she said softly. 'I don't want to think you did this, but now, I just can't be sure.'

'She never came back to us after that night,' Alec said. 'I know she ended up in some kind of hostel after she left the hospital, but that's about all.'

'Then why didn't you ask her?' Michael queried. 'It's no secret, Alec. When we first met she was seventeen and I was in my first year of uni. I'd worked a year before I went, tried to raise a bit of extra cash, so I was getting on for twenty by the time we met.'

Alec smiled wryly. 'You make twenty sound almost ancient,' he said.

Michael laughed. 'Did you never feel that old, Alec? Young enough to do anything and old enough to know the lot?'

'And you feel different now?' Alec asked.

'No, not so much. To be truthful, Alec, I hope I never do.'

He got up and crossed to the coffee maker, poured

them two cups of overbrewed but still warm coffee. 'Why did you come here?' he asked.

Alec took the coffee and stared into the black depths of it.

'Out of milk,' Michael told him. 'Sorry.'

'That's all right.' Alec glanced about him at Michael's tiny office in the law centre. Threadbare carpet, desk that looked like a badly put together flatpack and shelves laden down with books and files. A couple of spare chairs standing in the corner. He'd sat outside in the waiting room until Michael had seen the last of his clients, alone with his thoughts.

'I wanted to know,' he said. 'Where she went to. How you two met. What brought you together.'

'And what else?' Michael asked, his voice very gentle.

'It's about what I said to you the other night,' he said. 'No, it's all right, I'm not going to tell you. Not yet, anyway.'

Michael swirled the cooling coffee in the cup and regarded Alec thoughtfully. 'You must have guessed,' he said, 'that whatever you tell me here is confidential. I may not get to wear the fancy wig, but I don't betray a professional trust.'

'I did guess that. I know you wouldn't, but I can't do that to you. I just wanted to say that you were right. That I have to resolve this one on my own and do what, well, what my conscience tells me to.' He looked across at Michael, the pain in his eyes clear and unassumed. 'I've just begun to find my daughter, Michael, and I know I'm going to lose her again if she finds out what we did.'

Michael said nothing but listened closely, waiting for Alec to collect himself and carry on.

'I never laid a finger on that boy,' Alec said slowly, 'but I could have stopped him dying. I'm a coward, Michael, and for that I'm going to have to pay.'

For a moment the younger man said nothing, then he placed his empty cup on the table and leaned across towards Alec. 'You have to do what you feel is right,' he said. 'But one thing's for sure, you can't live with this any longer. You need to tell someone the truth.'

Jack heard Mary but the effort of showing it was beyond him. He was cocooned in a web of pain and drugs, his outer mind hazy and unresponsive. His inner mind raced and wove and built dreams.

In his dreams, Rebekkah called out to him as men held her down and raped her. Her fingers clutched sand. Her hair was filled with it, and as she struggled, throwing her head from side to side, the sand poured into her mouth, choking her until she could hardly breathe.

Becky! He wanted to call out, to make the dreams go away, but he was trapped inside with them. Inside this dope-filled, pain-racked cage.

'It's all right, Jack,' Mary whispered to him, feeling his restlessness as she clasped his hand, even though his body hardly moved. 'It's all right.'

Chapter Thirty

For more years than he could remember, Joe had kept his childhood in a wooden box tucked beneath his bed.

He bent awkwardly now, hooking it out with his stick and blowing the worst of the dust from its top, his mind resting on the day he had passed with Alec and Marcie and Michael, this strange assortment of family that had suddenly come into his life.

He sat down by the window with the box on his lap and his thoughts shifting to an earlier time and another family, long gone now but never really buried. He sat unmoving, watching through his window as the twilight deepened and all the ghosts Joe had collected in his long life gathered about him.

Finally, when the light beyond his window had faded into nothing, Joe reached out and switched on the blue-shaded lamp, then opened his wooden box.

He hardly needed the light to know the contents. The strange muddle of objects he had treasured when all else had been taken from him.

A photograph of his parents on their wedding day. Still and formal in their Sunday best. His father unsmiling and awkward and, by contrast, the wicked spark of humour in his mother's eyes.

Pressed flowers from his mother's wedding bouquet that his aunt had given him, sent to him in prison just before they'd finally locked him away. Pebbles, worn smooth, that he'd taken from the mill race where the water tumbled them, round and even, good to hold and twist in the hand. He'd kept them close to him, literal touchstones of freedom all the years he'd been confined. And there were the broken toys, cherished from a childhood that had little in the way of playthings.

He sorted through until he found what he was looking for. The only images he had now of his Becky. One staid photograph taken on their wedding day and one much older, taken of the entire school, all thirty or so of them, gathered in the school yard.

Boys in Norfolk jackets, worn and overworn by brothers and cousins before them. Tight collars, buttoned neatly to the throat, and hair severely combed, slicked down with water. And the girls, with their long hair fastened in ribbons, and aprons tied over their dresses to keep them clean. Most of them, Joe thought, would have only had the one dress. If they had a spare and one for Sunday they were considered well ahead of the game. He remembered his aunt washing out her daughter's clothes on a Saturday night after she had gone to bed and putting them to dry before the fire, her Sunday dress already ironed for the morning and her shoes given an extra brush.

They were all there. Himself and Jack, Mary and Alice and Rebekkah. She was standing in the third row, next to Mary and a half-head taller. Both looked directly into the camera, backs ramrod straight, both with silly, overlarge ribbons in their wavy hair. But there the resemblance ended. Mary, already aware of herself and the image she should project to the outside world, capable and stern and unyielding in the face of any adversity. And Rebekkah, lips parted slightly and a look in her eyes as though she questioned the photographer. Sought to look the other way through his long and awkward lens, see the world outside the little valley they inhabited.

'Never satisfied, were you, lass?' Joe said softly. 'I should have done what you wanted when we first wed. Taken you away from there. Emigrated, maybe. Canada or America. Made something for ourselves. But I was stubborn as Jack could be in my own way. Couldn't see it then that there might be a better life somewhere else, or that it could be for the like of us.'

He shook his head sadly at the thought, his gaze drifting from Becky's face and resting now on his brother, standing tall and stern in the back row. Given false height by the bench the boys had perched themselves upon so that they could be more easily seen. The old jacket he was wearing was stretched too tight across his shoulders and his collar did not quite meet where it should. His lips were pressed together in a tight grimace as he tried to look older than his years.

Joe recalled that day as clearly as the one he had just spent with Marcie and the others. It had burned itself into his memory. A point had been reached that day which, Joe felt, had set the pattern for the rest of their lives.

He looked again at the photograph, settling now on the little stretch of road running past the school and on a figure, shadowy and awkward, standing in the field beyond.

Benny.

It had been the last day of Benny's life, but no one had noticed him, standing in the background, gazing at the little group and the stranger come to freeze them all in time.

But, then, no one took much mind of Benny. The photographs had been printed and returned and two weeks had gone by before anyone even noticed he'd gone missing.

Two weeks and the flies had done their work well. They had not even tried to move the body, just dug a fire-break between the shack and the nearest trees and burned the lot to the ground.

The old man had lived in a tiny woodman's shack in the middle of one of the plantations about a mile from the village. The softwoods had been planted twenty years before Joe was born and he would see them felled the following summer. Interplanted with the oak and ash of the native woodland, the cover was thick. Poachers went there, Benny lived there, but that was all.

No one actively liked Benny. The adults tolerated him; he was considered mad but harmless and left alone. He didn't work, he had little to do with village life and he muttered constantly to himself as he walked along. The children laughed at him, following and calling names, and the women said that he was dirty, unclean.

How he kept himself fed and clothed was matter of great debate amongst the village children. Rumour had it that Benny had a treasure hidden somewhere in his dirty shack and even though they knew he fed himself by poaching and begged cast-offs to wear, the rumour was better. Much better.

On the day of the photograph, they had been let out of school early. A half-hour, no more, but it was free time. Not time for work or house chores. It had been Becky, always on the lookout for adventure, who had talked about the treasure.

'We could find it. Hide it till we're grown up, then all go away somewhere.'

'Like where?' Mary had asked disdainfully, but Joe could see the idea excited her.

'Travelling. Like our great-great grandkin used to. Oh, I don't mean like they did, fair to fair like the men do now. I mean across the sea. Maybe America! The New World. We could live there. Make our fortunes.'

Her eyes shone. They learned about America from the 'project readers' they studied in school. Books full of random chapters on history and maps and great battles, mixed without clear order into what were often dry essays. It had always seemed to Joe that these were books of fables. America might be as distant and mythical as the Golden Fleece, but to Becky it was something to be made real.

Her excitement was contagious. For a while they talked and argued. At not yet twelve Mary was already the realist. Becky, a little older, was still the dreamer and the rest vacillated between the two sides. Jack had been unusually silent. It was only after they had parted that he said to Joe, 'We could go and look. I mean . . . you don't know that he hasn't got a treasure hidden . . .'

They had argued about it before dinner while they'd

done their chores. Argued some more at bedtime, but it was clear Jack had made up his mind and equally clear that, as always, Joe would not choose to argue. He was far too afraid of Jack. The late night had found them creeping from the house and out of the village towards the plantation where Benny lived.

Sitting in his little room with the night shut out beyond his window, Joe recalled the tense excitement that had overtaken him then. The night sounds, familiar enough but so much louder this first time out so late without an adult. And the chill rising from the damp ground, making him shiver with more than cold.

They daren't speak much. The slightest noise seemed to carry in the stillness and it was not until they had reached the shelter of the plantation that Jack outlined his plan.

There was a good chance that Benny would be out. Poaching his supper and tomorrow's breakfast. If he was there, in the shack, then Joe would have to make a noise and lure him out.

'Why me?' Joe demanded.

'All right, I'll do it,' Jack stated angrily. 'Then you can be the one to go inside and search the place.'

Joe bit his lip and fell silent then. He was to wait outside, whatever happened, Jack told him. Keep watch and warn him if he heard Benny returning.

There was no sign of Benny. They stood holding their breath and listening for the slightest sound, but only the rising wind in the trees broke the silence. The door creaked as Jack crept inside. Joe watched through the tiny, dirty window as his brother crossed to the rough wooden table in the centre of the room and turned up the wick of the hurricane lamp Benny had left waiting for his return.

Jack looked up then and impatiently waved Joe away from the window. 'Go and keep watch!' he mouthed at him angrily.

Joe retreated into the darkness, reluctant to lose sight of the faint puddle of light spilling through the tiny window. He stood in the shadows, the night sounds growing louder all around him and the rising wind cracking the branches of the tall trees, willing Jack to hurry up and Benny not to return too soon.

Waiting seemed to last for ever and in the end Joe's watching did no good. Jack had intended for him to circle the shack, look all around for Benny's return, but Joe's nerve had failed him. The darkness seemed to grow more dark as he watched that bright flickering light against the window and the more he watched the light and the thicker the dark became the more reluctant Joe was to move.

'He won't come back, he won't come back,' he kept telling himself, willing it to be true.

But Benny did come back, rounding the side of the wooden shack, and the first Joe knew of it the door was opened wide, light spilling out on to the forest floor.

The breath rasping in his throat, Joe ran to the window and peered inside. The room had been torn apart in Jack's efforts to find Benny's treasure. He had thrown his bedding to the floor. Broken the few sticks of furniture Benny owned. Spilled food and water. Broken the wood-pile down and thrown the logs in all directions in his frantic search. And Benny stood there now, close behind the door, his shaggy head turning from side to side taking in the mess and destruction.

The low despairing moan rising from his throat clearly frightened Jack as much as it did Joe. The sound grew louder and Benny's arms began to move in time with the jerking of his head. He seemed, to Joe, to grow larger in the shifting light, his giant shadow thrown upon the wall.

He threw himself at Jack, knocking the boy off balance. Jack shouted something Joe could not make out and struggled to free himself from Benny's grip. Benny was shaking him now. Shaking him fiercely. Benny, throwing his head from side to side, his body following like some jerky marionette. His hands gripping Jack's arms, pinning them to his sides.

Joe stood frozen, knowing that he should help but unable to move.

Then the waiting was over. Jack pulled an arm free and hit out at the old man's head. Just for an instant Benny loosened his grip, but it was enough. Jack had something in his hand, Joe couldn't make out what, but it was a weapon. He hit Benny a glancing blow that sent him reeling.

Get out of there! Joe wanted to scream. Get out of there, we can lose him in the wood. But Jack had no intention of leaving now.

He raised his hands and Joe could see the piece of broken chair he held. He's scared, Joe told himself. He won't do anything, he's just scared.

Then Jack brought the weapon down on Benny's

head, smashing again and again into his head and shoulders until the old man lay still.

Joe stared. His feet were rooted. He couldn't believe what he had seen. Jack frequently got himself into fights, knocked Joe to the ground on a regular basis, but this . . . This was something else.

He was just scared, Joe told himself, didn't know when to stop. Just scared, that was all.

Then Jack turned towards the window as though he had known all along that Joe was standing there and he looked straight into his brother's eyes. A strange expression of exultation lit his face, demonic in the flickering light, and, as Joe watched, he saw his brother smile.

Chapter Thirty-One

*I tied the rope, binding it well so the eyelet ran free and
there was space enough for the rope to slide.*

*I can still recall the weight of it, the rope thinner
than it should have been and coarser, too. I remember
worrying about the way it would move against her skin,
grazing the softness of her flesh when it pulled through,
but it couldn't be helped. Some things just can't be
perfect, can they, Bird?*

*And her long black hair, so soft as I placed the rope
about her neck. The weight of blackness in my hands
as I pulled it free so it wouldn't snag against the binding.
But I didn't look into her eyes, my hands against the
softness of her throat.*

Dreaming, Jack remembered the texture of her skin
against his hands. The scent of Becky as she lay against
him. The child that had been Marcie sleeping in his arms.

The softness of her skin against his hands . . .

Marcie jerked herself out of sleep in sudden panic, her
breath caught in her throat.

She gulped air, hungrily, forcing it into her lungs, her
hands instinctively lifted to her neck and the marks,

almost faded now but which had begun to burn with a new intensity.

The dream, so frightening and so vivid... She glanced about, nervously, realizing that she must have fallen asleep on the sofa waiting for Michael to come home.

Her fingers touching the burning places on her neck, Marcie crossed to the mirror. The marks were still there, no worse, visible but hardly more than dark stains on her skin. 'Only a dream,' she told her reflection, then she stiffened as the image of the other woman joined hers in the glass.

'Rebekkah?' She half turned, her eyes fixed on the reflection. She felt no fear this time, only a strange kind of kinship, as though she and the long-dead woman shared a relationship that she couldn't quite define.

Even as she watched, the image faded and by the time she turned fully, it had gone.

But even as she disappeared from view, Marcie had been certain that she saw Rebekkah smile.

Chapter Thirty-Two

Alec left for Lincoln early on Tuesday morning. The phone book gave him the address of the local paper and at ten o'clock he was standing in the reception area.

'You normally need an appointment,' the girl said. But she rang through to the archivist anyway and told him to wait.

An hour later Alec found himself in the records section. 'We're a bit short-staffed,' the archivist, a neat young woman in her early thirties, told him, 'so I'm going to have to leave you to it, I'm afraid.' She ran through the way the drawers were coded, showed him where he'd be most likely to find the relevant information and taught him how to use the microfiche.

Alec sat himself down with a pad and pen and wondered where to begin.

February 1937. He found the right drawer and carried it over to the viewer. February's section was somewhere close to the middle. He pulled out the first slide and put it in the viewer, then frowned in annoyance. He hadn't realized just how much information could be packed on to those little plastic sheets. Impatiently, he began to move it around under the viewer, getting hopelessly lost in the process. Finally he got the hang of it, deciding that he almost had to think backwards to find his position. There was, he guessed after looking at a couple, a complete edition of the paper on each plastic slide. At first it seemed that would make his task easier until he began to check the dates. Nothing seemed to be in order. February the third began the sequence, followed by the sixteenth and then the twelfth and then something from the middle of May.

Sighing, Alec realized that he would have to work his way through the whole month, note down the dates to be sure of not missing any, and hope that there were no absences.

Methodically, he set to work.

After only an hour of staring at the screen, his eyes were aching, but he was beginning to get somewhere. The first reports of Rebekkah's death had appeared and Alec was astonished by what he found.

'Thought you might appreciate a coffee,' the archivist said. 'Getting anywhere?'

'Thanks,' Alec said. 'Yes, I am, actually.' He pointed at the screen. 'This,' he said. 'This is what I'm looking for.'

' "Tragic suicide",' she read. ' "The body of a young woman was discovered this morning in the coppice known locally as Bale's Wood, close to the village of Thoresway." ' She glanced at Alec. 'A suicide? What's your interest, if you don't mind my asking?'

'She was a relative,' Alec told her. 'And I'd always been led to believe it was murder.'

Silently, Alec read through the article. Rebekkah Armitage, aged only twenty-three, had been found by a farm worker. He'd realized that she was dead and that nothing could be done for her and had run back to the closest farm to get help. The reporter gave a sad and graphic account.

> This young woman, pregnant with her first child. Her features now bloated and disfigured by the rope and mercifully hidden from full view by her thick black hair hanging like a curtain over her face. Her dress soaked with the morning dew . . .

The report went on to speak of the shame and tragedy of the event. Of the shock her husband of less than two years had displayed when he had come to the scene, his utter grief and despair. When they had cut the body down he had thrown himself on to it, crying out his wife's name.

'He probably didn't see a damn thing,' the archivist said.

'Sorry?'

'The reporter – probably wasn't even there. Certainly not in time to see the body cut down, even if he'd had a car.'

'I'm not sure I follow . . .'

'We've got so used to on-the-spot reports these days it's hard to remember that a lot of local news was gathered second hand back then. *The Echo* wasn't a massive paper. We probably got most of our news from the local bobbies.' She laughed. 'You read some of this stuff and you can tell a lot of it's not much more than gossip.'

'A murder, though, that would have got more coverage?'

'Well, yes, especially when it came to trial. People

don't change, everyone likes a good murder, but suicide's kind of, I don't know, something that people get all holier than thou over.'

She looked back at the screen. 'Poor thing,' she said. 'And pregnant, too. That's really sad.'

It was another couple of hours – and the archivist had told him she'd have to throw him out while she shut up for lunch – before Alec found the next stage of the story. Three days after Rebekkah Armitage had been found dead, her husband, Joseph Armitage, had been arrested for her murder. Media interest had suddenly hotted up.

Alec returned to *The Echo* immediately after lunch, impatient now to find out why Joe had been arrested. The bare facts were supplied by the first report. Alec remembered what the archivist had told him about hearsay evidence. That seemed to be the case here, the reporter going into great detail about Joe's arrest, despite the fact that the arrest had been made just after dawn as though there had been some need for secrecy.

The arrest had not been made easily. Despite the earliness of the hour, Joe had been awake and partly dressed and he had tried to run. 'A sure and certain indicator of his guilt,' the reporter had intoned, causing Alec a moment's pause. He remembered Joe as he was now, an old man with a lifetime of regrets, living out his final days quietly and peaceably. Like Marcie, he couldn't perceive of Joe as capable of killing in cold blood a woman and an unborn child. But maybe in a fit of rage?

Alec shook his head. Somehow, that didn't seem to fit. People got stabbed or shot or even – he swallowed nervously – kicked to death when their assailant was enraged. Did they really get themselves hung, from an oak tree in the middle of an open, hill-top field?

He scanned the report again, aware that at this stage there was no indicator of why Joe had been accused.

The police had come to Joe's cottage just after five. Three officers from the local constabulary based at Louth, the local officer, a part-timer, who did the job when he wasn't tending to his farm, and a half-dozen or so other men, dragged from their beds to assist.

It seemed like a large number to arrest just one man.

He read on. The reporter obviously fancied himself as more than just a local hack. He'd given life and soul to purple prose. Alec could almost imagine him beating his breast and declaiming his right to preach the truth.

> They came upon the cottage just as the first light of dawn was breaking. There were ten men in all, their grim faces lit by the lanterns they carried and the torches of the constables. They had been warned that Joseph Armitage might not let himself be taken easily and his reputation locally as a fighter, both inside and outside of the ring, led them all to be nervous of the task the law had appointed for them.

They had approached the cottage from both front and rear, two officers and an unnamed man climbing over the wall and into the cottage garden. A light had been on in one of the downstairs rooms. Joe, maybe unable to sleep, or, just as likely, getting himself ready for work.

He would not, Alec guessed, be a man willing to sit inside his house and grieve. He'd be far more likely to solve things by working. By keeping busy . . .

The local constable hammered on the door. 'Open up, Joe, we know you're there, open up now.'

There was no response from inside the cottage. The light burned steadily and, looking through the kitchen window, they could see a hurricane lamp in the centre of the table. But there was no sign of Joseph Armitage.

'Force the door.'

Two men hurled their combined weight against the front door. It was old but very thick and still fastened with a locking bar on the other side. Their first attempt made a loud noise, bruised arms and shoulders but had no perceptible effect. They tried again, the local constable shouting at the men in the cottage garden to be sure to be ready in case Joe made a break for it out the back way.

Unseen by them, Joe crouched low on the upstairs sill, looking down at the men below. The room behind him was in darkness.

Further down the road, he could see lights coming on, people opening their doors to see what all the noise was about. They'd be in the street next, ready to assist in case the felon should try to escape, he shouldn't wonder. All ready to do their bit for law and order . . .

The rumours had been spreading almost from the moment he'd come back – before, most likely – and at first he'd been the object of both village sympathy and

ridicule. A child could have counted the months and
known the infant Becky carried wasn't his. It was a
tragedy. It was a joke, it was something everyone waited
with bated breath to see resolved.

And then they'd found her dead. Killed by her own
hand and taking the life of her unborn baby at the same
stroke.

There was little to laugh over any more. No one
knew what to say to him or what to do. He'd felt their
fear and their confusion even as they offered him kindness. It was a small village, hard to cross the road to
avoid another's pain, or escape the inadequacy of your
own sympathies . . . but there were many that had done
their best to try.

He'd heard them talking.

'It's a mercy, really . . .'

'Yes, but that poor little bairn.'

'Always the same, she was, all over the men. What
Joe thought he was doing when he married her, Lord
alone knows . . .'

And then the winds had changed direction. The
rumours of another sort had begun and Joe had found
himself shunned, the subject of questioning glances.

At first he hadn't noticed. Had been too wrapped up
in his own thoughts to listen close to what rumours they
were spreading. What guilt he'd been made to carry.

It had been Jack who had taken him aside and told
him.

'They're saying you killed her, Joe. Saying there's a
lump on the side of her head the size of a pigeon's egg.

That she was unconscious before ... before, you know ...'

'Before I strung her up!' Joe asked him angrily. 'God as my witness, Jack, I never laid a hand on her.'

Jack had nodded, patted his shoulder, but Joe could see the doubt even in his brother's eyes.

'You think I did it, don't you? Christ! You think I did it.'

'No, Joe, no, of course I don't, but there's plenty that will. Plenty. Maybe you should leave for a bit, go away. I've got a bit of money put away for when the baby arrives, but we'll give it to you. Best you go away.'

'No. I'm not running. If they've got something to say, something to charge me with, then let them come to me and say it. I'm ready for them.'

But that had been yesterday, when he'd been certain the rumours would blow themselves out. He'd been unable to comprehend how anyone could really think that he could hurt Rebekkah. Now, he was crouched on his bedroom windowsill, the bed he had shared with her taking up most of the tiny room behind him. The memories of her, of her laughter, of her love, the scent of her still clinging to the fabric of their home. Joe looked down at the men trying to break down his door and knew that they believed him guilty.

He knew he couldn't wait, he had to run, innocent or guilty. And the truth was that Joe wasn't certain any more just which was which. But he couldn't stay here. He had to run.

His cottage was the end one of three. To the right was a stone wall enclosing the side of his garden. Beyond that, fields and open space. Places to hide. Then he'd manage, somehow, to get to Jack. Ask him for the money. Ask him for help to get away. The window was not that high, the stone-built cottage being squat and settled into the ground, and it was set low in the upper wall above a supporting lintel.

And Joe was desperate.

He slipped the catch, balanced on the low sill, then, holding tight, lowered himself down and pushed off from the wall. Jumped almost over the heads of those still hammering at his door.

Pain in his ankle shot through his leg as he hit the ground, but it was nothing compared to his need to run. He pushed himself on, tearing down the road and towards the fields, but they were close behind. He could hear them, yelling and crying out. The hunt was on.

He fought as they came down on him. Felt the satisfying crunch as his fist met bone and was aware that his pursuers drew back. Confining him, but wary now. One man on the floor, with his hands covering a bloody face. Memories of the fights he'd won in his mind as he circled as best he could on his injured leg. His anger and grief fuelling the adrenaline that kept him on his feet.

'Come and take me then, ya bastards! Come and fucking get me!'

He hit out again as someone made a play for him, but it was only a feint meant to draw him on and the blow fell short, opening him up and throwing his balance for the merest instant. It was all they needed. Joe fell under the combined weight of three men, going down hard, his face grinding into the dirt as they dragged his hands behind his back and pinioned his arms tight.

'You'll fucking hang for this,' someone was saying to him, his voice muffled as his hands tried to divert the blood dripping from his nose.

'Oh, Becky,' Joe whispered. 'Oh, Becky, Becky. Why?'

Alec read the notes he had made out to them over the phone. Michael and Marcie huddled close, sharing the receiver, listening to the bare bones of the account Alec had managed to put down.

'Poor Joe,' Marcie said softly when he had finished. 'They'd found him guilty even before the trial. Have you talked to him, Da?'

'No, not yet. I'll try to go tomorrow. I've been at the newspaper offices all day. Finished when they finally chucked me out about an hour ago.'

'I saw her again,' Marcie told him. 'Rebekkah, I mean. She was here in the flat.'

'Are you all right?'

'Yes, yes. I'm fine. I had a bad dream and woke up with a real fright and ... well ... there she was. But the funny thing is, Da, I wasn't scared any more. Just sad for her, that was all.'

Michael hugged her to him. 'I wish we could help out,' he told Alec. 'I've switched shifts again for Friday, so we could maybe come over to Lincoln late afternoon.'

'That would be great, we'll take Joe out again. But look, I'll be back tomorrow night anyway and we'll talk about it then.'

'You want the sofa?'

'Thank you, but no. I'm still getting the lumps out of my back from the last time. Er, Adele's offered me a bed. I've told her thank you.' He paused awkwardly for a moment, then said, 'She's a nice lady, your Adele. Have you phoned the hospice?'

'Yes,' Michael told him. 'No change, Alec. I get the impression they're amazed he's hung on this long.'

'Right,' Alec replied. 'Well, I'll see you tomorrow night. Um, Marcie, kiss the babies for me, you know . . .'

He rang off then, leaving Marcie a little bemused.

'I want to like him,' she said. 'I *do* like him. There's just so much . . . I don't know, so much rubbish I've got to wade through.'

'I think he knows that,' Michael told her. 'I think there's a lot of his own dross he has to get rid of as well, you know. A lot of things he's not proud of.'

Marcie looked at him thoughtfully, then nodded. 'What is it they say in AA?' she asked. 'One day at a time?'

Joe ran, terrified of the look on Jack's face.

His only thought was that he had to get away. Hide before Jack turned on him.

Twice he fell, scraping his knees painfully on concealed branches. Twigs scratched at his face and tore across his eyes, dragged at his hair. In his mind it was Jack grabbing at him, pulling him down, grasping at his hair and clothes.

Jack trying to murder him.

He had no memory of fleeing Benny's shack, of leaving the wood or running back towards the village. Only the thought in his mind that he had to hide and that he dare not go back home.

The white shape of the wheelhouse loomed out of the darkness and in a moment Joe had wrenched the door open and was inside, his feet scrabbling across the narrow ledge behind the wheel and struggling to squeeze his body into the cramped space on the far side, the tiny work ledge used for maintenance.

He lay down on the ledge, willing himself small, struggling to control his breathing though his lungs burned and his throat was raw.

Joe closed his eyes, his body aching with shock. A little later he thought he heard Jack, his footsteps soft and steady, padding along the verge. He heard Jack's voice whispering his name before he passed by on his way home. But the way his mind was screaming with fear and pain it could have been a dog barking in the night. Or the wind, sounding through the wooden roof of the wheelhouse. Not his brother's voice at all.

Morning came, forcing itself through the cracks and under Joe's tight-closed eyes. He realized he must have fallen asleep despite his fear.

He had no idea of the time, but, since it was light, there would be people up and getting ready for work and Joe knew he had to move fast if he was to get away.

He squeezed his way back behind the wheel and pushed the door open, blinking in the sunlight, his eyes unfocused and his mind still confused. His uncle's roar brought him back to the present and a hand grabbing at his arms, fingers digging deep enough to bruise, made him yelp in pain.

'Stay out all night! Sneak out like a little thief and worry your aunt half to death! What do you think she thought when she went to wake you and there was no one there? I'll teach you what she thought.'

The beating was bad, but Joe had endured worse and he took it bravely, biting back the tears and apologizing to his uncle and his aunt for causing them distress. Clearly, they had put it down to some childish prank.

It was clear too that they had no notion Jack had been with Joe that night.

Glancing sideways under the shadow of his lashes, Joe could see his brother smirking at him from across the room.

Wednesday saw Alec back at the archive. The story of Rebekkah's death had remained in the news on an almost daily basis for the next ten days. Mostly a rehashing of events. Speculations in advance of the trial. Learned résumés from those who claimed to know both parties of what must have happened on the day Rebekkah died.

Items had been removed from the house that might have been used to strike Rebekkah. Common objects – pokers, rolling pins, a stone soda bottle. Things that could have been found anywhere. Others suggested that it must have been a blow from a fist or even a branch, citing the distance from the house to the hanging tree. A long way for even a strong man to carry an unconscious woman.

Alec thought about the loneliness of the spot. If Joe, if *someone*, had killed her – if Jack had struck that final blow, a thought he found unpleasant but, after Patrick Simpson, terribly possible – it would have been struck high on that lonely windblown hill. Not down in the valley where they would have been seen, or their raised voices overheard.

Joe and Becky had quarrelled. There were witnesses in plenty to that. But not on the day she'd died. When Joe had gone to his mother-in-law's house at Ludford and brought Rebekkah back to their cottage, her ill-kept secret had been impossible to keep hidden any more. They had quarrelled then, many people testified to that. But the next day Joe had been seen leaving the house early in the morning to work with Jack on the farm. From Rebekkah, even though many had knocked on her door, there had been only silence.

The morning after, she was dead.

Why, the paper asked, if Joe was innocent, why didn't he report his wife missing when he returned from work the night before? Was it, as he said, that he thought she had gone back to her mother's? That was why he had gone to Ludford that night, returning too late to continue his search.

The coverage grew less as nothing new was revealed. The trial date was set for almost a month distant and interest, though intense, could only be sustained for so long.

Alec moved his search to the trial date, then found himself backtracking again as something quite macabre turned up.

Jane Adams

Dr Fielding was asked by the preliminary hearing
to ascertain the exact age of the child, or at least
as close as such a judgement could be made. The
doctor in question was also responsible for con-
ducting the autopsy on the mother's body. It was
Dr Fielding who discovered the large bruise at the
side of Mrs Armitage's head that he believes at
the least rendered her unconscious and unable to
struggle when, it is alleged, her husband hanged
her from the oak in Bale's Wood.

'Alleged,' Alec laughed to himself. Getting all legal
and cautious, are we now?

It is stated for the record that Mrs Armitage was
underweight for a woman between the twentieth
and twenty-fifth weeks of pregnancy and that it was
impossible to tell from an external examination the
exact state of advancement of the foetus. The
doctor therefore undertook to remove the foetus
from its mother's womb, to assess its maturity and
to preserve it in case it should be required as evidence. The Prosecution's case hinges on the
assumption that the murder was provoked by evidence of infidelity on the part of Mrs Armitage.

This procedure was duly carried out, but was
not at the time made public knowledge.

On the evening of the twenty-sixth of March,
the evening that this paper described this rather
unfortunate necessity in its columns, person or
persons unknown broke into Dr Fielding's surgery

230

and from there gained access to his laboratory where the preserved remains of the foetus were stored. The doctor's laboratory was vandalised and many valuable items of experimental equipment smashed beyond use. Several preserved samples were stolen, including the unfortunate infant.

It should be noted that the body of Mrs Armitage, which had been preserved for evidence in the ice house of the Stafford Hotel, is now being kept under guard.

It was, thought Alec, an extraordinary twist. Who would want to steal Rebekkah's child? And what else was taken? The report had spoken of several other preserved samples. He searched until in an edition two days later he found reference to them . . .

Dr Thomas Fielding swept broken glass from the Turkey carpet that covered his laboratory floor. Laboratory was too grand a word for a room that held books and microscopes and assorted samples pickled in jars on high shelves. But it was the way he thought about it and he tried always to work within the parameters of science. His search for knowledge was genuine and he was deeply upset by the scale of the vandalism. Glass vessels he had to order specially from London, often having to wait for weeks until they were delivered, smashed into tiny pieces and thrown on to the floor.

The family had been eating their evening meal at the time of the attack. He knew that, because he had been working until just before and returned immediately after. His laboratory was built, like the surgery, as an addition to the main house, separated by several walls and rooms from the dining room. They had heard nothing.

'You can take the rug now, Millie. Shake it carefully, though – there may be fragments caught up in the threads.'

'Yes, sir,' she replied, averting her eyes carefully from the tiers of preserved tissue, of tapeworms and tumours and animal remains stacked about the room.

She made her escape swiftly. Fielding rarely allowed the servants into this room and they were distinctly glad of it, he knew.

A polite cough made him turn. 'Ah, Sergeant Willis. Come in.'

Willis, a thick-set man with a music-hall moustache, stepped through the door and looked about him with wary interest, his hands behind his back as though he was afraid of knocking something over.

'That list, sir, you said you should have some idea by now of what else was taken.'

'Ah, yes. I've taken an inventory, but I don't think I've anything to add. Just the three jars.' He laughed grimly. 'I don't think whoever broke in here knew quite what they were looking for,' he said. 'There were three preserved samples: the foetus you're interested in; another from a miscarriage of a slightly earlier maturity, about twenty weeks. She died, poor woman. Pauper's grave – it was a useful teaching aid.'

The sergeant nodded gravely.

'The other was the embryo of a pig.'

'A pig, sir?'

Fielding nodded. 'Bears a strong resemblance at an early stage,' he said. 'Though by twenty-five weeks, of course, the foetus of a human looks human. Very unporcine. My guess, sergeant, was that they took anything that had an umbilical cord and intended to sort out what was what later.'

'I see, sir,' he said, his large moustache twisting as he sought to keep the distaste from curling his lips. He found this cold discussion of what was, for him, the remains of a child, very unpleasant.

'They were in a hurry, I expect,' Fielding added.

'Not in too much of a hurry that they couldn't spare time to wreck the place.'

'No,' Fielding said heavily. 'That's why I think there must have been two of them. Anyway, the jars are heavy. Three would have been cumbersome to say the least. No. My guess is that you're looking for two people here. Though what the hell motive they might have is beyond me, Sergeant. The evidence has already been filed.'

'It could be the criminals didn't know that, sir.'

Three samples, Alec thought. He had only the most basic idea himself of the development of a twenty-five-week foetus. Would it look like a baby?

He thought back to recent hospital documentaries he had seen. There had been babies in a special unit that had been born at twenty-four weeks. And others at twenty-six. Even the slightly older ones had been fragile, wizened

Jane Adams

little things, with transparent skin and faces like aged monkeys. But yes, they had looked like babies.

It was puzzling. Had the thieves just taken anything that looked vaguely human? He shuddered slightly.

And then he thought of the teenage Marcie and the child she had been carrying.

Alec felt he had to get out. He packed away quickly, putting the film back in order and sliding the drawer away. He said goodbye to the archivist and left the building as quickly as he could.

Once out in the strong sunshine he felt better, more able to rationalize.

'I'm sorry,' he told his daughter, speaking out loud to her even though she was many miles away. 'I'm so sorry.'

The beating didn't stop him being sent to school. Joe walked in silence behind Jack, pretending Jack wasn't there, trying not to think about his bruises or the soreness of his backside.

He was still in shock from the night before, but an awareness was dawning that Jack would not let him off lightly. He had to act first, and make his actions good.

His chance came at lunchtime, when the class had gathered in the school yard. Jack was ready for him, as keyed up as Joe was himself. It took little goading to provoke him into fighting.

Within minutes a crowd had formed, arms linked to keep the fighters inside. The brothers were both known

234

to be scrappers, but Jack, the elder and heavier, had never lost to Joe. Still, it might be a good fight . . .

The boys faced each other, taking a measure they already knew, feinting and tapping, goading the other to throw the first punch.

Deliberately, Joe waited, leading Jack on, pulling him around the circle until his anger made him strike. Joe took the first hit square across the side of the head and nearly fell under it, but he'd been ready, knowing Jack's way of fighting, and as he came up he hit Jack square on the point of his chin, the entire force of his body behind the punch – and the force of his fear and hatred following it through.

Jack fell like a pole-axed pig and Joe, his anger spent and his strength suddenly gone, fell beside him.

His uncle beat him again that night. Beat them both for fighting in the school yard, but Joe, lying supperless and aching in his bed, the split knuckles on his right hand heavily bandaged, knew it was worth every bruise.

It was not the last time they fought, but Joe had got the victory he wanted. The night of Benny's death was never mentioned between them, not even when his body was found.

Joe had earned his brother's respect, for a time . . .

Chapter Thirty-Three

'I read about you,' Alec told Joe. 'Back issues of *The Echo*. Quite a celebrity for a while.' He laughed nervously.

Joe eyed him thoughtfully, then reached for the metal teapot and poured for both of them.

'And what conclusions have you come to, then?' he asked. 'Is Joe Armitage guilty of murder or no?'

Alec took the proffered cup. His hands were shaking and he slopped tea into the saucer.

'Blast!'

'Nervous, aren't we?' Joe observed. 'Worried I've spiked your tea, Alec?' He chuckled wickedly, then sobered. 'So, Alec, did I do it?'

'Did you?' Alec shook his head. 'No, I don't believe you did, Joe. I think that maybe, in a fit of anger, you could kill. But I don't believe you killed your wife.'

He looked across at his uncle as though asking for confirmation.

Joe gave him none but busied himself rearranging the tea things on the aluminium tray.

'You tried to run away,' Alec went on. 'I mean, I don't understand. Why did you try to run away?'

'Bastards had decided I was guilty,' he said. 'Wasn't so sure by then they weren't right. I mean, had I driven her to it or summat? She were a high-strung lass, my Becky.'

Alec gazed at him sadly. Joe's voice was thick with emotion and the fall into dialect seemed evidence of his grieving.

'The lump on her head . . .' Alec pursued. 'They think she was struck first.'

'Ay, I know what they say. But I never hit her, Alec, and I never put that rope around her neck either.' He shook his head. 'I was there, remember. I was there listening at the trial to what they said about me. What they claimed about me and Becky.'

'And they found you guilty.'

Joe nodded slowly. 'Found me guilty and locked me away. But I didn't hang, though there was plenty of folk thought I should. The judge thought there was reasonable doubt. Allowed my lawyer to plead it was manslaughter. Or didn't your precious newspaper tell you that?'

'I didn't read that far,' Alec told him. 'Not yet.'

Joe sighed, then drained his cup and poured himself another before speaking. Alec glanced around the little room that Joe lived in at Hill Grove. Small and neat and tidy and almost devoid of personal possessions. Almost.

'The photo,' Alec pointed. A picture of Marcie's children in swimsuits, playing in an inflatable paddling pool, was propped up against the bedside lamp.

Joe's eyes softened. 'In the post this morning,' he said proudly. 'She said she'd send me one, but I didn't think she would.'

'She's a good girl,' Alec said, as though speaking of

Marcie as a child. The child he felt he had never really known.

'I let my lawyer make stuff up about what might have gone on. Present it as though it was truth,' Joe said. 'And I wasn't called to the stand, so I didn't have to lie. I was past caring then. Wanted to die, but they said no. I shouldn't die for something they weren't certain I'd done.'

'Then why not just acquit you?'

'Circumstantial evidence, they said. Too much of it and too many folk crying for blood.'

'So what did they say?'

'That I'd hit her. Not known my own strength, then realized that she was dead and panicked. Tried to make it look like she killed herself.' He paused. 'It was Elizabeth that made them do it. Made them doubt I was guilty, I mean.'

'Elizabeth?'

'Becky's mam. Said she didn't believe I'd killed her girl. I'd got an alibi for the day. Working up at Strawson's farm. I hadn't gone home that night. I couldn't face it. I'd gone to Ludford to see her mam. I wanted to know who she'd been seeing. I thought Elizabeth must know, but she wouldn't tell me.'

'Did she know?' Alec asked.

Joe nodded. 'I'm certain of it, but she wouldn't tell. She spoke up for me at the trial. Said I'd been with her that evening and that I'd been a good husband to Becky. But there was the travelling time. There and back. I'd seen no one and spoken to no one. I'd had time to kill her there or back and still make my journey. There'd have been no blood. Nothing to hide. But I'd have had to be a cold bastard, don't you think so, Alec? To kill my wife then go visiting her mother.'

'So they put in a plea of manslaughter.'

'Not everyone agreed, but the judge couldn't sentence me to hang and keep his conscience clear. That's what I was told, anyhow.'

'You were lucky,' Alec said.

'Was I? Fifteen years they kept me locked away. Then they let me out. Everywhere I went I had to explain where I'd been the past fifteen years. Who wants truck with a killer, Alec? Even one that's served his time.'

He pushed himself to his feet and reached for his stick. His arthritis was bad today and he limped slowly towards the cupboard beside the window.

When he came back to Alec he was carrying a large brown envelope, sealed up and addressed to 'Marciella' in large black letters.

'You'd better be off now, or you'll hit the traffic,' Joe said, handing the envelope to Alec. 'Tell them I'm glad they came. You too,' he added. 'Even if you are Jack's blood.'

Joe picked up the photograph of Marcie's twins and gazed fondly at the two children.

A small sound made him look up. She stood by the window, gazing out across the lawn.

'I thought you might come,' Joe said quietly. 'I've seen you, time to time, but I've always thought it was just me wishing till I found out others saw you too.'

Becky glanced across at him, smiling, though her eyes were still pained.

'It's nearly done now, isn't it, lass?' Joe asked her. 'Is it revenge you want, girl? If it is, I'd say you've got it. He'll lose her at the end, just as surely as I lost you.' He shook his head as though disbelieving. 'And even after all this time, Becky love, I can't find it in my heart to pity him.'

Alec took a wrong turn coming out of Lincoln and found himself, at five o'clock, trapped in the multi-lane tidal flow of traffic that led out of the city, heading down from the cathedral. It took a full half-hour, slipping the clutch, breathing a toxic mix of hot, summer air and traffic fumes, before he reached the final sweep of the hill and a clearer road – only to find that at some crucial point he'd failed to move into the correct lane and was headed out towards Melton, in the opposite direction from the one he wanted.

He found a phone box and called Marcie to let her know he'd be late.

She'd just arrived home. 'Couple of hours, I should think,' he told her. 'I've a lot to tell you both. Yes, yes, I talked to Joe. Look, I'm out of change. Talk to you soon.'

He got back into his car and pulled out his road map, not certain how to get himself back on the right route. The package Joe had given him earlier tumbled out with it. Alec picked it up. An ordinary A4 envelope, sealed up and obviously crammed full of something.

'I want her to open it when you're all together,' Joe

had told him. 'And I'll check up on you, Alec. You've been making decisions for that girl for far too long. I don't want you deciding which of these she should see and which she shouldn't.

'Tell them both, her and that black man, that I'm looking forward to seeing them on Saturday. And if they can bring those pretty children that would make me very happy.'

Alec glared at the brown envelope, wondering what the mystery was. He was suspicious of anything kept secret. There had been altogether too many secrets in this family so far. He sighed deeply as he realized there were still some that he himself was as yet unprepared to tell.

He spent a minute or two studying the map, then started the engine and resumed his journey, thinking of the reports he had read earlier that day and of what Joe had told him that afternoon.

He hadn't talked to Joe about the theft from Fielding's surgery. He wondered if Joe knew about it, but assumed that he must. It was hardly the sort of thing that could be kept quiet.

Who had taken the child? What had they done with it?

Alec tried to relax, wriggling his shoulders back into the driving seat and concentrating on the winding road ahead of him.

And how long, Alec wondered, did they leave Rebekkah's body lying in the hotel ice house? His mind wandered, imagining her lying there, skin blue with cold, the colour drained from her body, wrapped in a shroud waiting for burial.

It would have been so cold, lying there. Cold death, like that of Patrick Simpson, his blood reddening the snow.

'That's Jack's writing,' Marcie said.

'Doesn't look as if they were ever posted,' Michael commented, examining the envelopes. He flicked his long hair back from his face and detached the envelope from Liam's small hand. 'Can't have that, lovely. Not for Liam.'

'Joe mentioned that Jack gave them to him when he left prison,' Alec said. 'But he wouldn't tell me anything else. Just said we had to all be together when I opened the envelope.'

Marcie opened the first letter and looked at the date. 'August 1938,' she said. 'What's yours?'

'March '39.'

'Right, well, let's try to get them in order.'

'Delaying tactic?' Michael asked her.

Marcie frowned. 'Maybe.' She surveyed the mass of envelopes covering the little table and spilling over on to the floor. 'How many are there, for goodness' sake?'

They worked in silence but for the reading of dates, separating the letters from their envelopes and fastening them with paperclips. Sorting them into date order.

When they had finished, Marcie picked up the first one. She glanced nervously at the others. 'It must have been written just after they moved.' She read aloud from the faded page:

I wrote and gave you our new address, not that
you write much, but in case you want to be in
touch. It's pleasant here, Joe, but it's not what
we're used to. Never thought I'd be able to settle in
a town, but Mary couldn't bear it back there. Too
many memories.

I don't need to tell you about memories, do
I? I think of you, inside that place. You, who
couldn't bear to be inside for more than an hour,
and I could weep.

Always the gypsy, weren't you? The wanderer.
You'd never have been a husband to her. Not in
the real sense. You'd have been like our granddad,
always on the move, following the fairs in
summer and the auctions all winter. Coming home
long enough to get his wife pregnant again and
then off on the road. Was that any life for a woman
like Rebekkah? She needed you there. Needed a
man to care for her. I suppose that's the only
excuse I can make for what I did, Joe.

Fact is, I can't live like this, keeping the secret
from you. A man has a right to know. So, I came
to a decision today. I'll write to you about all the
things I want you to know and tell you about
our lives and our news. Imagine I can keep you in
touch with the outside, ready for when they let
you go. And they will, Joe. One day you'll be a
free man again. And we can forget all of this, put
it behind us.

She broke off. 'He thought Joe could forgive him,'

she said, incredulous. 'That he could confess his sins and everything would go on as though it didn't matter.'

'No wonder Joe wants nothing to do with him.'

Michael nodded slowly. 'Confession can be a very dangerous thing,' he said softly.

Mary sat with Alice beside Jack's bed and talked about the past and the people they had once known.

'Do you recall Mother Atrie?' she asked. 'More than eighty, and travelled all her life. Only came home when she knew she was going to die.'

'Yes, I remember,' Alice said. An old woman with a wizened face, skilled in the arts of healing and brewing and birthing. 'But she'd had a good life, Mary. That's one woman went with nothing to regret.'

Mary's face was softened by a smile. 'You know what she said? "I want to be at me own wake," she told everyone and, my goodness, she managed it too. Drank everyone else under the table and died with an empty glass in her hand.'

She'd been kin to Jack and Joe, Mary thought, calling to mind how they'd come to give their blessings to her once she'd gone. Joe had been sixteen then and Jack a few years older. Both almost grown and already working all hours God sent.

'Joe fought that afternoon,' Alice said. 'Put three men twice his size to the ground. Tough as any of the travelling folk.' She stared into the middle distance, picturing that hot afternoon, the men bathed in sweat and Jack cheering his brother on – and taking bets on the side.

And at the end of it, Joe's eye half closed and the bruise rising. Spitting blood from cut lip and loosened teeth.

Mary laughed suddenly. 'Oh, and how the old folks glared at him in church the next day. Coming in with his face all bruised and his knuckles looking like some great dog had chewed them raw.' Her laughter faded as she remembered Rebekkah's face when she had looked at Joe, admiration in her eyes.

'They weren't like the rest of us,' she said aloud, knowing Alice would need no explanation. 'They were fey and wild, like. Not like Jack and you and me. I was glad of the choice I'd made when I married him. An honest, hard-working man, I thought.' An honest man . . . until I found out about Jack and that woman. Joe, coming out of jail and thinking the world owed him an explanation. Lord, but I thought they'd be fighting again that night, Joe as mad as he was. But even then, knowing about them, I swallowed my pride and stood by you, Jack. And here I am, still beside you . . .

She gave herself a little shake, aware that Alice was speaking again.

'They burned her wagon that night. Flames higher than the trees. And I remember a funny thing, Mary. I remember Joe looking at Jack in that odd way and saying to him it was like that time old Benny died. They burned that shack he lived in after he was gone. It seemed such an odd thing to talk about, I thought, and Jack looked so angry at Joe. I never did understand why.'

Chapter Thirty-Four

Alec returned to Lincoln on Thursday and spent the day at the archive. He telephoned Marcie and Michael in the evening, but his call did little more than confirm what Joe had told them about the trial.

Marcie's own day had been long. She had worked overtime and had not arrived home until close on eight o'clock. Michael, after work, had been involved with the twins. The main portion of Jack's letters still remained unread.

'I'm working until three tomorrow,' Marcie told him. 'Michael finishes at two. He's doing an extra evening session next week to make up for the Saturday. We should be with you just after five.' She hesitated, then added, 'It's going to be an expensive weekend, Da. And I'm not sure about that bed and breakfast place, with the twins.'

'Already sorted,' Alec told her. 'I drove out to the coast this afternoon, managed to get a chalet at a place called Anderby Creek. It's a bit out of the way, but it's right on the sea front. The french doors open practically on to the beach.'

'Sounds great, but how did you manage it at this time of the season?'

'It took some doing,' Alec confirmed, 'but I phoned around a bit and this place had a last-minute cancellation. It's cheaper than bed and breakfast and a lot more practical. Anyway, you let me worry about that. Oh, and I've bought buckets and spades, is that all right?'

Marcie laughed. 'Just great,' she said.

They arranged to meet at the chalet after Alec gave them directions. Marcie was smiling as she put the receiver down.

While her optimistic mood still held, she called the hospice. Yesterday was the first time she had missed in the last three weeks. Her feelings towards Jack had been severely challenged in these past few days, and yesterday she had felt so choked by them that her daily call had been left unmade. Dialling the number, she was afraid, guilty. What if Jack had died and no one had told her? What would the receptionist and nursing staff say to her? Would they hold it against her that she'd neglected him?

Angrily, she shook herself. 'Don't be such a prat, Marcie.' Forced a smile as the reception answered the phone and put her through to the ward.

'He's much the same, dear. Your gran and aunt have hardly left him, so if you've tried to get them at home . . . It must be hard for you, being so far away.'

'Yes,' Marcie agreed automatically. 'It is hard.'

'To be really honest, dear, we're surprised he's hung on this long.'

'I might be away for a couple of days,' Marcie told her on impulse, 'but I can give you a number to leave a message, if that's all right?' Marcie gave Adele's number. 'I'll call her a couple of times a day,' she said. 'And I'll phone you from here as well.'

She was aware she sounded over-anxious, but presumably the nurse was used to that. She must see so much pain, thought Marcie, so many anxious relatives and friends, afraid to miss the end.

She rang off, but stood looking at the telephone, wondering if she should have asked to speak to Mary or to Alice. Then decided that she could face neither of them. When Jack died she would try to make her peace. But that, she felt, would be soon enough.

The nurse told Mary and Alice that Marcie had called when she came to check on Jack. The morphine pump sighed and wheezed spasmodically. Jack never moved. He lay still, his eyes almost closed and his lips parted, a crust of salt grooved at the corners.

The nurse clasped Mary's hand soothingly. 'Why don't you go home and get some rest?' she said. 'Or if you'd rather, we can make up a bed for you. People often do, you know. You look worn out.'

'I'll be all right,' Mary told her. 'Thank you, but I'm fine just here.'

She sat in the high-backed chair, Alice in another beside her. Alice, her hands never idle, knitted with blue wool, the needles clicking softly against the silence.

'What's he waiting for?' Mary whispered, gazing at Jack's face with a mixture of love and resentment. 'Why is he hanging on like this?'

'Marcie,' Alice almost sighed the name. 'He's waiting for Marcie.'

'Then he'll wait a long time,' Mary said harshly. 'She'll not be back now.'

Alice said nothing, her hands pausing briefly while she counted her stitches, then continuing.

Children of my own, a house, a husband, work maybe, she was thinking. I could have had those things. Mary could have enjoyed those things. But it wasn't too late for them to live their own lives instead of just enduring Jack's. He would be gone soon ... and then what?

She shifted her thoughts away briskly, packing them carefully as though afraid another might hear them and know. Tell Jack. Tell Mary.

The silence closed about them, and the women waited.

Friday seemed to drag, the last hour of work extending impossibly. Three o'clock and Marcie made her escape.

'Have a good weekend,' her supervisor told her. 'We've put in a request to have you back again, by the way, so we'll probably see you next week.'

'Thanks,' Marcie grinned. 'Nice weekend.'

Michael was already outside, illegally parked and watching out for traffic wardens. 'Hi,' he said. 'I was just thinking I'd have to go around the block again.'

She kissed him and glanced into the back of the car at the twins. 'Sleeping?' she said, surprised. Hanna and Liam rarely napped mid-afternoon.

'Morning in the park playing havoc with the ducks,' Michael said. 'Hanna got chased by a goose and yelled all the way back to the crèche. Gwen said that Liam joined in as well, just to be included, so they've worn themselves out.'

'Did it hurt her?' Marcie asked, turning around to examine the sleeping child.

'No, she'd been feeding it. It thought she'd still got more, I suppose, but she's just fine now.'

'Did you have a good morning?'

'Not bad, but I'm glad to be away.'

They drove in silence then for a time, each busy with their own thoughts. It would be another hour or so, Marcie knew, before Michael's attention shifted from the work he'd left behind. Her own thoughts were occupied by Joe and by Jack and the letters crammed into her bag. She reached down and fished them out. They had read no more than the first few, the night Alec had brought them home. Jack talked at length in them about himself and Rebekkah. Spoke of their meetings and their love-making. He phrased his telling as confessional, but that did nothing to mitigate the cruelty as he unfolded the depth of his relationship with his brother's wife.

To come out of prison, hoping to begin again, and then be faced with this, Marcie thought. The sensible thing would have been for Joe to burn the letters as soon as he realized their content. But he had kept them, read every one – from the number of folds in them, probably read them many times – unable to put them aside. Ordinary human curiosity would have been enough to make him look at each page, open each sealed envelope; the self-destructive side of Joe, which Marcie recognized in her own make-up. In Jack. Maybe in everyone, that tendency to probe wounds, see if they still cause pain, would have been enough to keep him reading, and remembering.

But he had never ceased to love his wife. Only learned to hate Jack.

She turned back to the letter she had begun.

'Read it to me,' Michael said.

'It's about something that happened when they were both kids, I think,' she said. 'But I can't make much sense of it.'

> I know you were angry with me about George,
> but there was nothing to be done about it. He
> was old and wouldn't have lasted much longer. I
> know we argued, Joe. That you believed he was
> in no pain and should be allowed to finish his life
> naturally, but what use was he? He couldn't hunt,
> he was stiff and arthritic and just costing food to
> eat. It's not merciful to keep useless things alive.
>
> I did feel for him, though, you must know
> that. He'd been around since we were babies, the
> pair of us, but he was fourteen. Old and had a
> lifetime of work behind him. I hanged the cat
> when he went blind and got too old to catch
> anything. But I couldn't kill the dog that way. I
> felt for him, you see, though you could never
> understand that. I got old Bill Haines to put a
> bullet in his head, then buried him up in the top
> field.
>
> Merciful, really. No sense keeping useless
> things alive.

Marcie shuddered as she folded the letter and looked at Michael.

'He hanged the cat, had the dog shot,' Marcie said slowly, her voice echoing her disgust. 'He drowned the kittens. Did he kill Rebekkah?'

'Horrible as it is, Marcie, it's quite a step from an animal to a woman he claimed to be in love with.'

'You don't think he could do it?'

'Do you? Look, darlin', I don't know about your granddad. I don't believe Joe's capable of it, but Jack?' He glanced sideways at her, noting the change of expression on her face. The sadness about her eyes and mouth. 'What are you thinking of?'

'About Patrick Simpson,' she said. 'About not knowing about him. About what I accused Jack of doing to him.'

Michael said nothing. He stared at the road ahead, silent, afraid to say too much and yet not wanting to lie to her, if only by omission.

Damn Alec, he thought. Damn him for what he's almost told me. For making me share in his secrets. For taking this circle of lying and deceit and making me carry it on.

Chapter Thirty-Five

Joe was captivated by Liam and Hanna. His eyes flooded with tears as Marcie brought them into his little room.

'You've brought them with you,' he said. 'I got your photograph. Look.'

Alec glanced across at the picture, enthroned now in a cheap gilt frame. 'This little lady's Hanna,' he said, 'and the quiet one is Liam. He has to get used to you first, but Hanna's ready to create chaos any time.'

Marcie laughed. 'We thought we'd take you out, if you like,' she said. 'It's a beautiful day.'

'I'd like that,' he said, his eyes still fixed on the twins. 'I don't get out much.' He looked up quickly. 'Can we go to the cathedral? I haven't been there in years.'

'Sure.'

'I'll take you in my car,' Alec said. 'There's more room in the front. Marcie's packed a picnic, is that all right?'

'Perfect,' Joe told him. 'Give me your arm, lad,' this to Michael. 'I'm ready when you are.'

Liam was reaching to be picked up. Marcie swept him into her arms and, not to be outdone, Hanna clung to Alec's trouser leg. 'Granddad, up,' she demanded.

Alec swung her high into the air and she squealed and shouted, 'Again!' He felt devastatingly happy. Almost able to believe that this was an ordinary family outing with an ordinary family that had more than blood kinship in common.

He glanced back as they went out to the cars. Michael and Joe were deep in conversation and, as she watched, the younger man threw back his head and laughed. The sound was free and unrestrained.

Alec sighed and cuddled Hanna close, suddenly afraid that this interval in a lifetime of strife was going to be all too short. That he was going to lose everything even before it was properly begun.

'I love you, sweetheart,' he whispered to Hanna, astonished to find just how much he meant it.

By the time they arrived at the cathedral, Hanna had decided that Joe was all right. She insisted on holding his free hand as he leaned heavily on his stick and walked slowly into the great nave.

Progress this far had been slow. Joe liked to walk, he said. He was fine if he wasn't rushed, but the brief distance from the car park to the cathedral close had taken them almost half an hour.

'The ankle didn't mend right,' he said. 'I broke it jumping from that bloody window and then ran about a quarter-mile on the blasted thing. It's given me strife ever since. Hadn't been for that then I'd have been home free.'

'Then what, Joe?' Marcie asked him.

'Oh, I dare say I'd have boarded a ship somewhere down the coast. They didn't make the checks then they do now. You could sign on as an unskilled hand and no one asked for papers. Just an honest day's work. Course, it was illegal to carry on like that even then, but no one bothered. Another year, of course, and we were winding up towards the war. Things must have got tighter then.' He shrugged awkwardly. 'I missed that show, not like Jack.' He turned a sharp glance upon Marcie. 'You read those letters yet?'

'Not all of them. I don't know if I want to read them all, Joe.'

'But you will,' he predicted. 'You will. Like me, you see, you have to know. Otherwise, why would you have come looking?'

He paused again, gazing up at the high vault of the ceiling arching over their heads. 'We used to sing here,' he said. 'In the choir, Jack and me. Beautiful voice, Jack had, sang solo. I hated it, but our mam and dad thought it was an honour. They never came themselves, mind.' He chuckled at the memory. 'It was the war that finished it for Jack, I'm convinced of that. Oh, he was mad enough before, but the war really brought it out in him. Made it all right.' He shook his head. 'You read about that poor woman yet?'

Marcie nodded. 'Last night,' she said. 'I could hardly sleep, Joe. It was a dreadful thing to do, to have to see.'

Joe looked sideways at her. 'War's full of dreadful things. The death camps were a dreadful thing. The blitzkrieg. The firebombing of Tokyo and the Burma railway, all dreadful things. I don't doubt there were precious, honourable, decent things came out of it too, but I'd have a hard time naming any far as Jack was concerned.' He led Hanna to a seat left from the last service and eased himself into it. 'Your Uncle Joe's got aching feet, my lamb,' he said. 'Have you the letter with you?' he asked.

Marcie dug into her bag and gave it to him. 'He gets her mixed up in his head, Joe. She'd got tangled up with Rebekkah in his mind. I don't know if he can tell the difference any more.'

Joe said nothing. He slid his glasses from his jacket pocket and perched them on his nose, held the letter at arm's length and peered thoughtfully at it. 'It was this one told me he'd really lost it,' Joe said. 'I wondered before if he'd killed her. It would have been the best thing, far as he was concerned. Get rid of her for good before I knew what he'd done.'

'He offered her money to go away,' Marcie said slowly. 'One of his other letters says so.'

Joe nodded. 'Just like he offered it to me under the guise of brotherly love,' he said.

'Maybe he meant it?' Marcie asked.

'My brother never offered me anything that didn't profit himself,' he said. 'No, not Jack.' He looked back at the letter. 'One death amongst so many,' he said. 'He felt it wouldn't matter.'

'It played on his mind,' Michael pointed out. 'Otherwise, why write about it?'

'Trouble shared is a trouble halved. That what you mean?'

Slowly, Michael shook his head. 'No,' he said. 'I don't mean that.' He thought of Alec. No, he definitely didn't mean that.

' "The night was so cold, you wouldn't believe it," ' Joe read slowly,

and the stars were so bright it reminded me of
those cold nights waiting for the lambs to be
born. Huddled in the shack, back of the crew yard,
keeping warm among the sheep. When you
looked outside and the sky was so clear, hanging
with frost, you could see right the way to heaven.
She hung there, Joe, her feet kicking the stars like
Becky had done, and for a minute I thought I
was seeing it again. They'd not set the rope
properly, see. Left it to pull tight across her throat
instead of slipping the eyelet close beside her ear.
It took her time to die, kicking the stars, Joe.
Kicking at the stars.

Joe broke off and turned bright eyes on Marcie. 'You
said you'd read this thing,' he said.

Marcie looked at him sadly, the implications of it
sinking in for the first time. ' "Like Becky had done",'
she repeated. 'He was there. There when she died.'

'Seems like it to me,' Joe said. Then, 'I'm sorry, love.
Maybe I should never have shown you this. Maybe it's
better to doubt than to know for certain.'

Marcie didn't know what to say to him. She swallowed and got to her feet, walking away from the others.
Was it better to doubt? She had suspected Jack of many
things, of killing Patrick Simpson, of murdering
Rebekkah and her child. But always, there had been
space to excuse, to let the love she still had for Jack
worm him free of her questions and her accusations.

She walked slowly down the length of the nave,
through the angel choir. There was a chapel set aside,

which she had seen before, set with large stoneware pots like Ali Baba jars. They were filled with sand and set with candles lit in prayer. Marcie found herself there almost without realizing it, staring at the candles, her tears reflecting and refracting each tiny flame, transforming into hundreds the light of dozens.

Joe's footsteps behind her, the tapping of his stick marking the rhythm of his steps, made her wipe away the tears. He came to stand beside her, the letter rolled up and clasped in his hand.

'Why did you tell no one, Joe? You could have cleared your name,' she managed, her voice shaky and uncertain.

'Why? I don't know, lass, I don't know. Maybe I thought no one would care any more. Maybe, I don't know, maybe I thought there'd been enough suffering over this. Enough for Alice and Mary. Why take Alec's father from him?'

He reached out, the letter rolled up in his hand, and planted it like a candle in the sand. Took a small white candle from the box and offered it towards a flame, then turned it to the letter.

'No!' Marcie laid a hand on his. 'No. It'll change nothing, Joe. It's too late for that and I won't let you do it.'

Gently, she took the letter from the sand, smoothed it out and placed it back in her bag. Then she took the candle from Joe's hand and lit another from the same flame. 'For Rebekkah,' she said, 'and for Patrick.'

'Patrick?'

'Something else I couldn't quite believe,' Marcie told him.

Chapter Thirty-Six

It was hard to put things back on the level after that, but they tried. Alec suggested they went back to the chalet and Joe agreed enthusiastically. They drove back and spent the rest of the day on the beach, Joe resting in a beach chair at first, then, to please Liam, rolling up his trouser legs and paddling in the shallows, listing somewhat as his walking stick sank in the wet sand.

Marcie left the men to play with the children and busied herself with setting out the picnic, making tea and cold drinks, stealing the time taken by simple tasks to get her thoughts under control.

Just like Alice, she thought wryly. Maybe that was how it had begun. A way of stealing time for thought. Or time to be absent from it. She ran through what she knew.

Fact one was that Jack had killed Patrick Simpson. She no longer had any doubt about that.

Fact two, Rebekkah had been another victim, her baby too. He had killed them both that night, then stood aside, prepared to let Joe take the blame.

What if Joe had hanged for the crime? Would Jack have let it go that far? The thought made Marcie shiver despite the heat. She felt like winter inside.

Abandoning thoughts of Jack, she looked out across the beach, watching the others. Joe had Liam by the hand, who was kicking the water, watching the sunlit spray as it sparkled in the brilliant light and squealing with pleasure. Michael and Hanna played near by, though she refused to hold anyone's hand. Both hands and feet were in the water as she crawled through it on all fours. Alec stood a little apart, shoes still firmly in place, standing on the drier sand further up the beach. He was laughing, looking relaxed and happy. Away from Jack, she thought. Away from Mary and her demands. Away from everything.

Poor Mary. The thought came almost unbidden into her head. When had she found out about Rebekkah? Had she read the letters, or had Joe confronted his brother in her presence? Marcie had no doubt that her gran had known. Her reaction every time Rebekkah's name was mentioned, the sudden removal of the harvest photograph that Alec had said once resided on the sideboard, told her that. Joe must have shown her the letters when he came out of prison.

Marcie sighed. Why does anyone stay married? Maybe she still loved Jack in spite of everything. Looking at her own, mixed-up feelings for her grandfather, Marcie could sympathize with that.

She thought of Alec's sister, the baby that had died, and the carefully tended grave in the little churchyard. Who placed fresh flowers there and, after all this time, why?

There was, she remembered, a service at the church that Sunday, the one in three for which a vicar could be found.

Crossing the beach to call the others in to eat, Marcie decided that the next day that was where they'd be.

They brought her to me and I slipped the rope around her neck. She was shaking and crying and her eyes seemed to look everywhere at once, unable to focus on anyone.

I tried not to look into her face and I wanted to tell her that it would be quick. That I knew well how to do these things, had learned to do them properly.

The hands, remember, Birdie. The hands know.

I eased her black hair free of the noose, stroking down the length of it past her shoulders. They had torn her clothes and left her shoulders bare. The skin was soft beneath my fingers, the roughness of my own hands dragging against its smoothness.

I wanted it to be easy for her, the way it should have been for Becky, but the preparation should be slow, Birdie. Death is a thing the senses should be a party to, not a thing to be rushed.

But Mills didn't understand that and he grabbed her from me before I had a chance to set the eyelet right beneath her jaw and they threw the rope across the tree branch and hauled on it until her feet came off the ground and her body jerked and twisted like a puppet dancing, kicking at the sky.

It wasn't easy to find somewhere to park. Cars had been pulled up on to the grass verge, but what little space there was had been almost filled. They were glad that they had chosen to cram everyone into the one car, Marcie wedged not terribly comfortably between the twins' car seats.

The Sunday service had already begun by the time they arrived. They slipped quietly inside, aware of the curious stares as the congregation turned to look at the latecomers. The vicar smiled, indicated them to sit down and carried on with his announcements. They had arrived in time for the first hymn and, just as they had seated themselves, had to rise to their feet again.

Marcie didn't know the tune. Vainly she tried to match words to melody but in the end she gave up and turned her attention to Liam, who was eating a hymn-book and Hanna, who was trying to escape by sliding through the little gap in the wooden pews.

'Monster,' Marcie whispered, as she removed the book from Liam's mouth and ducked down to pull Hanna out of her hole. She tried to remember the last time she had been in a church like this. It had been a Sunday tradition all through childhood, but the last time ... it was well before she had finally run away from home.

Since then she had been with Sophie Lee on odd occasions, enjoying the singing and the pure pleasure the congregation had taken in praising. But she had no religious feelings these days. None at all.

The hymn ended and they sat down, Michael with Liam on his lap and Hanna on a hassock on the floor, her fingers twisting the fringing, watching it spring unwound again. Marcie carefully lowered the baby bag on to the floor so that Hanna could reach the toys, checking to make certain nothing too noisy had found its way inside.

Then she took the time to look around, her mind wandering while the minister intoned the lesson for the day.

There were no more than twenty people in the church besides themselves. Mostly elderly, but with a few young people and three or four kids, sitting quietly with their parents. Fresh flowers decorated the altar and the side chapel, and light streamed in through high windows, broken into tiny diamonds by the glass.

Was one of these people the one who put flowers on Margaret's grave? she wondered, playing games with herself, imagining the elderly lady in the black hat kneeling to pluck weeds from the close-cropped grass, or the young man in the blue suit arranging the tiny vase of flowers. The old couple sitting with linked arms halfway down the row – were they the ones?

The service dragged. The hour that Marcie had been used to every Sunday, seated without thought of complaint between her grandparents, now seemed to stretch into eternity.

Finally it came to an end, with a hymn that Marcie actually remembered. She sang this time, fervently as though in apology for her inattention. Hanna decided that she would join in too. She climbed back on to the seat and stood beside her mother seriously intoning 'Baa, Baa, Black Sheep' against a background of 'There's a Wideness in God's Mercy'.

Marcie let it go. Beside her, Michael was trying hard

not to laugh. Alec stared, eyes strictly forward, pretending not to hear.

'I loved your version,' the vicar told Hanna as they left the church. 'You sang with real feeling.'

Hanna stared at him, then hid her face in her mother's skirt.

'Are you on holiday here?' he asked.

'Just up for the weekend,' Marcie replied. 'Our family came from around here. In fact, you've my father's little sister buried in the churchyard over there.'

'Really?'

Marcie pointed to the child's grave.

'Oh,' he said. 'Little Margaret Armitage, now isn't that interesting? You'll want to talk to Helen.' He called out to a young woman shepherding her children towards the door.

'Helen, these are relatives of Margaret Armitage.' He turned to Marcie. 'Helen's on our committee. We try to keep things up to the mark here. The committee split the work. Margaret Armitage is one of Helen's charges, isn't she? Always makes sure there are flowers. So sad, a child's grave, especially with no family living near by.'

Marcie's heart sank. So that was the solution. Just a church committee to keep the graveyard tidy, and a kind-hearted woman who could not bear to see a child's grave neglected.

The young woman was smiling at her and holding out her hand. 'I'm pleased to meet you,' she said. 'I hope you like what we've been doing?'

'Oh, I think it's lovely,' Marcie managed. 'Have you been doing it for long?'

'Oh, yes,' Helen said. 'I enjoy it.' They moved slowly towards the little grave, her children trailing behind, calling out to friends who were now leaving the church.

'It's odd, really, but my family have always looked after this grave, and when the vicar suggested we got a committee together, well, I couldn't let anyone else do it, so I took this section over.'

'Always?' Marcie asked her, puzzled.

'Well, yes, though I don't really know how it came about.' She smiled, looking slightly embarrassed. 'My gran used to do it and then my mum. I couldn't let it get overgrown, it wouldn't be right somehow.' She glanced curiously at them and asked, 'If you don't mind, how are you related to Margaret?'

'She was my sister,' Alec said quietly. 'My parents moved from here the year after she was born.'

'Oh, really? I hope you don't mind, then. I mean, after all, she was your sister . . .'

'Please,' Alec said hastily. 'I think you've done a marvellous job, just marvellous. Er, if you'll let me contribute towards flowers . . .'

'Oh no,' Helen told him. 'Mostly they're from my garden anyway. I'm sure the vicar would be grateful if you want to send something to the church.' She turned back to Marcie. 'You might like to remember me to your grandparents,' she said. 'Tell them the grave's looked after. They must have known my gran and my mum. Tell them, let me see, they would know my gran's name, that was Lacey. Elizabeth Lacey.'

*

It was time then to go back to Joe. They had talked further to Helen, but it had been obvious that Rebekkah's story was not familiar to her, though she knew the name. 'Oh yes,' she'd said. 'I think she died in childbirth. Quite common then, my mum says.'

They found Joe as they had first seen him, in the garden with the chess board set out in front of him.

'I know,' he said, as Marcie confronted him with what they had been told. 'Or at least I knew that Elizabeth tended the grave. It's good that someone still does.'

'But why?' Marcie asked him. 'Did she feel guilty, or what?'

It seemed as though Joe didn't want to answer, then he sighed deeply and said, 'She couldn't bear it. Bad enough that her daughter was dead, but to cut her open like that, you know . . . The police wanted to know for certain how far gone she was. They kept it quiet, like, as long as they could, but then some newspaperman let it slip that the child had been preserved in case they needed it for evidence. That's what they said, anyway. But I ask you, Marcie, they could have looked at the poor little bugger, figured out how old it was and let it go at that. Given it a decent burial. Bad enough she couldn't bury her girl, but to think of her grandchild, pickled like a side of pork in brine, it was more than Elizabeth could take.'

'The break-in at Dr Fielding's,' Alec said.

Joe nodded. 'She came to me, told me about it. Got special permission to see me in the jail. Desperate, she was, and I was scared as hell that she might get herself caught. But she was a determined woman, Elizabeth. She

took someone with her, I believe, though she didn't tell
me who, and they broke in through a back window.
Took the child away.'

'What happened to it?' Alec asked.

'They buried it in Margaret's grave, didn't they, Joe?'
Marcie said.

Joe nodded again. 'That's right, lass, they did. Seemed
just, somehow. Two innocents buried together. It wasn't
hard, she eased the turf from off the top and then dug
down. It didn't take much of a hole. Took the spare earth
and scattered it in a new-dug grave. Watered the turf
back down again.'

'And Elizabeth knew about Jack?' Alec asked.

'She knew. Becky told her when she realized she was
pregnant. Thought she could get Jack to leave his wife
and go off with her, but he wouldn't have it. She felt she
couldn't tell me. That it was Jack's baby, I mean. Then
when I found out, I went to her. Wanted to know the
truth and that's when she told me. All of it. She told no
one else. I'm certain of that.'

'And she believed that Jack was guilty of the murder?'
Alec asked him.

'Believed that all along,' Joe confirmed. 'Spoke up
for me in court, but she could prove nothing about Jack,
you see. She'd only Becky's word. And there were plenty
willing to call Becky a whore. She didn't want her name
dragged further through the mud than it had to be.'

'Did you show her the letter?'

'Yes.' Joe nodded slowly. 'I was mad as hell. Took it
and showed her. She said the same as you, that I should
try to clear my name with it, but I'd no faith in the law

and no money to fight my case anyhow. It was lost before I even started.'

'Oh, Joe,' Marcie whispered, taking the old man's hand. 'What a waste. What a terrible waste.'

Chapter Thirty-Seven

'They say we should go now, if we want to be there,'
Marcie said. She sounded undecided, as though going
back to see Jack would be too hard.

'Then you'd better be on your way,' Joe said. The
last letter Jack had sent to him, the one he had chosen
not to let the others see, burned in his waistcoat pocket,
folded tight. He had read it so many times he knew the
words by heart: *The night she died was so clear and so
cold . . .*

He had carried it there so long, unable to act, to
change anything. He blamed Jack. Jack had taken Becky
from him. Taken much of his life, too.

'You'd best go to him,' he said, and this time Marcie
nodded.

'We'll be back, Uncle Joe,' she said, kissing him sadly.

Joe smiled. 'I know you will,' he said contentedly. 'I
know you will.'

He watched them walk away across the parched lawn
and smiled again. The one thing Jack had truly valued,
truly loved, he thought, looking at Marcie, and he'd lost
her.

Joe patted the letter in the pocket of his waistcoat
and nodded, satisfied. He could have shown it to her.

But he chose not to. Something was owed, Joe felt,
and Marcie and her family would well do in payment.

As Marcie turned to go up the ramp and into the house she paused, stepped back and then stood still as though something had caught her eye. Joe followed her gaze.

Beneath the trees, where the children had played a little time before, a figure stood in half-shadow. Black hair fell about her face and a hand protectively touched her swollen belly.

'Becky,' Joe whispered. 'Becky.'

He looked back sharply to where Marcie stood and their eyes met for a moment, and he knew that she had seen her too. Then she turned and walked away.

When he looked towards the trees there were only shadows. Long branch shadows, laying themselves across the dried-out grass.

Marcie had expected trouble when she reached the hospice; had expected that Alice and her grandmother would deny her wish to see Jack. But nothing happened. Mary and Alice had grown too tired to argue. They joined Alec and Michael in the waiting room and Marcie went to Jack's bedside alone.

'I've talked to Joe,' she told him without preamble. 'And he showed me the letters you sent to him, about you and Rebekkah.' She paused, finding words hard. 'How could you, Jack? How could you do that to someone you loved?'

Jack could barely open his eyes. He felt so tired, and the light, dim as it was, hurt. But he didn't need to look to know that Marcie was there or to hear her voice.

Becky, he thought. She was talking about Rebekkah.

'How could you kill her?' Marcie said. 'She was pregnant, Jack, pregnant with your baby. What was it, too inconvenient for you? Did you think she would tell Joe whose baby it was? Were you scared of him? Scared enough to kill them both and pin the blame on your brother?'

She shook her head, still half disbelieving, the enormity of Jack's crime overwhelming her. 'How could you, Jack? How could you . . . ?'

And then there was Patrick, Marcie thought, and her own ruined teenage years and the hurt he had caused to Alec and to Mary and to Lord alone knew who else.

Marcie found she couldn't bear to be there, beside him, any more.

In his half-conscious state Jack could hear Marcie's words.

No, he wanted to tell her. It wasn't like that. It wasn't like she said, but they were all there now, crowded round his bed. All hating him and judging him for what he'd done and what he'd been.

They were all there, Becky and the child and the woman he'd seen hanged on a cold desert night in some place he could barely remember. And that boy who'd got Marcie into trouble.

Jack knew they were waiting for him, but the fear of losing Marcie was the worst of all.

It wasn't like that, he wanted to say, as he saw Becky take the child by the hand and slowly walk away. It wasn't like that ... as the others faded slowly from his vision, leaving empty space filled only with Marcie's voice.

'I'm going now, Jack,' she said slowly. 'I'm sorry, Jack, but you must understand that I have to go.'

Joe held Jack's final letter in his hand. The letter he had decided Marcie would never see.

> The night she died was so clear and so cold and there was a bright moon, two-thirds towards full. I'd missed you, Joe, up at the farm, and so I'd kept watching the house, waiting for you to come home. It wasn't hard. We could see the corner of your place and the road you'd come by from the kitchen window and I'd sat there, reading while Mary prattled away, keeping a lookout.
>
> It was Mary's idea. We'd hardly seen you since you got back and she wanted you to come in for supper. Family, like. Rebekkah, too, if she had to. I'd told her we should stick together, show solidarity.
>
> I thought it would soon pass. The trouble, I mean, and the village gossip. It wouldn't be the first child born with an awkward birthday and folk forget in time, or at least put their memories away.
>
> It was a strange thought I had as I watched

the door open and Becky slip through, that at
least the child would be family. It made me smile
and I had to take care that Mary didn't see and
wonder why. She could be sharp at the oddest
moments.

But I admit I was scared. What if Rebekkah
had told someone about us? What if you found
out in some way? A moment's carelessness or anger
and that would be that.

When I saw her go out I took a chance. I
wanted to talk to her. To make certain that things
would stay secret. Mary was a good match. I loved
her. Not like I loved Rebekkah, but still, I loved her.
And her family were not people to offend.

So I made an excuse about trying to meet you
on the road and I slipped out after Rebekkah.

I almost lost her. I'd been carrying a hurricane
lamp, but turned it low as I'd left the village,
afraid she'd see the light. There was something in
the way she moved that made me feel strange and
I was worried, anyway, that we might be seen if
we stopped too close to the houses.

But she never looked back. Just walked with
her eyes fixed straight ahead and her coat collar
pulled up high. She carried no light and moved
like an awkward shadow.

I almost lost her when she turned off the path.
I'd gone by the gate and kept on up the road,
thinking she was ahead of me where the road bent.
But then, when I reached the straight and had a full

view of the road as it went on up the hill, I knew
she'd left it and cut across country.

So I went back.

There was a gate about a quarter of a mile
back up the road leading off to Bale's field. She
must have gone through, there was no other place.
I climbed the gate and skirted the field, following
her.

Joe sat in his favourite place by the window, watching
the evening creep across the lawn, Jack's final letter to
him clutched in his hand.

He looked up as she came into the room and he saw
this time that the smile reached her eyes.

'Becky.'

She sat down opposite him, leaning back in the chair
with a sigh, her hands resting lightly on the chair arms.
She looked satisfied with herself, he thought. Happy after
all this time.

'She's left him, then,' Joe said, his eyes soft as he
smiled back at her.

Chapter Thirty-Eight

Marcie waited outside for Alec, aware that he couldn't just abandon Gran and Aunt Alice at a time like this, but feeling herself apart from it all now.

She watched Michael playing catch – or, usually, miss – with their children and thought . . . nothing. Her mind felt numb and tired. She wanted to go home and there was still luggage left at the chalet to collect. It would be as easy to drive back there tonight as to go home and make the longer trip the following day.

Alec came out eventually with his mother holding his arm.

'We've sorted things out here,' he said. 'They don't think Jack will last the night.'

Marcie nodded.

'You'll do all the arrangements for us, won't you, Alec?' Mary said to him, a touch of her old control returning.

Alec shook his head. 'If I can,' he said. 'If not, you'll have to ask Marcie and her husband if they'd mind giving you a hand.'

Mary was clearly dumbfounded.

Alec didn't give anyone the chance to question. Instead, he looked straight at Marcie and continued to speak, his tone calm and unhurried.

'There's something I have to do,' he said, 'and I don't quite know how it'll go.'

Marcie gave him a puzzled look. 'I don't follow you, Da.'

'It's about Patrick Simpson,' Michael ventured.

Alec nodded. 'You were right,' he said. 'I have to grow up some time. Decide things for myself.'

Marcie hesitated, looking from her husband to her father. Then she reached out and took her father's hand.

'This time we're coming with you,' she told him.

With Rebekkah beside him in the dimly lit room, Joe read on.

I didn't see her until I'd reached the top of the hill and then I knew. She was standing there on that low branch, her arms around the trunk, and I remember thinking how hard it must have been for her to climb up there with her belly swollen and throwing her balance the way it must. But it had always been a good climbing tree, that one. Even a child could do it.

Then she threw the rope over the higher branch and I understood. She'd thought it out well, made a loop in the other end, so all she had to do was thread the noose end through and pull it tight, and I remembered how I'd showed her how to bind a whip handle with thick cord, pulling it through so it made a noose, then hauling the free end to make it neat and safe. She'd bound her death noose the same way. Made it secure so it wouldn't fail her.

You know, Joe, I remember I was proud of her then. Not many women would have gone to such trouble to get it right.

I had to respect her choice, Joe, you do know that. I had to let her go.

I sent you that letter, Joe. Told you, but you did nothing, so I knew you understood. What else was there to do?

But she haunts me, Joe, and I know she's waiting for me. Like that other one. They've found each other, stand each side of my bed and wait.

She saw me. She saw me. Just as I came over the rise and she'd already got the rope round her neck, was standing there, her feet planted on that big branch and her hands resting on the trunk to steady her.

She saw me, Joe. Looked straight into my eyes and there was this look, like she'd hoped I'd come. Not thought I would, but hoped I'd come. That I'd want her so much that I'd somehow know what she had in mind and come and make it right. Make it possible for her to go on living.

Tell me you'll leave her. Tell me you love me. You want me. Her eyes, fixed on mine, they said all those things, but I couldn't, Joe. I couldn't lose everything, she must have seen that.

Next moment, she'd thrown herself forward, her hands reaching for me and her skirts and hair billowing around her like a wave. Just for an instant, she seemed to be held there against a starry sky, beautiful as an angel, her hands reaching out in blessing.

Then the rope jerked her back. The force of it yanked her head sideways and cracked it against the tree. Then it was all over. Just her legs dancing some obscene dance and her body swaying in the wind, like a rag blowing across the moon.

Fade to Grey

By Jane Adams

What follows here are the opening scenes from Jane Adams's new novel, *Fade to Grey*, which reintroduces Detective Inspector Mike Croft and retired detective John Tynan.

It is published in hardback by Macmillan (priced £16.99) in September 1998.

Prologue

She took a good photograph, anyone would say so. She had that look about her, that little bit of self doubt, or not quite innocence, that men found so appealing. Some men.

She'd always resisted Jake's attempts to make her look even younger than she was. The schoolgirl look or the baby doll just wasn't her style, she said. Though it was amazing what you could do with the right software package these days.

In the end he'd turned her out pretty much any way he wanted and she hadn't said a word about it.

He turned the pages of the latest magazine. Computer porn might be the new thing, but personally, he preferred the finished article to be one he could roll up and carry in his pocket.

Which he did now, tucking the magazine into the inside pocket of his coat.

It would be a collector's item, before long. This edition. In certain circles anyway. Those that were in the know . . .

Not because it was anything harder than you could pick up from the top shelf of any news-stand. Nothing more than soft porn in this edition – the other stuff, the stuff he could have been arrested for if he'd been caught prancing round town with it. That was elsewhere. Already distributed on the multi-media wave.

No, it wasn't the content that made this little package rare, but the scarcity of the commodity.

There would be no more centrefolds, not of this little lady. Not unless, of course, you liked your meat well done . . .

Chapter One

Stacey hesitated before squeezing through the next to the park gates. It was dark in there but it was also the quickest way of getting home. Besides, turning around and walking back the way she'd come would mean running into Richard again and she just knew he'd be standing around, waiting for her to come back to him. And Stacey wasn't going to apologize for anything. Let him stew for a while.

Once inside the park she stopped and groped in her bag for the little penlight torch she had attached to her keyring. The thin beam of light showed her only a few yards of the muddy path before it was swallowed by the thick darkness. She slid her finger through the ring, posting the key in between her fingers the way the man in the self-defence class had told them to. Nervous now, her mind niggling about those reports in the papers.

Maybe, after all, she should go back and find Richard. Not apologize exactly, just open the discussion enough for him to give her a ride home.

She glanced back over her shoulder one more time startled by what sounded like a footstep.

'Richard? Is that you?' No reply. 'Richard. Oh for Christ's sake, if that's you . . .'

She shone the torch back through the wrought-iron

gates but could see nothing, no one at all walking along the lonely street.

Stacey walked swiftly down what she could see of the slimy, leaf-covered path. The silence seemed to close in all around her, only the heels of her boots clacking with a reassuringly steady beat as she walked and the jingle of loose change in her pocket breaking the quiet.

Stacey shivered. It had begun to rain and the air was damp and clammy against her skin. Thinking she would be driven home she had only worn her denim jacket and left her umbrella on the table in the hall. She quickened her pace now, as the rain fell more heavily, desperate to be home.

And then it happened, footsteps, the sound of someone running making her look behind. Richard's name half spoken before one hand was clamped around her mouth and a second hand grabbing at her breasts, the man's body pressed tight against her back. Then he had shifted sideways and she was on the floor even before she realized that she was falling. The hand away from her mouth now, Stacey screamed in fear, then pain as the fist came crashing down at the side of her head.

Only half conscious she still tried to wriggle away from him. Felt the sudden chill of air on her legs and stomach as he wrenched her skirt up above her waist. Hard fingers bruising as they grabbed between her legs.

Stacey tried to scream again, but he was on top of her, his body heavy on her chest and breath hot in her face. He was saying something but Stacey was too stunned to understand the words.

The torch, the keys, somehow she had managed to

keep hold of them, the ring still tight around her finger. She brought her right hand up, striking into the man's face. Her left hand reaching up and grabbing at his hair, winding her fingers tight and pulling as hard as she could. Adrenalin and fear had overcome the pain of her bruised and bleeding head and half-closed eye.

The man was yelling now, loosening his grip on her just for an instant. Stacey hit out at him again, fighting for her life as he came back at her, his hands tightening on her throat.

Mike sat uneasily between Maria and her sister Josie watching as three wise men, bearing gold-wrapped boxes, slow marched across the stage. Enthusiastic music, played on a slightly off-key piano helped to keep them in time, left feet, right feet, lifted in unison like a dissociated caterpillar making its way towards the manger.

He tried desperately not to fidget, the hard plastic of the chair was digging into his back and there was no room to stretch out his long legs. A tall man who liked space to move around, Mike felt over large and over conspicuous wedged in between proud parents and grandparents. His body cramped and his mind over-whelmed by remembrance of another time when his son Stevie had been one of the three kings. Wearing his father's old plaid dressing gown and holding his gift high as he presented it to the little girl cuddling the baby doll.

'Doesn't she look lovely?'

It was Maria, smiling happily at her niece. Little Essie was grinning so much she almost forgot her words. Her thick black hair, braided tightly and threaded with blue and yellow beads, swung around her face as she strutted forward with her arms outstretched to take the presents from the kings. Mike didn't have to look sideways to know that Josie dabbed at tears, watching her little girl up on the stage.

He tried hard to smile, knowing he should feel grateful to be included in such a family event, but it brought back so many morbid thoughts and, since Stevie had died, he'd always found it hard to cope with this pre-Christmas rush of emotion.

The angels were just about to break into a new song when the beeping started. Mike grabbed at his pocket to silence it, aware of Maria's glare as he peeked a look at the number on the LCD screen. He unfolded himself awkwardly from the little plastic chair, trying hard not to catch her eye as he headed for the door, apologizing as he went and horribly conscious of every inch of his six-foot-two frame.

Maria caught up with him at the outer door.

'I thought I told you to leave that bloody thing behind.'

'Well no, actually it was the phone you told me to leave behind . . .' He smiled sheepishly, 'it's work,' he said.

'Isn't it always?'

'Um, I need the car keys, the phone . . .'

She sighed in exasperation and dug into her pocket for the keys. 'You'd better take the car,' she said. 'I'll get a lift back with Josie.'

'Thanks.' He paused, wondering if he should risk

a kiss goodbye. He reached out and caught her hand instead.

'I'm really sorry.'

'You're always really sorry.' Marie shook her head. 'God! Never get yourself involved with a policeman. Well, what's keeping you? Phone's in the car.'

He watched her as she stalked away, shoulders set. This was the third time in as many already scarce evenings off that he'd been called away. He could understand her getting mad at him. Mike was relieved when she glanced back from the door, not quite smiling, but her expression softened enough to let him know he was off the hook . . . almost.

Then he got into the car, rummaged in the glove compartment for the phone and called the office. 'DI Mike Croft.' He listened in silence as they told him about this latest attack.

'They've taken her to the Royal and District, Mike. Price is interviewing the boyfriend.'

'Is she badly hurt?'

"Bruising, shock. They'll be keeping her overnight though. You'll want to speak to the boyfriend?'

Mike signed off and turned the ignition key, listening to the low purr of the engine for a moment or two before pulling away, his mind already cataloguing the new information, he turned the car towards the hospital.

JANE ADAMS

The Greenway

Pan Books £5.99

Even in her dream Cassie could feel the exertion of that run... Then, the sudden shimmer, like a displaced heat haze; the feeling of heaviness cloaked around her shoulders, the ground shifting beneath her feet. Dimly, as she fell, she heard Suzie's distant voice calling her name.

Cassie Maltham still has nightmares about that day in August 1975 when she and her twelve-year-old cousin Suzie took a short cut through The Greenway, an ancient enclosed pathway steeped in Norfolk legend. For somewhere along this path Suzie simply vanished . . .

Haunted also is John Tynan, the retired detective once in charge of Suzie's case, still obsessed by the tragic disappearance he failed to solve.

Then another young girl goes missing at the entrance to The Greenway. And Cassie's nightmares take on a new and terrifying edge . . .

JANE ADAMS

Cast the First Stone

Pan Books   £5.99

Ellie Masouk never knew who cast the first stone, but suddenly and inexplicably her world descended into madness . . .

Life in Portland Close was pleasantly uneventful for Ellie and her neighbours – until Eric Pearson moved in. For within just a few short weeks he had become the focus of violent intimidation.

Pearson claims he is being persecuted because he has the journal of the late Simon Blake JP, which details some sinister crimes. Crimes that could topple powerful figures . . .

Detective Inspector Mike Croft is asked to investigate, although at first it seems Pearson's allegations are simply the work of a bitter, obsessed man.

But then a terrible discovery is made on the outskirts of Bright's Wood . . .

All Pan Books are available at your local bookshop or newsagent, or can be ordered direct from the publisher. Indicate the number of copies required and fill in the form below.

Send to: Macmillan General Books C.S.
              Book Service By Post
              PO Box 29, Douglas I-O-M
              IM99 1BQ

or phone: 01624 675137, quoting title, author and credit card number.

or fax: 01624 670923, quoting title, author, and credit card number.

or Internet: http://www.bookpost.co.uk

Please enclose a remittance* to the value of the cover price plus 75 pence per book for post and packing. Overseas customers please allow £1.00 per copy for post and packing.

*Payment may be made in sterling by UK personal cheque, Eurocheque, postal order, sterling draft or international money order, made payable to Book Service By Post.

Alternatively by Access/Visa/MasterCard

Card No.   ☐☐☐☐☐☐☐☐☐☐☐☐☐☐☐☐☐☐☐

Expiry Date ☐☐☐☐☐☐☐☐☐☐☐☐☐☐☐☐☐

Signature   _____

Applicable only in the UK and BFPO addresses.

While every effort is made to keep prices low, it is sometimes necessary to increase prices at short notice. Pan Books reserve the right to show on covers and charge new retail prices which may differ from those advertised in the text or elsewhere.

NAME AND ADDRESS IN BLOCK CAPITAL LETTERS PLEASE

Name _____

Address _____

_____

_____

_____

                                                    8/95

Please allow 28 days for delivery.
Please tick box if you do not wish to receive any additional information. ☐